"Vanity, celebrity, murder, and fabulous shoes!

Revenge for Old Times' Sake has all this and more. Kris Neri's cool-under-pressure protagonist and her witty narrative voice are the reasons this series is an award winner. The clever plot twists and vivid characters bring to mind what might result from the unholy coupling of Mel Brooks and Janet Evanovich. But I'll take Tracy Eaton over Stephanie Plum any day of the week."

— Bill Fitzhugh, author of *Pest Control* and *Highway 61 Resurfaced*

"Wacky, witty, wise and wonderful.

With the show-biz savvy, funny and punny Kris Neri as producer and director, readers will laugh their way through non-stop action, zany characters and a madcap plot worthy of the silver screen. (The secret? This is a smart, solid and well-written mystery -- that reveals a lot of heart.)"

— Hank Phillippi Ryan, Agatha-winning author of *Prime Time*

"A delightful mystery with a witty, feisty, fresh heroine.

Tracy's wildly outrageous family will make you thankful for your own! I found myself laughing out loud. Can't wait for the next one!"

—Deb Baker, author of *Ding Dong Dead* and *Murder Talks Turkey*

"A witty glimpse at insider Hollywood with a spunky, no-nonsense heroine, the movie-star mother from hell and cast of big egos. A fun and fast-paced read."

— Rhys Bowen, author of *Her Royal Spyness*, Molly Murphy and Evan Evans mysteries

"A hysterical mix of incompatible personalities, unexpected plot twists, unorthodox methods of detection. Absolutely delightful! The interplay between Tracy and her aging sex goddess mother alone is worth the price of admission."

— Chassie West, author of *Killing Kin*

A TRACY EATON MYSTERY

REVENGE
FOR OLD
TIMES' SAKE

Kris Neri

Cherokee McGhee

Williamsburg, Virginia

ISBN 978-0-9799694-5-4
0-9799694-5-X

First Edition 2010

Cover illustration by Braxton McGhee

Published by:
Cherokee McGhee, L.L.C.
Williamsburg, Virginia

Find us on the World Wide Web at:
WWW.CHEROKEEMCGHEE.COM

Printed in the United States of America

To Joe, from his "Red Hair and Ruby Lips." It's not every woman who gets songs written about her.

REVENGE
FOR OLD
TIMES' SAKE

Kris Neri

PROLOGUE

I never thought sex would kill me, but it nearly did.

Oh, not at that moment. Bathed as I was in the afterglow of coital bliss, death was the last thing on my mind. And it's not often a mystery author admits that.

Snuggling under the down comforter, I ran my fingers over my husband's chest. With his wavy light brown hair sleep-tousled and his dimples flashing, Drew was extra easy on the eyes this morning. But it takes more than looks to make a marriage. As different as we were, people often found us an unlikely pair. I never thought it should be that hard to grasp what kept us together. Quite simply, Drew was my rock, and I was his fun, his spirit of adventure.

Sure, I kept things from him at times, for his own good. And mine. And, yeah, rocks do crush adventures, when they fear they'll go too far afield. As if such a thing were possible. Mostly, it worked because we both knew Rock Guy needed a dash of enjoyment in his life, and though I hated to admit it, Fun Girl needed some stability.

Besides, we'd always been dynamite between the sheets.

If it ain't broke, don't be a jackass and break it — that's my motto.

Elsewhere in our rambling wreck of a house, I heard the faint sound of footsteps. Our houseguests were stirring. I braced for the inevitable frown that should cross Drew's face. He didn't understand why we needed to house a steady stream of visitors. While I hadn't exactly chosen our current companions, I'd been raised to welcome the chaos guests bring with them. It was the circus come to town. What's not to like?

To cover the sounds he obviously hadn't heard, I produced a contented sigh and looked past him to the time flashing on the nightstand digital clock. "This is sure a red-letter day."

"We were great, weren't we, Trace?"

Sure, but that wasn't what I meant. "It's not like you to lollygag around here at the lazy hour of six-twenty in the A-M when your case has gone to the jury." He generally paced the halls of the courthouse hours before the jury reported, getting in the way of the cleaning crew.

His naked shoulder peeked out the top of the comforter in a shrug. "Let's be honest, babe. The Sullivan case hasn't exactly been mine."

Too true. Drew worked as a junior partner at the prominent Los Angeles law firm of Slaughter, Cohen, Rather, Word & Dragger. He, like most people, shortened its name to "Slaughter, Cohen," while Mother referred to it as SCREWED. Hers was clearly the more accurate version. Not just who they are, but — after you see the bill — what you'll be.

Some months before, we accidentally exposed the involvement of one of Slaughter, Cohen's bigger clients in a crime. That's not how they spell *teamwork* at SCREWED, and it put Drew in deep shit with the bigwigs. I'd encouraged him to join another firm, where maybe they weren't so picky about their associates' extracurricular activities. But until his career took a detour through the sewer, Drew had been the office rising star, on the fast track for senior partnership. Since he's nothing if not hopelessly misguided, he vowed to stay the course.

They made it rough on him at first. They pulled him away from his beloved estate practice and made him work on a criminal case, the last thing he knew anything about, despite my efforts to educate him. They gave him the scut work to do. Eventually, Drew seemed to be winning everyone over again, until a few weeks ago, when Ian Dragger, a senior partner and first chair on the case, started tormenting him again. Since they didn't have a prayer of winning the case that had just fallen into the jury's hands, things didn't look promising for Drew.

"I guess Ian didn't let you do the good stuff," I said.

"Maybe not, but I took some independent action on my own during the trial. Radical, even. You'd have been impressed, babe. Why should Ian get all the glory?"

What? Words like *independent* and *radical* weren't in Drew's life description. They needed to come with the warning: *Stodgy guys, don't try this alone.* Did he need me to perform damage control?

I blamed sex for derailing my focus. Unless that was his knee rising up to meet me under the covers, I had a feeling we were headed for round two. I'd intended to ask him what he did, I swear. But then he nibbled on my ear, and we were at it again.

Who knew an ear nibble could turn into such a nasty bite on the butt? If I'd questioned him, rather than letting the idea float straight out of my mind, I might have gotten to the ugly truth much sooner. Instead, that quickie claimed two lives, and cost others loads of heartache, not to mention nearly condemning both my love monkey and me to an absolute eternity of canoodling. And eternity threatened to begin way too soon.

CHAPTER ONE

Three days later the unraveling had already begun, though I didn't know that at first.

But then, *someone* kept distracting me.

"Murder's my beat," my mother intoned with great drama.

On a busy corner in Century City, L.A.'s Westside business district, Mother struck a pose against a lamppost. A very mystery-ish pose, very noir. Tugging down the brim of her smoky fedora, her blue-violet eyes narrowed in a fierce scowl, sure to stop any would-be bad guys in their tracks. From the looks of things, that Friday rush hour sidewalk was full of bad guys. Didn't those silly suits have anything better to do than to gawk at the bane of my existence?

Mother's hat hid most of her wavy blonde hair, but the too-short skirt of her navy suit exposed enough of those pinup girl legs to stop traffic. Literally — drivers came to a halt in the intersection and stared. Wouldn't you think a woman her age would wear longer skirts? And shouldn't my legs look half as good?

The photographer from *Starz* magazine, who'd come for a photo shoot that morning and parlayed it into a daylong media bonanza, just encouraged her. "That's the stuff, Martha," he cried with glee, as his camera clicked off frame after frame of Mystery Mother for posterity.

He was a gaunt man, dressed entirely in black, who looked as if he should be reciting profound, if atrocious, poetry on the Left Bank — not instructing my mother to "work it" on crowded Los Angeles sidewalks. He told me his name when he showed up at my door, but given my resistance to the media zoo just beginning with him, in a fit of adolescent spite, I chose to think of him as Pierre.

Worse yet, I had no one to blame but myself. Since Mother had inadvertently influenced the plot of my last mystery novel, I named her as co-author. I knew that would mean taking a book tour together, and I was prepared for it. Well, I figured I would be when the time came. But I hadn't anticipated that my publisher would send us on the talk show circuit to build interest in the book — fully eight months before the *Deadly Shadows* publication date. Though we weren't set to leave for another ten days, Mother kicked off the insanity today with the *Starz* shoot.

Just kill me now.

In the throng behind me, I heard the inevitable murmur swell through the crowd as people recognized Mother. "That's Martha Collins, the movie star," people whispered.

Mother didn't acknowledge them, but I knew she heard those awestruck whispers. Everything in her life was predicated on making sure that recognition never stopped.

Passers-by cast occasional glances my way. My resemblance to my famous parents, movie legends Martha Collins and Alec Grainger, is striking. But in my tattered jeans and the free T-shirt from the hardware store, that screamed in violent hues, "Painters do it in color," I looked like a rube from the burbs. Precisely what I was.

I began to think Pierre's finger must have fused to his camera's shutter. Yet even when he freed it, and Mother acknowledged the cheers of the crowd with a satisfied nod, we still couldn't move on. The last member of our little entourage lagged behind.

From a half-block back, Mother's new publicist, Vanessa Eccerly, called, "Hey, you guys, wait up, willya? Why's everyone walking so fast?"

Considering the *Starz* guy had shot enough film to replicate half the movies Mother had made during her long career, I guessed walking wasn't Vanessa's thing. I just wished I could figure out what was.

Vanessa loped across the street and tripped at the curb. She was a big, gawky girl, who wore mostly granny dresses and Doc Martens, like many kids near her twenty-something age. But while she seemed to be shooting for trendy, that style just contributed to Vanessa's tendency to resemble a quaint, oversized doll. Her little Dutch girl bob was another strikingly old-fashioned touch; although her hair was colored cotton candy-pink, its sheen resembled a doll's vinyl hair. Even her bright blue eyes often seemed as fixed and unnaturally wide — and just as vacant.

That this empty-headed plaything, Mother's new publicist, had planned our talk show tour, made me dread it even more.

Vanessa leaned against Mother's vacated lamppost to catch her breath. "Whew! Why did we park so far from this party?"

"Tracy?" Mother asked with a devilish smirk.

"I will — if you will, Mother," I said.

That cryptic exchange referred to a set of questions Mother and I kept throwing at each other. She wanted to know why I always parked blocks away from any destination, while I wondered why she hired Vanessa. The trouble with our stalemate was, even if I didn't answer her question, she knew I was walking the extra blocks to take off the last of the weight I put on when I quit smoking. That was no secret — most days my stomach rumbled loudly enough to be heard in Dallas. I was down to the final five pounds now, but they were putting up a fight.

Yet I couldn't figure why Mother hired Vanessa. One of the city's leading media consultants had always handled her film publicity. Why had she passed over him in favor of this gawky girl? Curiosity is my curse — I had to know what she was up to.

Since Vanessa's wide eyes hadn't yet blinked, I realized she was still waiting for an answer. Talk about having a breezeway between your ears. Mother often suggested I missed Vanessa's hidden depth, reminding me that there's little difference between genius and stupidity. The only difference I could see was that genius had its limits.

I gestured to the cars crawling past. "Knowing there would be a parade eyeing Mother, I figured I couldn't get any closer."

"Oh...right," Vanessa said with a slow nod.

The *Starz* guy snickered. Mother gave my wrist a nasty pinch. I gritted my teeth and pressed on.

We were bucking the exodus from the office towers around us to attend an impromptu party at Slaughter, Cohen, celebrating their accomplishment of the impossible. They'd actually secured an acquittal for a defendant who had the poor sense to commit his crime live on cable TV, thus proving that: a) SCREWED had some damn fine lawyers, or b) they argued the case before an L.A. jury.

Though Mother hadn't put on any more shows on the subsequent blocks we trod, the crowds became quite dense as we approached Drew's building. When I saw the placards carried by the people spilling around the corner, I understood. A demonstration, and counter-demonstration, resulting from today's verdict had clogged the street.

"DOLT wins!" some placards read, while others said, "DOLT is dangerous!"

"What's a dolt?" Vanessa asked.

From beneath the brim of her fedora, Mother shot me a warning look that killed my smartass comeback right in my throat. Though she's not exactly a traditional parent, she can still produce looks that make it more than my life is worth to defy.

But how could anyone not understand those signs? DOLT stood for Decency and Order in Life and on Television, the organization whose founder, Skippy Sullivan, achieved victory in the courtroom today. I always thought Skippy should be jailed for not realizing what word that acronym would produce, but he was too busy embodying the concept.

Around the corner, the sidewalk became impassable. I took the lead, encouraging the others to wiggle through single-file. Yet I found myself agreeing with those counter-demonstrators. DOLT would have been dangerous, were it not so lame-brained.

At the garage entrance, I shouted to my companions, "We'll never make it to the main entrance. Let's cut through here."

"Will it lead to the same place?" Vanessa asked.

Never had I felt such a pressing need for an *I'm With Stupid* T-shirt. It was gonna be a long tour.

After the din in the street, the relative quiet of the garage seemed as silent as a tomb. But once my ears adjusted, I heard Drew shouting.

I ran to the other side of the garage, where I spotted Drew and Ian Dragger near Ian's forest green Range Rover. I jerked to a halt when I saw what was happening, only vaguely aware of the sounds of my companions' footsteps catching up.

Drew might be a hunk, but he's also such a stuffy young-fogy, who never accepts anything short of conventional perfection in his appearance. His business attire typically remains so rigidly unwrinkled, he looks like a living page in a high-priced men's catalog.

I gawked in disbelief at his shocking transformation. Drew's ever-neat wavy hair hung awkwardly over his forehead, and his face looked dangerously flushed. His suit jacket had been thrown to the floor. He'd yanked his tie down, and his shirt and pants looked like they'd been put through the spin cycle — with Drew in them.

Ian Dragger still seemed more pristine in his chocolate pinstriped suit and soft gold tie. But while Ian was also an attractive man, this wasn't his finest moment, either. His emerald eyes had narrowed into hard slits, while his thin lips twisted into a mean knot on his rigid face. His hands were clenched in fists at his sides.

Drew also cocked his fists, holding them before his chest, boxer-style. "I mean it, Ian," he shouted. "I want to know why you're riding me. I know it has nothing to do with the teamwork crap you keep throwing around."

"So you're going to push your claim, you son-of-a-bitch," Ian said, so softly I wouldn't have heard it, had it not echoed in the concrete garage. "I knew it. You're no better —"

Without warning, one of Drew's fists shot out. It smashed into Ian's nose, sending him reeling into his SUV, as blood showered both of them.

I stood there, too stunned to move. That wasn't my Drew. He was up to the wazoo in impulse control — and believe me, I've tested it.

Not everyone was stuck in a stupor, though. Pierre snapped a picture just as Drew's fist and Ian's nose achieved intimacy. A photographer for a national magazine caught Drew at the most damaging moment of his life. And I'd brought that photographer there. Boy, was I in trouble.

And I didn't know the half of it yet.

CHAPTER TWO

The party was surreal. Well, mostly because we attended it after what happened.

I had to admit Slaughter, Cohen put on a classy show. That they'd thrown it together at the last minute wasn't apparent. If anything, it looked as if weeks had gone into the planning.

Though most of the space on that floor was taken up with offices and cubicles, they squeezed in a large number of revelers to share in their triumph. A string quartet played softly where the corridor bent at one corner. And an impromptu bar did a booming business. Legal secretaries passed out trays of hors d'oeuvres that looked no less yummy for having been tossed together by some caterer called in at the final hour.

But it was so weird. I kept pinching myself to make sure what I saw wasn't just the nuttiness of a dream.

After the prizefight in the garage, when Ian had stomped off, leaving a trail of blood drops, I'd said to Drew, "Dude, did the pod people come for you?" When he gave me a blank stare, I made it clearer. "What happened here?"

"After the verdict came down, Ian's abuse of me spiked." He'd shrugged. "I couldn't take it anymore. I followed him down here to talk, but..."

Go figure. I'd written off Ian's treatment of Drew as the result of trial stress. Shouldn't the verdict have mellowed him?

"You'd have done the same thing," Drew insisted.

Not me. It's a point of honor with me that I can trick anyone into doing anything. But rigid people do snap. Was it any wonder I wanted to loosen him up?

Naturally, I tried to talk Drew out of going the party. Even I wouldn't have been nervy enough to show up if I'd creamed the host. But drunk as he was on his own testosterone now, Drew insisted he had every right to be there.

Now he claimed half the space as his turf, relegating the other part to Ian. Drew floated around his territory as if he were the conquering hero who delivered Skippy's syrupy testimony or Ian's stirring summation, instead of the guy who did the grunt work. He didn't shake hands with anyone, though — since he kept his right hand thrust into a plastic bag full of ice. He'd put on his jacket again, but it was streaked with dust. And while he had adjusted his burgundy tie, his button-down shirt was liberally spattered with blood. Even odder for my fastidious sweetie, he'd resisted my efforts to clean him up, flaunting his present state as a badge of honor. What had this creature done with my husband?

Ian's duds looked spiffier, apart from the blood that also soaked his shirt and tie. But he kept his icy drink glass pressed to a nose ballooned beyond recognition.

The *Starz* guy kept snapping pictures. Mother continued to strike her version of mystery author poses. And Vanessa wolfed down whole trays of canapés by herself.

Apart from those pesky concerns, it was a perfectly normal party.

I figured Drew's days there were numbered: one, if we counted today. I was still too stunned to take in what it meant for him to be suddenly unemployed. But I had enough sense to know that we ought to try to mend some fences, so when he went on the job market, interviewers wouldn't duck if he extended his hand.

Since Ian now lapped his scotch like a dog at his water bowl, I decided this might not be a good time to approach him. But Ian's wife, Kathy Right, was another story. Given her slight smile, as if she had a secret nobody else knew, I was guessing she wouldn't be as quick to even the score.

I always found Ian and Kathy an odder match than people said Drew and I were. She was in her late thirties, Ian's age, but her lanky gray hair and the earnest expression she generally wore on her long, unmade-up face made her look a decade older. The child of hippies, Kathy still dressed as her mother had decades earlier, in ankle-length, knife-pleated skirts, that made her hips look as wide as a bus, and the ever-present Birkenstocks, which exposed her French manicured toenails. Since Kathy never met a progressive cause she didn't embrace, I always wondered how she justified life with her high-priced hired gun of a husband.

I approached her with caution. "Kathy, I don't know what to say." I bent my head at a humble angle. Unaccustomed to the pose, my neck ached. How do people keep that humility thing going?

Kathy gave her hair an emphatic shake. "No need, Tracy. Men are natural brutes. It's their nature."

While I didn't agree, I could hardly deny it now, given what my caveman did to hers. But my bullshit meter told me Kathy was not unhappy with the pounding her husband had taken. I suspected her secret smile was one of satisfaction.

"I believe in the power of women," Kathy said, giving her chin a smug tilt.

I glanced at Mother and Vanessa. "Me too. But I prefer to pick my own team."

While drifting around after I left Kathy, I noticed the DOLT followers were the only ones more overbearing than Drew in flaunting their victory. One particular DOLT, whose jaundiced white hair looked too greasy to have been shampooed lately, had taken over Drew's office. I wondered which Drew would regard as the greater offense, that he pressed his icky hair against the desk chair, or that he'd propped his shoes on Drew's stark black leather desk blotter.

The hair, I decided, since the shoes barely showed signs of wear. They were caramel-colored wingtips with dress uppers, but whose rubber soles were patterned like workout shoes. Come to think of it, they also looked like Drew's shoes. He'd ordered them for his midday walks, but found them uncomfortable. Drew kept a full change of clothes in his office for emergencies. But I didn't think he would mind if this guy appropriated his stuff. If today didn't qualify as a clothing emergency, nothing would. Besides, it didn't look like Drew was going to be pulling any more pre-trial all-nighters at SCREWED.

I wandered to the largest of the firm's many conference rooms, where I found the victorious defendant, Skippy Sullivan, holding court. When I was a kid and Skippy a popular stand-up comic, I always considered him a funny-looking guy. He'd been so skinny, his baggy pants drooped, and his big craggy honker dominated his scrawny face. Along the way, he had filled out nicely; I'd heard he started lifting weights. Today, at fifty-six, Skippy's tanned face had taken on attractive proportions. The pleasant crinkles that formed around his milk chocolate eyes and his engaging smile captured more attention these days than a nose that now fit his face. The silver strands at the temples of his dark hair were such a perfect touch, I suspected Skippy's hairdresser of having manufactured it.

The fleshing out of his body wasn't the only change Skippy had experienced. In the middle of by-pass surgery, his heart had stopped. During that time-out, Skippy claimed to have had a near-death encounter with his Maker, in which the Big Guy ordered him to rid the airwaves of smut and tastelessness. Considering that Skippy's ribald routines had provided a good bit of it, it seemed only fair that he clean it up. He formed DOLT, whose first objective had been the elimination of the trash tabloid shows proliferating most cable networks today.

Though Skippy knew Drew, I'd only met him once when I was a kid, and I wasn't sure if he'd remember me. But when I approached with my hand extended, Skippy crushed me into a hug. His spicy cologne tickled my nose, and I sneezed, leaving tiny wet smears on his charcoal silk shirt.

To make up for the snot spots, I said with as much enthusiasm as I could muster, "Congratulations, Skippy."

His prominent nose twitched as if it detected a bad smell. His own cologne? "Please, Tracy — it's Skip. How many times do I have to tell people that?"

I see, he'd not only gotten religion, he'd gotten dignity. Pardon me for not considering a fifty-six year-old man called *Skip* all that dignified. And this guy believed he should decide what I watched on TV? Not a pretty thought.

"It wasn't my victory, but all of mankind's," Skippy said.

Right. Skippy's target had been *Scarlet Stories*, a show that exposed the sexual peccadilloes of prominent celebrities. He and his cohorts had stormed the studio where the show taped and taken the employees hostage. They replaced the *Scarlet Stories* tape with one of Skippy lecturing the audience on the evils of bad taste, in a delivery that demonstrated his expertise in that area.

Though that studio shared space with a radio station's transmission tower in the hills above my house, I didn't watch the assault in person, but like everyone else, on TV. *Scarlet Stories* might just have been a sleazy show that barely penetrated beyond our local market, but Skippy had invited network news crews along to tape his big moment.

Despite the gravity of the charges, the D.A.'s office offered him a knuckle-slapping deal. But Skippy demanded his fifteen minutes of legal fame. Especially since it seemed unlikely that he'd get another chance to create such a sensation. *Scarlet Stories* and the other cable shows that once taped at that studio now used a more secure facility in Hollywood. *Nobody* thought Skippy would walk.

"When the cause is just, right prevails." The way Skippy's chiseled chin stuck out made him look like a moral prig, not the kindly, all-knowing father figure he seemed to be going for.

"Tracy, have you met my savior?" he asked.

He was here? I thought they only communicated during surgical blackouts.

Skippy led me around the long walnut conference table, where he liberated a small man from a cluster of reporters. The center part in the little guy's brown hair mirrored a gap between his front teeth. And when he grinned, his hazel eyes beamed so brightly, I'd have sworn they were slicked with Vaseline. He wore a rust sweater vest over a rose shirt that still retained the new-shirt folds. High on one side of the vest, he'd pinned a yellow silk boutonniere.

I beamed back at the guy — I love it when someone else's fashion sense makes mine look good.

"Tracy, this is Juror 490," Skippy said. "He convinced eleven lost souls to see the rightness of my cause."

"Riley," the little guy said, cracking his gum and sending a Juicy Fruit wave my way. "Just doing the job the people asked me to do."

They asked him to find Skippy not guilty? "Something Riley or Riley Something?" I asked.

"Yeah." Crack, crack.

Okay.

When the chitchat died — and that happened fast — Skippy led me to the conference room door to give me the boot. I'd monopolized him long enough. Long enough for both of us.

Along the way, Skippy said, "I understand you moved into your mother's old mansion in the boonies."

Mother had given us her former country home in the northwestern corner of the San Fernando Valley, a smidge past the Los Angeles city limits.

"I was invited there for a party once," Skippy said, "but I can't remember whether I went."

He went, all right, but he hadn't been invited. According to Mother, he crashed. Skippy topped her ultimate shit list, though I'd never managed to learn why. One of my friends speculated that Skippy must have groped her or something, but that generally guaranteed them lifetime tenure in her inner circle. Whatever Skippy had done, he'd made certain Mother would wear red to his funeral and dance on his grave.

He spotted Mother across the party, where she had gathered Riley's reporters. "Is that Martha? Tell her to come and see me."

"I sure will," I said with a grin. Hah! Fidel Castro would sleep in the White House before Mother would mingle with Skippy.

At the conference room threshold, I glanced back over my shoulder. Without their reporters, Skippy and his Savior only had each other now. While locked in earnest conversation, Riley pulled a brown card case from his pocket. But Skippy didn't reach for Riley's card. Instead, he frowned so hard, he looked like he was trying to squeeze those silver temples together. Maybe Riley Something had made the mistake of talking about himself. If he wanted to stay in Skippy's orbit, he'd better learn all conversational roads lead to the head-DOLT's favorite subject — himself — and usually sooner than later. When Pierre's flash went off next to me, blinding me peripherally, I made my escape.

Once I returned to the main party, I saw Ian disappear into his corner office. A short time later Skippy also headed in that direction, distractedly slipping the brown card case into the pocket of his black leather jacket as he walked. Not Riley's card, but a gift? Who cared, I thought, as I watched Skippy shut Ian's office door behind him.

That Drew was the only one of the combatants left on the floor meant he had won, didn't it? He could leave the ultimate party from hell now, right? I gathered our motley crew together and decided to put an end to this bizarre nightmare for all of us, before anything worse happened.

But how much worse could it get?

CHAPTER THREE

I sent Mother, Vanessa and Pierre off in Mother's Mercedes, while I dragged Drew to the parking garage for his car. He didn't object when I took the keys to his cinnamon-colored Volvo. He didn't even criticize my driving on the way home. A first.

I waited till we hit the 405 Freeway before returning to his new career as a pugilist. "How's the hand doing?"

He flexed it gingerly. "Still sore, but I would have thought punching someone would hurt more."

Just when you think you've heard everything. My parents' hands never ballooned up when they threw punches, but they'd been schooled by stuntmen. If I'd known Drew planned to pummel Ian, I'd have asked Dad to give him a lesson.

"Drew, do you think you might have handled it —"

He cut me off with a shaky sigh. All the pumped-up bravado he'd shown earlier had leeched away, leaving him horrified by his actions. "It was bad enough that I did, babe. Don't make me relive it, huh?"

Wait till he found out about the picture Pierre took. But I'm nothing if not persistent. After zipping around some slowpokes in the fast lane, I came at things a different way. "Did you get a chance to talk to CeeCee after the verdict?" I asked of his former girlfriend and the prosecutor on the case. "How's she taking her loss?"

"CeeCee's a pro, Trace. Neither wins nor losses throw her."

Well, bless her cold, black little heart. "Tell me this, Drew. What are you gonna do now?" I willed him to say he already had another job lined up. A good one this time.

Instead he said in a weary voice, "Wish for death."

He didn't say whose death.

While Drew seemed to regard his future as dismal, the more I thought about this new direction his life had taken, the more it tickled my Elmo. Now he had to leave SCREWED, where the quota for billable hours exceeded the hours in a week, even if sleep were not an option, and where backstabbing had become a gold medal event. Even better, word would spread through the legal community that Drew was a wild man. An exaggeration to be sure, but one that was certain to bring him cases I'd find more fun.

Once he secured a new job, that is. The only downside was it might take a while for Drew to find a good match to his new social skills. That meant I had to take the tour with Mother and Vanessa for the bucks they'd be paying us, even though I'd secretly hoped to blow it off. Someone had to put the bacon on the table, since, even while dieting, I knocked back plenty.

When I opened our front door, the sound of giggles cut through the sprawling house, despite its thick walls. Mother and Vanessa had beaten us there.

Drew groaned. "Why did you invite Martha and Vanessa to stay with us? Don't they have their own homes?"

You'd think he was the one making the sacrifice for our solvency. Besides, I didn't invite Mother, she simply showed up when we began planning the tour. I suspected she brought Vanessa along because Mother couldn't imagine living without at least one peon to push around. Without Vanessa, our only servant would have been me.

"Look at the bright side. Your Uncle Philly and my dad left yesterday."

Philly was my mother-in-law's black-sheep brother and a recovering con man. I'd promised to clean up Philly's act when he came to live with us. Talk about making the fox into the chickens' den mother. Fortunately, his tutoring of me had proven more effective than the other way around.

"That's two less people here," I said.

While my father, Alec Grainger, was a still a major Hollywood star, he was also handy with a hammer. He and Philly had begun updating the old place for us, which kept both Philly and me out of trouble. Mostly. Though they'd started out as rivals for Mother's affection, Dad and Philly had become buddies when they discovered they shared a taste for disreputable haunts and lowlife friends. They left this morning for a trek along Route 66. As to where they'd end up, it was anyone's guess when it came to those rolling stones.

A sudden shriek of high-pitched laughter ricocheting through the house seemed to dim the bright side for Drew. With a weary sigh, he said, "And they didn't see the benefit in bringing those two with them? Imagine that."

The sound of claws slipping on tile echoed in the staircase to our left, one of two that led to the second floor. Buddy, our dog, bounced into the hall and greeted us with a happy bark. Buddy was a stray Philly had picked up, whose genetic makeup was even more diverse than the architectural styles reflected in the eccentric design of our house. But he was pretty cute with his wavy black-and-tan fur and his giant nose.

Drew knelt on the Mexican tile floor and ruffled Buddy's mane. "Fella, you're still my friend, right?" His hand must have been doing better if he was able to use it like that.

Still, when I helped Drew up the stairs, I rustled up some aspirin for him from our bathroom and promised to bring him more ice.

Though the house was built in the late '60s, the master bedroom looked like a throwback to some film set decorator's garish idea of a '30s movie star's lavish bedroom. A huge padded headboard, the color of the unnaturally bright violet used in Colorized films, was attached to a bed large enough to hold the entire population of Canada, assuming a few of them didn't mind getting a little close. And big overstuffed chaise lounges, upholstered in pale lavender satin, filled most of the sitting area. There is a state at which kitschy taste actually becomes fine art, but this room proved there was also a point of diminishing return.

Our house is located on a huge rocky knoll in the Simi Hills, the sandstone mountain range edging the northwestern San Fernando Valley. I took Buddy downstairs and let him out the backdoor. Buddy ran to the back of the knoll and barked a few times, probably at some critters. Though our only connection to the main street was a rutted dirt road, anyone who wanted to do a little climbing could access any part of the property, and animals frequently did. I couldn't tell which kind had invaded Buddy's turf tonight, since I hadn't replaced the burned out floodlights at the back of the yard. That this was mountain lion territory made me nervous. I whistled for Buddy, who came loping back.

When I headed up the staircase with an ice bag, I met Drew on his way down, carrying the cordless phone. "Some woman who works for Kathy Right called to say Ian is on his way here to talk to me," Drew muttered, thrusting the phone at me.

"Ooh, what woman? What does she do for Kathy?" It always cheered me to learn Kathy was more of a hypocrite than I thought.

Irritation at my detour into trivia made Drew snarl, "How do I know what woman? Her voice sounded familiar, so I must have talked with her before when I called over there."

"Want me to referee?" I asked, maybe a shade too eagerly. I didn't want some eleventh-hour reconciliation wrecking my plans for him now.

Drew lowered his head. "It won't come to violence this time, I promise you. I'd rather not have a witness to my embarrassment."

Too bad he hadn't made that choice before the *really* embarrassing encounter.

"Babe, if he's just leaving now, Ian won't be here for a while. I'm gonna take a walk to clear my head." He accepted the ice bag.

I nodded and continued up the stairs. Drew often took walks when he felt agitated, the length of the outing determined by the level of his turmoil. After his title bout today, he'd need to stroll to Cleveland.

I tried to wait up for him, but I'd had a tough day, too, what with Mother and Vanessa and Pierre, and I fell into a deep sleep. I did hear some noises during the night, but not enough to pull me all the way to consciousness. Until around four, when Buddy nudged my arm with his cold, wet nose. Must have been too busy chasing gophers to do his business when I let him out earlier. I looked to Drew to see whether I could push the chore off onto him, but the slow rise of his chest, which I saw in the moonlight streaming through the window, convinced me he was sound asleep.

I gently shifted our cat, Harri Houdini, off my hip and was rewarded with a nasty feline snarl. Then I took Buddy downstairs.

To make sure he really answered nature's call this time, I stopped in the kitchen for a flashlight. I opened the sliding door in our living room and let Buddy out.

Though barefooted, I followed him as far as the edge of our glitzy Art Deco pool and pointed the flashlight toward the rear of the yard.

Buddy returned on his own, and pretty quickly. As I directed the flashlight away from the back of the property, the beam spilled onto the center of the wide gaudy pool. I nearly dropped the flashlight when I saw what was there. A man floated face down in the middle, surrounded by a swirl of reddish water.

And I'd swear the guy was wearing Ian Dragger's chocolate-colored suit.

CHAPTER FOUR

Finding Ian's body must have rattled me more than I knew. What else could explain the member of my household with whom I chose to share the news?

"Mother!" I hissed. "Mother, wake up."

Gimme a break. We had a serious shortage of sidekicks here. If Philly had been home, we'd have been poolside already, watching Ian drift across the surface and quietly communing together on the brevity of life. Or maybe working out a neighborhood pool on the precise time when Ian bought country real estate. Philly's homemade lotteries brought in a tidy sum. But without my kindred adventurer, Mother seemed the best bet.

Her eyelids fluttered open. "This better be something big."

It was that, all right. I tried dragging her to the door, but she stopped before the shadowy mirror over the black oak dresser.

With its sedate Mission-styled furnishings, the guestroom Mother had chosen was decorated in a fairly conventional manner. If you could overlook the small angels painted across its robin's egg-blue walls. Only with closer scrutiny was it apparent that they all resembled Mother's film contemporaries from her heyday, the people who had actually occupied that room when they visited. Even knowing they were real people, I might have found the sight of those angels peaceful — if one celestial spirit, who looked suspiciously like a leading man with whom Mother reportedly carried on a torrid dalliance, hadn't been flashing me.

"Mother, there's no time to waste," I whispered.

"Darling, there is always time for what matters." With no sign of urgency, she ran her fingers through her sleep-tossed hair.

Though she must have brought a dozen blonde wigs for her stay, her naturally wavy hair only needed a good shaking to fall into place. In mere moments she created such an artfully tousled look, it was clear why she aced out every other contender to become

AARP's favorite cover girl. Glancing over her shoulder, I saw that my own golden blonde pillow hair had formed a ledge that tilted up and to the left.

Mother took another few days to cinch the sash on her dressing gown. But then we finally crept through the darkened house and out to the pool. There we knelt at the edge, and I pointed the flashlight toward the ornament floating in the center.

"That's Ian," Mother said. "Is he...?"

"Deader than disco."

When she frowned, I took that as a comment on my flippancy. Then she clarified. "Really, Tracy — don't you keep up on trends? Disco's making a comeback."

"Ian won't be."

My mutt slipped through the open door. Buddy-the-watchdog finally noticed the intruder and let out one baritone bark. Having him there made me feel so safe.

Mother clicked her tongue in disapproval. "Ian Dragger was not a good man. We reap what we sow."

"Whoa! *Reap what we sow?* Where'd you get that?"

"I might have heard it in *The Ten Commandments*."

If it weren't for movies, she wouldn't know anything. "How am I going to break this to Drew?" Though his relationship with Ian ended badly, they'd worked together for years.

She arched a brow. "So...we're operating under the assumption that he doesn't already know because..." She slashed her index finger across her throat.

"Mother! No!" Despite my protest, an unwelcomed suspicion knocked on my mental door. I refused to answer it.

Mother shrugged. "I didn't say I blamed him."

I lifted my face to the predawn sky, and a scent tickled my nose. "Do you smell something?"

"Really, darling." Mother jabbed her head toward Ian.

"Not *that*. It smells like...maybe smoke."

She leveled those velvet eyes on me. "You're not turning into some anti-smoking evangelist now that you've quit, are you, darling? Just because you've gained weight —"

"I'm not anti-anything except straight-laced," I snapped.

"I only wanted to be sure because, really, Tracy, you don't know the meaning of the word *moderation*."

How could I? She'd banned it from my vocabulary at birth.

"Someone's barbecuing," Mother added with a dismissive sweep of her delicate hand, weighed down by the huge pear-shaped diamond my father had given her for one of their engagements. "You haven't lived here long enough to realize how far odors and sounds travel in the canyon."

Barbecuing at four in the morning? Besides, it didn't smell like meat, it smelt like... Well, now that the scent had drifted away, who could say?

Mother crossed her legs in a lotus position and pressed her forearms to her slender thighs, which gave her a purposeful look. "Forget the odors, Tracy. We have more important concerns. What are we going to do with Ian?"

I sat back on my heels. "Do...?"

I heard the flip-flop of Drew's slippers approaching through the living room. So much for breaking it to him gently. Rubbing his puffy eyelids with his fingers, he said, "Will you two keep it down? Some of us are trying to —" He gaped. "That's...Ian. So that's why he never showed up last night."

They never saw each other last night. A wave of relief swept through me.

"I'll call the police." Drew disappeared through the door, and after a moment, the lights went on inside the house.

I struggled to get to my feet, while Mother jumped quickly to hers — shouldn't arthritis or something be overtaking her at this point? I started after Drew.

Mother yanked my wrist. "That's why I wanted us to handle it. Drew's too conventional. Why didn't you stop him from calling the police?"

"When someone dies, you have to tell them. It's the law."

Mother stomped a tiny foot clad in a fuzzy turquoise mule. "Since when do you follow rules? Next time, Tracy, be bold — don't tell them. It just makes it harder on everyone."

Next time some stiff bobbed up in my pool? "Mother, don't you think Ian's family would want to know?"

She rolled her eyes. "It would be a loss either way."

And people say she has no compassion.

"Hey, check that out," Vanessa said from behind us.

I whirled around to see her big doll eyes widen more than usual, as she stared into the pool with undisguised excitement. I hadn't heard her approach; for a clumsy girl, she could drift into places when she wanted to.

I ignored her, concentrating instead on building a comfortable theory. "Ian must have come back here to gather his thoughts. Maybe he slipped and hit his head." Too bad that as the morning sky brightened to a paler gray, I couldn't see a trace of blood on the pool's trim.

"Sure, that's what musta happened," Vanessa said. "Unless Drew pushed him."

CHAPTER FIVE

When visitors arrive at this house, the doorbell plays a random selection of old tunes. I had yet to locate the ancient contraption responsible for it, though when I did, I was considering exchanging it for my CD player. Sure, the CD changer played songs with modern efficiency and less scratchy noise — but not with the same jagged sense of humor. This morning's selection, when the cops arrived, was "Anything Goes."

Drew threw the door open to admit the law. Standing behind him, I panicked when I remembered the little automotive shell game Philly and I had been playing. Around the time we moved into this loony bin, Mother had invested in a business that bought discarded cars from junk dealers and fixed them up enough to sell to movie companies, so they could be wrecked again on film. Naturally, she volunteered my private lane as a storage yard. There must have been fourteen cars out there now, some of which had been cannibalized to such a degree, their makes couldn't be determined on a bet. There was even a huge horse trailer whose wheels wobbled worse than Jell-O in a storm.

Since my pickup had bitten the dust during our last caper, until I decided to buy a new car, I put the truck's license plate on whichever of the wrecks I drove on a particular day. If the fuzz ran that plate, I was toast. Not only wouldn't it match that car, all of those tin beasts had been struck from the D.M.V.'s rolls. But I bet they had more on their minds today than whether the plate on the yellow Duster-Camaro combo was strictly kosher.

Not that I sensed any urgency in their approach. When Drew opened the door, only one representative of the L.A. County Sheriff's Department stood there, a woman in her early forties, with short chestnut-brown hair that fell over her forehead. The eyes that looked out below the fringe of hair were kinda hazel — a little brown, a little green, with golden glints. She wore black knit slacks topped by a black-watch plaid sweater.

The fingers of one of her hands drummed against the doorframe, while the other held out her shield. "Detective Patti Garcia," she said. The faintest of twinkles appeared in the golden specks in her eyes. "We heard you got a live one here."

Twinkles, gallows humor — yes, a kindred spirit. But the sparkle vanished so fast, I questioned whether it had just been a trick of the early morning light.

Detective Garcia shouted over her shoulder, "It's the right place."

Other cops and technicians meandered up our drive, weaving around the junked cars. Nobody seemed in a hurry, but their experience probably told them Ian wasn't leaving anytime soon.

While Drew led them toward the rear of the house, Garcia shouted instructions over her shoulder, making me think they might not be as low-keyed as I first believed. I began to feel as if an invading army had overtaken us. Apparently, I wasn't the only one who felt under attack. Harriet Houdini, our small silver-and-white tabby, who possessed the world's shortest fuse, puffed and hissed.

Garcia said, "Dangerous cat. Where was she when the vic went in the drink?"

I glared at the poufy silver tail escaping into the kitchen. If only it were that easy.

Hours later, there were so many cops and crime scene techs swarming out back, it looked more like some of the parties Mother must have thrown when she owned this house — apart from the stiff in the pool. Though now and then she must have had a guest who was on the quiet side, too.

They had placed Ian's body on the patio. I couldn't see much through the kitchen window, especially with all the people bent over the body, but it looked like Ian's wheat-colored hair had been parted along a deep red gash. Someone must have knocked him unconscious and tossed him into the pool to drown.

Someone?

Not Drew. Punching out Ian's lights was one thing, but giving him a permanent blackout was a different ballgame, one I felt sure Drew didn't play. Still, I'd have sworn yesterday that Drew couldn't be pushed far enough to rearrange Ian's nose, either.

I glanced around the kitchen, empty now apart from me and our pets. Shouldn't Drew be here to sell his innocence? We'd huddled there together from the time the police arrived. Only I made the mistake of telling him about the photo Pierre took of him hitting Ian. He harassed Garcia until she agreed to let him go for the newspaper. But he'd been gone so long. Was the news so bad that he just kept going?

At least I didn't have to keep up a brave front anymore. While Harri was on the counter doing her toilette, Buddy remained vigilant at my side. Naturally. Though my stomach roared louder than the MGM lion, I hadn't an appetite for anything more than the bottomless mug of coffee I'd guzzled since I awoke. Finally, something that put me off my feed; if my husband stayed neck-deep in buffalo chips, I might lose the last of those pounds clinging to my hips. But when my gut began to feel acid washed, I grabbed a box of crackers from the pantry. Even then, to set aside my fears, I started tossing them into the air and trying to catch them in my mouth. That I didn't catch many probably explained Buddy's devotion.

Rock Guy was about to cruise up the river, but Fun Girl still knew how to play the game.

I'd been about to toss up another Sociable, when the door from the outside started opening. I held my breath. Sensing my distraction, Buddy snatched the cracker from my fingers. If that mutt hadn't saved my life once, he'd be in big trouble.

Yeah, right. Discipline isn't a concept I can get behind in the best of times. Now I scarcely noticed the crumbs Buddy was spreading over the new ceramic tile floor Dad and Philly had laid in that room. All I saw was Detective Garcia, standing in the doorway, and judging by the scowl she wore, she was a mite peeved.

With her fists planted on her slim hips, she snapped, "If the kid with the pink hair doesn't get out of our way, I'm gonna arrest her for obstruction."

Vanessa. I should have realized I hadn't seen her around since the cops showed up. I debated whether it would be fair to throw her to the wolves. What did we know about her? She'd acted awfully eager when I invited her to come along to the party yesterday, giddy almost.

I shrugged to Garcia. "You'd be doing me a favor."

"Yeah? I'm not in the favor business. How 'bout if I pull you in, too?"

No fair. If everybody in my life kept landing in cow pods of trouble, they had no business dragging me in with them.

"What's it gonna be?" she demanded. "What do you want me to tell her?"

Mother pushed through the swinging door and said, "That her employer requires her to monitor the news."

There she was, Martha Collins in all her splendor. Fully made-up now, she wore a royal blue crepe lounging outfit of the sort Marie Antoinette might have chosen when advising the peasants on their dessert options.

I had to give Garcia points for not blinking. Her only acknowledgement that she recognized Mother was a slight widening of those enigmatic eyes. She wouldn't surrender her objectivity easily, dammit. With a brusque nod of thanks for Mother's solution to getting Vanessa out from underfoot, without having to make it too official, she went off to put it into effect.

Mother crossed to the far end of the kitchen. Cabinets and tan tile counters lined most of the perimeter of the large room, with a big butcher block island plopped in the center. The cabinets had been too dark for my taste, so Dad and Philly had lightened them to a pale honey. And they covered the vinyl floor with ceramic tiles that matched the counters. I'd added a maple table to the space beyond the island, where Buddy and I now performed our cracker act.

Though my things didn't fill a fraction of that cabinet space, I refused to let Mother's belongings crowd them. I'd boxed up all her old dishes and crystal, and I wrapped the boxes in bungee cords and stacked them on the floor. But Mother hadn't even acknowledged those boxes, much less have them removed.

On her way across the kitchen, doing the cutest little sidestep around that stack of boxes, she asked, "Anything new?"

I shrugged. "Hard as it is to believe, they don't recognize their obligation to keep me in the loop."

Though the coffee maker rested below the cabinet that held my vast mug collection, Mother went to the other end of the room where I stored the gold-rimmed bone china she'd bought us for our wedding. She helped herself to one of the cups and saucers we never used, and went to the pot and filled her cup.

After taking a sip, she said, "Now that's why I resisted making it official. Promise me, darling, that next time this happens, you won't."

So she was still on hung up on that. It seemed a safe enough promise. What were the odds of this happening again? "Sure thing," I muttered.

Mother responded with a satisfied nod. What that woman knows about the real world wouldn't fill a thimble.

My little tabby traitor made an excited whir and rushed toward Mother. I used to believe that cat liked her better. But I'd decided it was just that I wanted to win the cat's approval, while Harri needed Mother's. More self-possessed than a cat — now, that was saying something. While Mother fussed with Harri, the cordless phone on the island rang.

"Don't answer it." I ran to check the Caller ID display. "Charlotte," I said with a groan when my stuffy mother-in-law's number appeared. Our nighttime pool guest must have made the national news. "Just let the machine get it. Drew doesn't need to deal with her hysterical I-told-you-sos now."

And neither did I, since most of what Charlotte told him had to do with me. I turned the volume down on the answering machine, so we wouldn't have to hear her message. Life was bad enough without that.

"You know the phone company offers voicemail with the cost of the phone, don't you?" Mother said.

But you can't screen voice mail like a machine. When Caller ID failed to identify a caller, my backup was listening to the message.

With as many calls as I avoided, no way would I give that up. But I didn't explain that to Mother, since the calls I screened were often hers.

I glanced out the window in time to see one of the cops pointing to something where the property dipped off in a shallow ravine. If anyone had approached our backyard from the rear, that spot would have been the easiest climb. Was that how Ian had come? He wore the same suit and dress shoes he'd had on yesterday. Even if the grade was shallow at that point, the rocky ground would have made it a tough hike in business shoes.

Mother looked around. "Where is poor Drew?"

I explained about his getting the paper. One downside to the house was its remoteness. We were a half-mile away from the main road, where the neighborhood mailboxes and newspaper boxes were clustered. A good distance, but Drew had been gone long enough to take it twice. Was he retracing last night's walk in search of something that would clear him? An awful thought drifted into my head against my will: He could also have gone out to destroy evidence that would implicate him. But I beat that idea down with a stick.

From beyond the closed kitchen door, I heard the sound of the living room sliding glass door open. After a moment, the television came to life in a flash of sound. Had to be Vanessa, monitoring the news as ordered. I pressed my finger to my lips to remind Mother to watch what she said.

But not everyone was so circumspect. Drew pushed open the swinging door. "I'm screwed," he said from the doorway and tossed the paper onto the table. From the way he said it, he didn't mean it in the good way.

The *Starz* guy sure took a great photo. Plastered across the front page of the *Los Angeles Courier*, under the banner headline, "Legal K-O," was Drew's infamous punch.

From the TV beyond the open door, I heard Nick Wickerson, the anchor of a popular tabloid cable news show, *Nick Wick's Sin City*, promoting tonight's show. "They don't get up after they've been K-O'ed by this legal eagle," he hyped, proving he was not above stealing from headlines.

Drew's face paled. "No, it can't be. I'm so screwed," he repeated.

A figure came up behind him, though he blocked most of that body from my view. But she was shorter than Vanessa, and the hair, peeking over Drew's shoulder, was chestnut, not pink.

Garcia. Detective Garcia, not Vanessa, had been watching the TV.

"More screwed than you know," she told Drew.

CHAPTER SIX

I'd say the day spun out of control at that point, only the control vessel had set sail at four o'clock that morning, and it was long gone by the time Garcia dropped her bombshell.

They found the bloody shirt Drew had worn yesterday where he'd tossed it in a trashcan out back. Drew insisted he'd thrown it away since he assumed it couldn't be cleaned, but Garcia preferred to think he'd been hiding it.

The cops also showed us an old hammock in navy-and-white stripes that they insisted had to be ours, since it resembled the faded lawn chair cushions in the pool house, and they maintained Drew used that hammock to drag Ian onto the knoll from the back of the property. I hadn't yet begun to sort through the stuff Mother had left in the pool house, the garage or the storeroom off the garage, so I couldn't say whether it was ours or not. And since Mother wouldn't remember what she wore last night, expecting her to know how she furnished her patio thirty years ago was really out of the question.

Drew told them he wasn't on the rear road above our house last night, and certainly hadn't taken Ian for a hammock ride. But they seemed to have found something that placed him there, which they refused to divulge.

The Coroner's crew took Ian for his last ride, except for the one he'd take to the cemetery. But the cops stayed on, tearing the house apart. I'd heard there was another crew creating havoc at the SCREWED offices, and at Ian and Kathy's house, but they weren't my problem.

Mother called a French restaurant to deliver some food. She'd been doing that since she moved in. Having to make do with meal deliveries was probably her idea of roughing it. Since it was my idea of luxury, I didn't discourage it. But when the doorbell rang, playing the theme from *Psycho,* I thought about passing the delivery guy and escaping from this pressure cooker.

Only when I opened the door, I saw that reporters had filled all the space left on our private road. Though a deputy kept them away from the house, a few had climbed on the horse trailer to improve their camera angles. The crowd of media hounds seemed subdued as they milled around the junk vehicles — until they spotted me. Then they started shouting questions that mingled together into noise. No escape there, though.

The delivery guy was a teenage wise-ass whose jeans had slipped so far down his hips, they threatened to warm his ankles. "Why don't you hire me to handle that bunch for you?" the kid suggested, jabbing a thumb over his shoulder. "I could be your spokesman."

Wasn't that Vanessa's job? "Work cheap, do you?"

"I figure you couldn't possibly pay worse than you tip," the snotty kid said.

"Don't believe it." I slammed the heavy door shut.

I carried the take-out bag up the hall, pausing in the living room just long enough to announce that lunch was there, but neither Mother nor Vanessa stirred. How did I get stuck with the servant chores?

While I placed the containers in the stainless steel wall oven to keep warm, Mother drifted in, followed by Buddy.

"Mother, there's a crowd of reporters out on the road. Why isn't Vanessa dealing with them?"

"Because I haven't told her to, darling. What do you think she is? A mind reader?"

To read one, she'd probably need to have one. Mother opened the oven and inhaled deeply, drawing in the tantalizing aroma wafting from the containers. Then she closed it. Was that how she stayed so thin — by smelling, not eating?

She grabbed a fork from a drawer in the island and opened the oven door again. She coaxed one container open with the fork's tines and picked at rice kernels. Once two or three grains of rice took the edge off her hunger, her good mood was restored. "Tracy, darling, let's hope we can find food this good when we're on the road next week."

I choked. "The police are upstairs at this moment, tearing my home apart. Do you think I care about some stupid TV tour? I have no intention of leaving town now." How could she think I would?

Her large eyes grew so wide, I thought her eyeballs would pop out and roll around on the floor. She seemed shocked by the idea of my canceling the tour.

Mother flicked her scarlet nails at me. "This business with Drew will blow over before then. The police will see he doesn't have what it takes to be a killer."

I remembered once when she tried to convince me of the exact opposite — that he was precisely the type that snaps. Of course, she did that for the self-serving reason of directing my attention away from her life, which couldn't stand much scrutiny at the time. But I began to fear there might be some truth to it.

Stuffing herself now, one grain of rice at a time, Mother said, "Here's how I think we should sell our writing partnership..."

I slammed the oven door shut, startling her so, she dropped the fork to the floor. Buddy was on it like rice on pilaf.

"Mother, get this straight — we're not writing partners now. We're not partners of any kind." One mistake like that was enough for a lifetime. "And if you hear nothing else, hear this — the tour is history."

Before she could argue any more, Drew pushed through the kitchen door. Though the scent of food could only be a memory now on Buddy's fork, he was really getting into its toy potential. He'd perfected the art of flipping the fork into the air with his big snout and letting it fall to the tiled floor with a clatter. Drew stared blankly at the mutt's shenanigans, as if he couldn't understand what he was seeing. When he finally brought his golden brown eyes back to me, despair had turned them to a flat muddy brown.

"Uh, Trace, the police are ready to leave now. But Detective Garcia wants me to go along for questioning," Drew said.

Acid crested in my stomach in surfer-sized waves. I gulped hard. Mother rested her hand briefly on Drew's arm, before slipping out the door behind him. At the table, he slumped into one of the wooden chairs.

He could never read me the way Mother could, but I plastered my most positive expression on my face anyway. "Okay, first thing, we have to find you a good lawyer," I said, pacing before him. "Who do we know?"

Drew's head popped up in outrage. *"I'm* a good lawyer. Why do I need anyone else?"

I'd been trying for years to interest Drew in criminal law. But I hadn't expected him to provide his own training case. "Drew, this is your life. You know what they say about lawyers in jail having had fools for clients."

Anger flashed in his eyes. And hurt, too, I saw. Thanks to Ian's discounting of his ability. Drew needed to do this, to prove to himself that he still had it. But he didn't have it, not now. When I suggested that I should go along to run some interference, he vetoed that with a downward cast of his eyes; he didn't want me there to witness his humiliation.

All I could do was try to build him up. "You're right. Who could handle it as well as you?" Hah! A high school kid who watched *Law and Order* would have more on the ball.

The phone rang, and I leaped to the island to check the Caller ID. Charlotte again.

"Doesn't identify the caller. Probably a reporter on a cell phone," I lied. Thankfully, the volume was still down, so he couldn't hear her message.

Not that Drew would notice if his mother walked into the room right now. Naked. His vacant eyes stared off into space. "Know what's the hardest part? That I was trying to do what you would do? And I blew it. Let's face it, Trace, I'm too uptight. But you take the wildest chances, and I wanted to show you I could, too."

He'd said that before, but thanks to our having nooky, I failed to pay attention. Cautiously, I asked, "Drew, what did you do?"

Garcia pushed the door open and tapped her finger against her watch. "Time, Mr. Eaton."

I wrapped my arms around him for a moment, drinking in his scent, the feel of having him close. I wished I'd held him more this morning.

Then Drew headed for the door. But he paused in the doorway.

"Tracy, things are such a mess — I need to know you won't do anything to further upset the applecart while I'm gone."

"How about if I just pick up a few apples?" There was no shortage of them on the ground.

"I'm not kidding, babe. I can't handle any more," Drew said. "Promise me you won't try to solve this — and really mean the promise this time."

Ooh, crap! A double-promise. Did that mean I had to cross fingers on both hands to break it?

Raw desperation filled Drew's haggard eyes. He really needed to know that I wouldn't make things worse. How could I deny him that? I gave my head an emphatic nod. With a sigh of relief, Drew followed Detective Garcia out. I continued standing there, still as a statue, till long after I heard the front door slam behind them.

Mother came through the open door, inching up to my side. "You didn't mean what you told Drew, did you? About not solving Ian's murder."

So she'd been eavesdropping, exactly what I would have done. "Yes, I did."

"But, darling, we could fix this. I know we could."

Her "we" didn't escape my attention, but I didn't react to it. "I promised Drew I wouldn't try to solve this case, and I intend to keep that promise."

"I see," Mother said, obviously peeved.

We were quiet for the longest time. Then I said, "Fortunately, tweaking is a whole different thing — because I'm gonna tweak the hell out of it."

"Hallelujah!" she cried in glee.

CHAPTER SEVEN

T hough I vowed to go alone, by the time I actually hit the road, Mother had become my partner in tweaking. She reminded me that I didn't have any wheels, apart from those wrecks in the yard, and that this probably wasn't the time to break any laws that wouldn't benefit Drew. We even stopped calling what we were doing "tweaking," once we chose our first stop, a condolence call on the widow. That was comforting, not tweaking.

Were it not for rationalization, I'd never survive.

Before we left, we changed into outfits more appropriate for a bereavement call. I chose a pair of gray pants, which buttoned more easily than the last time I wore them. Yes! I topped them with a navy blazer. For me, that was downright formal.

When Mother appeared, it was in a white knit dress, as stark as virgin Arctic snow, if it wasn't too ironic to apply a word like *virgin* to my mother. I know some countries consider white the color of mourning, but as this was not one of them, I suspected she made that choice to guarantee that she'd stand out among people wearing black. Ya gotta admire someone who never loses sight of the ball, but being a narcissist gave her a leg up.

I slipped behind the wheel of Mother's tan Mercedes, and we headed over the hill to the exclusive Brentwood neighborhood where Ian Dragger and Kathy Right had made their home.

I remembered when they built their house. The guts of the place, with its ecologically friendly insulation, had been the subject of many national news stories. Now that it was completed, however, apart from the native plants and the solar panels on the roof, it was indistinguishable from the other vaguely Spanish mansions on the block. But I bet Kathy never let anyone forget how they built it.

Mother had a similar thought. "Did it ever strike you as funny that Kathy's name is *Right,* when she's so far *left?"*

"Yeah, I bet she hasn't heard that more than a few thousand

times. Try to behave yourself in there."

"As if that's ever been problem for me," Mother sniffed over her shoulder, as she marched toward the door.

No, it was always a problem for *me*.

A middle-aged Hispanic woman, dressed in a smart red pantsuit, answered the door. Despite her stylish presence, she was obviously the housekeeper. Leave it to Kathy to have a maid who couldn't dress the part, even if she did perform the functions.

The woman showed us into a family room, whose floor was made of inexpensive terrazzo, covered with a priceless Navajo rug in a rainbow of greens and coral tones. We found Kathy seated on a sofa of some colorful rough-spun fabric, facing a giant plasma TV whose picture was tuned to the local news, while the sound was muted. The hand that gripped the remote looked rigid and white.

I slowed. With my own husband in such jeopardy, I felt a mere fraction of the pain Kathy had to be experiencing now. How could I make it worse? Fortunately, Mother was made of sterner stuff — she hurled me into the room. To my surprise, when Kathy's vague sherry-colored eyes focused on mine, they brightened.

The knobby sofa surface stuck to my pants when I sat next to her. Before I could adjust my position, Kathy's body sank against mine. I wrapped my arms around her. "Kathy, I'm so sorry," I whispered.

Her gray head quivered. "I don't blame you, Tracy. I don't even blame Drew. Men lose control of themselves. If he pleads guilty, I'll testify for him at the sentencing."

Whoa! Don't let the cell door hit you when it closes behind you *forever.* I shoved myself away from her so fast, the sofa fabric caused enough friction under my butt to spark an inferno. Felt kinda toasty.

Before I could object to her remarks, Mother stepped in and took Kathy's slack hand. "Kathy, darling, it must be hard to know who to trust. A man like Ian had to have scores of enemies."

That was her idea of behaving herself?

The muted TV screen flashed an image of my house. With obvious effort, Kathy's unfocused eyes traveled from the screen, to Mother. "Everyone loved Ian," Kathy said with unexpected force.

Sure. Was he a trial lawyer or a priest? Where were all the people who'd loved him? Apart from the housekeeper who let us in, and the occasional sound of children's voices coming from upstairs, Kathy was alone.

Guilt overcame me again. "Is there some friend we can call to stay with you?"

She gave her straight gray hair a sharp shake. "They're all at the MAT rally at the Federal Building on Wilshire."

Our expressions must have conveyed our ignorance.

Kathy's forehead contracted with irritation. "Mothers Against Tyranny. My friends wanted to stay with me, but it was essential that we have a good showing at the rally."

Why? Were there actually mothers *for* tyranny? Well, other than mine?

Arranged on a bare wooden étagère was a collection of Native American artifacts. Mother strolled there and absently ran her slender finger around the intricate pattern carved into a shiny black bowl. Over her shoulder she said, "You're handling this so well, dear. Rising above the rumors."

Rumors? What rumors?

Anger stiffened Kathy's slack face. "They're not true."

I know you've seen what Mother can do on the screen, the way she conveys volumes with the barest of gestures. Well, she was equally effective in life. She gave one of her brows a skeptical lift and held it — until Kathy's head fell in defeat.

"People don't understand how it was with Ian and me. They think he sold out because of this." With a throw of her arms, Kathy indicated the expansive room, humble by choice not price. "They think he sold his soul. But *I* was Ian's soul. As long as he had me, he held on to his values."

Mother's nod convinced the agitated widow she understood. Which meant she knew more than I did. While it pained me to admit it, Mother was worming good stuff from Kathy. Maybe she'd pick up even more if I left. I faked a cough and said I needed a drink of water, and insisted I would get it myself. I wandered around till I found the kitchen.

The woman in the red suit stood before the sink, chopping an onion for a casserole in progress. Shouldn't the MATs be making food for the bereaved family? What kind of friends were they? The maid stopped chopping long enough to point the knife blade at the refrigerator when I asked for water. I yanked open the door of the big Sub-Zero, whose doors were covered with panels that matched the hand-carved, distressed pine cabinets, and I grasped a small bottle of Evian. While I sipped, I tried to hook the woman into conversation, but she wouldn't bite.

My vision drifted to the rough-hewn pine table at my elbow, where I saw some muddy ropes in yellow and blue that had been knotted together, along with some unusual aluminum clamps. Kathy had written her name on them in black ink. I'd seen ropes like that before, but I couldn't place what they were used for.

When I returned to the family room, the front door flew open and clusters of women blew into the house. The MATs no doubt. Mother made a tiny motion to indicate the door. I expressed our sympathies again, and we left.

I waited till we were alone in the Mercedes before saying, "Some delusion there, huh? Ian didn't sell his soul, he *bought* it. For the right price, Kathy provided it for him."

Mother nodded. "But maybe it had become too much of a burden for him. Surely you understood my exchange with her?"

I wouldn't admit it, but I didn't. Too bad my silence ratted me out.

"Tracy, where's your sense of subtlety? Ian was involved with another woman, one who didn't reflect the values Kathy wanted to believe he wouldn't abandon."

"How did you know that?" I cranked the engine but let the car idle.

"I didn't *know*, I guessed. And Kathy confirmed it. Now we have another suspect," Mother said. "Kathy wouldn't have killed him for his money. But rather than see him abandon his last hold on the beliefs they shared, she might have."

Outraged at being one-upped, I stared at her.

Mother didn't even try to control the superior twitch of her full red lips. "You're going to be glad you included me in this caper."

I threw my annoyance into shifting gears, causing the car to buck forward. I might be glad at that — but she'd never hear it from me.

CHAPTER EIGHT

Mother wanted to *"cherchez la femme,"* as she described it. The scent of scandal lured her. She wasn't too specific about where or how; filling in the details seemed to be my function. To Mother's annoyance, I insisted on returning home.

"Drew might be there now, already cleared of suspicion, for all we know," I said. "Unearthing the truth about Ian's dalliance would be someone else's problem then."

"Darling, wouldn't he have let you know?"

"How?" I demanded.

Like every other Angeleno, I did have a cell phone. Unfortunately, I'd mislaid it somewhere last week and hadn't had a chance to replace it. How do other people keep track of their stuff?

With a superior sigh, Mother took her own phone from the tiny white bag she carried. I should have thought of that. She was as attached to her cell phone as her nails were to her fingers. She placed several calls to my home number, but Vanessa let the machine get it every time.

When I groused about that, Mother said, "Be fair, Tracy. You didn't tell her to answer it."

"Doesn't she have any professional instincts? What if an emergency popped up on the Tour from Hell?"

Mother frowned at my description, but didn't rise to the bait. Once again I wished Philly hadn't gone off with Dad. I could always count on him to find the most amazing solutions to problems. If he was along now, he would probably con some operator into giving our phone such a unique ring, Vanessa wouldn't be able to resist answering it. But since he wasn't here, I had to wait till I arrived home to find what I needed to know.

Once there, I threw open the door and raced down the hall. The décor of the sprawling living room was one of the least objectionable in the place, if you could overlook the slick '60s feel to it. The rear wall was glass and looked out over the flashy Art Deco pool and the craggy sandstone hills behind it. A baby grand piano filled one corner, and clusters of white woven sofas and brass-and-glass tables were scattered through the rest of the space, along with the occasional black leather chair.

Too bad that one semi-tasteful room had also become the repository of all the atrocious decorating samples Mother had been foisting on us for weeks. Every seat, every table and most of the floor space was given over to ugly wallpaper patterns, paint charts in putrid colors, and samples of tiles destined to be sold off in outlet stores.

Worse still, Mother, the last one in the world to discover Post-it notes, had embraced those little slips with a vengeance. Post-its in a rainbow of colors, Post-its stuck to other Post-its, filled with her rambling, hand-written opinions, had been attached to all those decorating samples. As if I didn't get enough of that right from the horse's mouth.

Vanessa had cleared enough room for her own wide behind on the sofa before the TV armoire. I shoved more wallpaper sheets aside so I could sit next to her. Unfortunately, by toppling the pile, I sent one sample that I'd hidden in the middle of the stack to the floor, where it was displayed now in all its vile glory. The Post-it on that swirling freeform pattern in a collection of browns indicated it would be ideal for the powder room, though frankly, I thought it looked like what you go in there to do.

"Is Drew here, Vanessa?" I demanded breathlessly.

Vanessa's big doll eyes drifted away from the TV. "Tracy, don't you remember? Drew left with the police." She half-hid the sigh my stupidity seemed to warrant.

I tried counting to ten, but Vanessa kept making me start the count from scratch.

"Boy, the phone hasn't stopped ringing since you left." Her big empty eyes flashed with annoyance.

Before I could hit her, Mother slipped between and asked Vanessa what she had been doing.

"Monitoring the news, just as you told me, Martha," Vanessa

assured her.

So why was my TV tuned to a soap opera? That might be the fitting setting for my life, but we wouldn't learn what happened to Drew there. Why was his questioning taking so long? I reached across Mother and grabbed the remote from Vanessa, but she snatched it back.

With a pout, Vanessa said, "Martha lets me work the remote."

I directed a scowl Mother's way, but she gave no indication she noticed, other than an amused tug at her mouth. Mother really liked it best when men fought over her, but in a pinch, other women, whole countries, dogs and even corpses would do. I refused to give her that satisfaction and just snapped for Vanessa to tune it to the *News!News!News!* station.

Vanessa was pretty quick with that remote, I noticed. *Find what you're good at and stick to it* — that's my motto. Too bad Vanessa hadn't discovered that remote-thing before she signed on to set up hellish talk show tours.

Considering the local *News!News!News!* had only appeared on our cable company's lineup in the last six months, it'd picked up a huge viewership. Mostly because its headliner show, the nightly *Nick Wick's Sin City,* gave juicy updates all day.

Once Vanessa tuned it, a pretty Asian woman appeared behind a shabby anchor desk that looked as if it had been fashioned from scrap motor home paneling. She aimed two rows of elegantly capped teeth at the camera and announced, "Now let's see what Nick Wickerson is working on for tonight's *Sin City.*"

Mother leaned forward, as she usually did when a good-looking young man promised to appear. While Nick Wickerson was neither as young nor attractive as her usual fantasy object, his cocky grin did give him a boyish look, which his short brush haircut enhanced. Yet he had to be over forty. His lean face was starting to sag, making him look like a frat boy with a hangover. What put me off, though, was the calculating expression in his cool gray eyes, which always seemed to be appraising whether you were buying what he was selling.

Nick Wick directed those scheming eyes at the camera, while

the word *Live* flashed on the screen. "Here's the latest on the murder of a prominent local attorney." His voice had a breathless quality, as if he'd just run into the studio to share his scoop.

"How can this guy investigate anything, when he's always in the studio doing these updates?" I snapped.

"Hush, Tracy." Mother ran her tongue along the bottom edge of her front teeth. "I've heard they pay the earth to their sources."

Naturally. Just because they chose not to waste money on sets, didn't mean they wouldn't spend it on the stuff that really dug up the dirt.

"This reporter has uncovered a witness who'll show the chief murder suspect, one of the attorneys on the Sullivan defense team, Andrew Cord Eaton, had been stalking his employer, murder victim Ian Dragger, for weeks before the murder." After a pregnant pause, Nick Wick went on with, "For more on this story, tune in tonight to *Sin City.*"

Mother took the remote from Vanessa and snapped it off. "I don't think I like that young man anymore."

A first for her. Drew should feel flattered. "That's just stupid. Drew wasn't stalking Ian, for chrissakes, they worked together. If I know Drew, he was keeping out of Ian's way." But did I know him? Smashing Ian's nose wasn't how to keep a low profile.

Vanessa took back the floating remote. "Now that's why I prefer *Scarlet Stories.* They don't wreck people's lives by accusing them of nasty stuff like murders."

"No, just by exposing their affairs," I said. "Much better."

"*Scarlet Stories* is serious investigative journalism," a testy Vanessa insisted.

"Really, Vanessa," Mother said, as I snapped, "Get out."

But at least *Scarlet Stories* wouldn't be trashing Drew. While their taped tabloid reports aired at night, in the afternoon, *Scarlet Stories* ran reruns.

Only not today. A live broadcast was underway when Vanessa switched the channel.

"...today's special show," the anchor, Lorna Larson, announced.

While Nick Wick seemed the quintessential contemporary guy, former actress turned trash anchor, Lorna Larson, looked more like a throwback to the forties. She wore her auburn hair in the old-fashioned pageboy Mother had once made famous. Her classic body-hugging dress was also of the same era, though the body beneath that green dress, with its gym-sculpted arms and grapefruit-sized breast implants, was strictly today's.

I had to hand it to Lorna in one respect. While Nick Wick always seemed to be checking whether you noticed yet that he'd picked your pocket — Lorna managed to give the impression to the thousands of woman on the other side of the camera, that you were just a pair of girlfriends getting together to trash another friend. For once I was grateful for the show. As tacky as it was, the *Scarlet Stories* format wouldn't lend itself to taking a stab at Drew, the way *Sin City's* did.

Wrong again. When would I learn?

Lorna gave her sleek head a seductive tilt. "Today we're taking an in-depth look at the background of murder suspect and celebrity son-in-law, Andrew Eaton. Here's my special report."

I groaned. A tape began to roll that showed Lorna slowly strolling down what looked like the corridor in an office suite. "We're here to visit an earlier victim of Mr. Eaton's callousness." She paused at a doorway, and then entered an office. A law office, judging by the spines of the books caught by the camera. "Meet Drew Eaton's victim of the heart, Los Angeles County Assistant District Attorney, CeeCee Payne."

"Crap! It's The Pain." That was my private name for Drew's former girlfriend.

The camera panned down to where CeeCee sat behind her desk. When she smiled for the camera, bringing her prominent cheekbones and pearly white teeth into focus, it was easy to see why juries usually let her have her way with them.

Mother's pouty lips twisted grudgingly. "She is a beautiful girl."

Well...almost. While she was as strong as a body-builder, CeeCee's tall form and ropy muscles made her look as lean as a model. I didn't feel too dumpy in comparison. Her best feature had to be her lustrous black hair, which was as shiny as polished coal and fell in waves to her shoulders. The only feature that robbed CeeCee of true beauty was her narrow hooded eyes. They were as dark as a moonless night, and just as impenetrable.

"Did he do it? Did Drew Eaton kill Ian Dragger?" Lorna asked in a breathy whisper.

Though CeeCee hesitated, her answer was strong enough when she finally delivered it. "Absolutely not. Drew doesn't have it in him to kill anyone. I'd be more likely to kill Ian Dragger. I'm the one he stole the Sullivan conviction from." The Pain laughed, an effortless jingle that reduced her suggestion to a joke.

"And yet Drew broke your heart, didn't he? When he severed your engagement and married the daughter of a pair of major motion picture stars?"

"The name, darling," Mother muttered to the screen. "Give them my name."

While Mother addressed the important concerns, Vanessa glared at me. "Tracy, you poached another woman's man?"

I kicked the poopy wallpaper. "It wasn't like that, dammit. They weren't engaged. They only had a few dates in college. I never even heard about her till just before Drew and I were married."

Mother turned away from the screen once she realized they weren't going to detour to her favorite subject. "Vanessa, you should have seen Tracy and Drew together at the start. As different as they were, they had such chemistry." With a satisfied sigh, she crossed her hands over her heart. "If only someone could have captured it on film."

Then it would have been real. But she was right about our chemistry. We met near the end of Drew's last year at Stanford Law School. He'd come along with his roommate when the guy came home to L.A. for the weekend. The roommate seemed a nice enough guy, but he didn't drive like any Angeleno I ever met. When he stopped at a crosswalk to let a little old man hobble across, naturally, I smashed into his bumper. Who could have predicted that he would stop?

But when we climbed from our cars to inspect the damage, while I noticed the roommate was attractive, it was Drew who had pushed my buttons.

Mother took Vanessa's large hand in her smaller one. "Tracy wisely told them she lost her insurance card, so they'd have to call her."

Wisely, right. I *had* lost it. I'd lose my head if it weren't attached.

"And she gave them my number, so the young men would meet Alec and me and be impressed with her family," Mother said.

Did she really believe that? I didn't *want* Drew to meet her, but I had no choice. I'd mislaid my phone bill and forgotten to pay it. The phone company shut off my service. Just like that — can you believe it? I had to give them my parents' number.

In those days I never wanted men to know I was their offspring. This was L.A., after all, where it sometimes seemed as if there are only two kinds of people: actors and actors who really want to direct. In intimate moments, guys were more likely to slip me their headshots than the tongue.

Granted, there was no chance of that with Drew. But it still amazed me that my parents didn't scare him off. He couldn't claim he didn't know what he was getting into.

"Ooh, Tracy, what a terrific story." Vanessa flushed a rosy shade that complemented her pink hair. "If only Raul would see that it could be that way for us."

Raul was Vanessa's guy-pal. He stopped by to see her enough evenings, but I guessed those visits never ended the way she hoped. I didn't know what they discussed when they pressed their heads together and whispered, but Raul always looked too serious to have romance on his mind.

The Pain's taped interview ended. *Scarlet Stories* switched to the live Lorna Larson, behind her studio anchor desk, where she promised more to come on this fast-breaking story. When the credits began to roll, Vanessa switched the channel in a flash.

"Let's get rid of this show. It's hurting Tracy," she said.

As if that horse hadn't bolted long before she shut the barn door.

I walked to the window and stared out at the pool. While searching the tiles for bloodstains, I kept hearing updates on Drew's situation as Vanessa surfed the channels, each more dramatic than the last.

I'd hated the media my whole life. Well, almost. When I was a toddler, my parents and I were featured in a spread in *Life* magazine, and the public's reaction turned my little head. Strangers called me "America's sweetheart." What's not to like? But in the years since I'd learned that the press always extracts a price many times the worth of whatever it gives, and when you least expect it.

The only good that had come from a lifetime of watching my parents dance to the media's quixotic tune was that I'd developed an intimate knowledge of how those bloodsuckers worked. The speed of all this reporting now struck me as strange. Sure, I'd expected the story to build, to feed the habit of a sensation-addicted population. But not *this* fast. I started to wonder whether there was someone powerful behind the scenes packaging and pushing it. But who would have that kind of power? And why had he targeted Drew?

CHAPTER NINE

M y observations about the speed of the news coverage spiked my anxiety into the stratosphere. But I gave up watching the TV coverage when the tabloid shows passed the baton off to the network news. Aging anchormen, awash in dignity, solemnly reported rumors that Nick Wick and *Scarlet Stories* had dug up.

Tapping my foot against the tile floor, I glared at one tanned somber face that stared out from the screen. "Slumming with tabloids was more fun when they were the scourge of journalism, not the vanguard," I announced to the world at large. Neither Mother nor Vanessa reacted.

Though crime scene tape still roped our knoll, without the cops there to enforce the barrier, the reporters outside became progressively bolder about crossing it. It didn't help that, as the afternoon wore on, Mother began taking their calls on her cell phone and waving to them from the front windows. She never misses the chance to beg the media to respect her privacy. Privacy — sure, that was what mattered most to her.

I wanted more elbow room than the cozy relationship she'd developed with the fourth estate would allow. Besides, for all she knew that caller could be Charlotte. Charlotte had given up on our house phone — her name hadn't shown up lately on the Caller ID. But she was crafty enough to call from, and to, another phone. Nothing diverted that woman; she was almost as persistently annoying as I was. Fortunately, Mother's attention span was shorter than the lifetime of a gnat. When the news anchor mentioned her name, that so stole her focus, I snatched her cell phone and returned it to her room.

I knew the reporters outside wouldn't leave until another story claimed their interest. But I could make it harder for them to approach the house. We kept the keys to all those junked vehicles on a ring hanging from a hook in the pantry. All except for the horse trailer key, which had its own ring. I grabbed the car keys and headed out the door.

They descended on me instantly, but I pushed through them. One-by-one, I shifted those cars until they had ringed the property more effectively than the crime scene tape, threatening life and limb of so many of those snoopy souls out there, I had my first laugh of the day.

With that accomplished, I stuffed the key ring into my pocket and escaped to my study. For my writing room, I'd chosen the round room perched atop the second floor, which Mother had once used as her office. I hopped up the winding metal staircase and zipped through the curved wooden doorway.

Originally, the entire room had been round, doorways and windows alike. But Dad had built a huge oak bookcase along one side of the circle to hide something Mother didn't want anyone to know about. I discovered what was hidden behind that bookcase by accident, and while I vowed never to tell anyone about it, I did tap the bookcase for luck whenever I came to the room to write. This time I blew it a kiss. I needed all the luck I could get.

I sat behind the small Scandinavian desk Mother had placed there years before, which my MacBook and printer nearly covered. While booting up the computer, I stared out the west-facing windows. The sun had moved well across the sky. How could Drew's questioning be taking so long? He didn't know anything.

To calm my frantic nerves, I decided to make some notes about Ian's murder. But other than what Mother learned from Kathy, I didn't know anything. Not the woman Ian had been seeing. Nor why he'd been riding Drew. And especially not the other people who might want Ian dead — judging by the way he treated subordinates, there must have been scores of them. Skippy and the DOLTs were the only ones I could say for certain had been thrilled with Ian, since he secured Skippy's acquittal.

My mind drifted off. I couldn't say how long my jaunt had taken, but when I came back, I noticed my fingers had involuntarily typed one word over-and-over across the screen:

CeeCeeCeeCeeCeeCeeCeeCeeCeeCeeCeeCeeCeeCee

Whoa! Was my subconscious having a little fun with my former rival? Or trying to tell me something? I remembered what The Pain had said in her *Scarlet Stories* interview. That she would have been more likely to have killed Ian than Drew. Was she toying with the interviewer? Or did I just *want* to believe she could be the killer?

I had to admit CeeCee cut a daring presence in the courtroom. But in life, she wasn't any more adventurous than Drew. The only bold move either of them had ever made was abandoning their place in New York society for life out here in L.A. Drew did it for me. CeeCee was already established in the Manhattan District Attorney's office when she chucked it all, after she'd divorced the husband she had married shortly after Drew and I got hitched.

When she first moved here, I felt sure she'd realized her marriage was a mistake and decided to try to win Drew back. But Mother, an expert on stealing other women's men, swore whatever ember once burned between CeeCee and Drew was long dead.

If The Pain had wanted him back, she would have given me a fight. She was a tough competitor — I had to grant her that. And that was why I didn't buy Drew's theory that CeeCee was such a pro, she didn't care about trial losses. Yet care so much about losing that she'd *kill* the opposing counsel — even I couldn't buy that.

Slow, heavy footsteps beat against the stairs outside the room. A moment later, Drew appeared in the doorway.

I rushed across the room and threw my arms around him. "Jeez, Drew, I didn't think you'd ever return."

He offered me a wan smile. "Babe, maybe you ought to operate on the premise that I won't."

Kidding, right? I slipped my arm around his waist and guided him to the couch. The smudges below his golden brown eyes looked so dark, it looked like he'd taken to using charcoal concealer.

"They have some kind of witness..." My voice trailed off. I didn't know how to tell him they thought he'd stalked Ian.

Drew ran his fingers through his hair. "The nail in the coffin." He spit out a dry laugh.

My gaze remained fixed on his face. He looked so lost, I couldn't believe I ever allowed myself to doubt him.

"Remember when I said I tried to be adventurous? That witness, Toby Newton, was the result. Skip was smart to target a cable station. Since they're locally franchised, actions taken against them result in local charges." Safe in the arena of legal mumbo-jumbo, Drew's voice, raspy from strain, took on a calm, disinterested tone. "But that cable company rented space from a radio station that had a small studio on the site, though it wasn't often used. I'd heard the radio station put an engineer out there that night and went to a live feed when DOLTs stormed the property."

I nodded to show I understood, even if I hadn't heard anything daring yet.

"I decided to talk to that engineer, to see if I could forestall any charges against Skip the FCC might bring."

"This Toby Newton-person?"

Drew nodded. "So I set up a meeting with Newton. Two meetings, actually. He stood me up the first time."

"And this was wild and crazy because…?" I asked.

"I told you, babe. It was my own investigation. Independent, like yours always are. Believe me, during a trial nothing happens without Ian's approval."

A meeting? *That* was what he considered reckless? If that was what he thought I'd do, he didn't know as much about my thought process as I feared. I'd have set up a meeting with the guy, too — but only to be sure he wouldn't be home when I shook down his house. To think I worried about forgetting to pursue this. It couldn't have had any bearing on our present crisis.

"We met in a coffee shop near his apartment in Studio City, attached to one of those funny motels," Drew continued.

He wasn't being silly. Some of the motels in that area displayed lodging schizophrenia. For years they'd been the kind of slummy dives that rent by the hour. Then some smartened up their exteriors and solicited the Universal Studios tourist trade. Yet they still maintained their adult business. I always wondered whether they had two sets of rooms and counted on their desk clerks to put visitors into the right ones. Did they ever get it wrong? Did the family folks ever wonder about the mirrored ceilings?

"Newton agreed to the meeting readily enough, but he tried playing it cagey when I got there. As if he suspected me of something nefarious." Drew's snort sounded outraged — ironic when you considered the mess he was in. "I assumed he was holding out for a payoff." He shrugged. "Well, he works for K-LIAR. What can you expect?"

K-LIAR was our pet name for KLR, the local shock talk radio station. Like most discerning people, Drew deplored their programming. Naturally, I only listened when they featured a top newsmaker. And when Drew wasn't around.

Drew crossed his arms over his chest and rubbed his own arms, as if to warm them, though it wasn't chilly. "The funny thing was Toby Newton wasn't good at securing a bribe. He leaked too much to me."

I slipped my arm over his shoulder and rubbed his tightened neck muscles. "Such as?"

"He confirmed that Skip and his pals never set foot on the radio portion of the property, which was what I wanted to hear. And he let me know someone spilled word of the DOLT assault to Nick Wickerson, who was waiting there in the radio broadcast booth with him."

"That's odd, since *Sin City* was one of Skippy's intended targets. Any idea who blabbed?"

Drew shook his head. "I assume one of the DOLTs told the radio station, and Toby Newton called Wickerson himself."

Mother said *Sin City* paid its sources well. If Toby collected something from Nick Wick, maybe he assumed everyone else would pay for information as well.

"And now he's claiming you stalked Ian. Because he was pissed that you didn't pay him?" I slumped forward till another thought perked me up. "But the cops let you go."

"Tracy, they're just getting their ducks in a row." He gently touched my nose with his fingertip.

"And what will they have then, besides orderly ducks?"

Drew's weary brown eyes found mine. "They'll have a murder charge."

Jeez, what a nightmare! The phone rang. I ignored it until static came through the built-in intercom beside the door. Intercoms had been installed in all the rooms when the place was built, but most didn't work anymore. Vanessa's voice, sounding far too excited for my taste, followed the electrical crackling. "Tracy, pick up the phone. It's the police, for Drew."

With a sigh, Drew rose and crossed to my desk, where he identified himself into the phone. He listened in silence until he concluded with, "Yes, I understand."

I sure didn't. I went to his side, but remembering how I'd typed CeeCee's name across the screen, I turned the laptop away.

Drew slowly hung up and turned to me. "I have an hour to turn myself in."

Now *that* was why I avoided the real world with everything I had. It was crazy out there. How did anyone survive facing that all the time?

The doorbell rang. Well, Frank Sinatra started wailing, "Fly Me to the Moon." Not a bad idea, actually. Our caller must have been stabbing the button, because the song kept starting over. Buddy began punctuating Frank's lines with his incessant barking.

"Doorbell," Mother called in a voice loud enough to project to the second balcony.

Weren't she and her pink-haired publicist closer to it? I stomped down the stairs.

When I passed by the living room, I shouted, "Nobody move."

Nobody did. Holy doomsday, Batman. Drew's whole life, and mine, was unraveling faster than we could gather the threads, but those lazy slugs couldn't tear themselves away from the idiot box.

Buddy danced at the door in joyous anticipation. He nudged me aside when I approached the door, as if he intended to open it himself.

"Tell me something, Buddy — when visitors come, are they ever here for you?"

But it was wrong of me to take my mood out on my loyal canine friend. The person on the other side of the door would make a better target. I grasped the brass doorknob, determined to dump all my fear and rage on whoever kept starting Frank's song. But I hesitated. What if our caller wasn't being obnoxious, but merely insistent? What if it was someone with information that would make things even worse?

Impossible. Things couldn't get any worse.

When would I learn?

I threw the door open. My mother-in-law, Charlotte, stood on the doorstep.

Now things really couldn't get any worse.

CHAPTER TEN

S tanding on my doorstep, Charlotte looked like a warrior. Okay, a middle-aged socialite warrior, but there was a militaristic suggestion to her ivory knit suit with its crisp navy braid and shiny brass buttons. And so much hair spray lacquered her chin-length, honey-blonde hair, it had to be as strong as a helmet. When she clapped the heels of her navy pumps together, I distinctly saw cannon fire flash in her stormy blue eyes.

Considering how tightly she had clamped her thin lips shut, it was a wonder she could speak without rupturing her jaw. "Tracy, since you didn't see fit to return my calls, I had no choice but to come and aid my son."

No fair. I figured with Caller ID and an answering machine, I'd finally nailed my telephone avoidance technique — and it still bit me in the ass. Bowing to the inevitable, I gestured for her to enter.

She charged in a few feet, unseeing initially. But that house was such a magnificent monstrosity, far less conventional types than Charlotte had run screaming from it. A brass wall sconce fashioned to look like a naked man who was...shall we say...really, really happy — finally pierced Charlotte's armor.

Her hand clutched at her heart. "Dear Lord, this is a chamber of horrors. Who would build such a place?"

At the other end of the hall, Mother stood with her hands on her hips. "*I* built it." There was something of the warrior about her, too.

"You!" Charlotte's voice dripped scorn. "I might have known."

Yowza! Watching those two square off against each other at opposite ends of the hall was like witnessing the showdown at the OK Corral. Female style. Which meant instead of the scent of rugged male sweat charging the air, expensive perfumes wafted at each other, warring for dominance.

Mother fired the first shot. "Bitch."

Charlotte shot back, "Crone." After holding Mother's glare for another moment, Charlotte gave her head a toss and turned away in an obvious attempt to rise above the bickering, now that she had the last word. "Tracy, I must see Drew."

Vanessa popped up behind Mother, peering over her head with undisguised curiosity.

"Drew is upstairs," I told Charlotte. "Vanessa, could you do the honors?"

Rushing faster than I'd ever seen her move, Vanessa appeared at Charlotte's side. "Ooh," she trilled, "it would be an honor."

Funny, she'd never before considered it such privilege to do my bidding.

Vanessa reached for Charlotte's arm. Charlotte took one look at that gawky pink-haired kid and veered away. But she couldn't outrun Vanessa's reach. Vanessa fixed her large hand around Charlotte's elbow and resolutely dragged her upstairs.

When I finally turned to shut the front door, I noticed a weary cab driver stood there. The poor slob must have parked way down the drive, beyond the car ring I'd established. Surrounding him was a mountain of well-seasoned brown tweed Hartman luggage that he must have carried there alone.

Please tell me visiting us was only her first stop on a round-the-world tour.

I told the cabby to drop Charlotte's bags in the foyer. Then I rushed to cut off Mother before she charged up the stairs after her nemesis.

When Mother finally stopped struggling she said, "Charlotte has had that bug up her ass so long, she's probably named it by now. Tracy, darling, you have terrible taste in in-laws."

What did she expect? Look at my taste in parents. "Can't you behave appropriately with her for once?" Since I wouldn't know appropriate behavior if it French-kissed me, maybe I wasn't the one to ask. But I'd be the one catching the blows if they started swinging at each other.

"You want appropriate, Tracy? Fine. The black eye I gave her at your wedding was nothing. This time, I'll probably have to kill her,"

Mother said with cheerful anticipation.

And people say she has no sense of proportion.

The minutes of the hour allotted to Drew ticked away. But neither he nor his mother — nor even nosy Vanessa — emerged from their meeting upstairs.

When I couldn't stand not knowing what was happening any longer, I grabbed a couple of Charlotte's smaller bags and dragged them upstairs. But I found Drew alone in our bedroom, slumped at the end of the big purple bed.

I forced a smile. "Bet your mother had something to say about this room, huh, Drew?"

Joining me in denial, a ghost of a grin flickered on his face, deepening his dimples. "She said this place would give her brain damage."

Not if she left very, very quickly. "Where is she?" I heard Vanessa's giggle through the closed door opposite our room. "You gave her the room across the hall? Drew, that's the chalkboard room."

He shrugged indifferently. "Would you rather I put her closer to Martha?"

I'd rather they send Charlotte to jail instead of him. "I can only barely tolerate having my own mother here. Now —"

Still avoiding his problem, Drew embraced a new line of conversation. "That's not true anymore. You're getting along with Martha awfully well."

"Bite your tongue."

Drew chuckled. "I thought having her around so much would make you crazy, but it hasn't. Even your cracks about her sound empty now."

Say it wasn't so! Had I thrown away thirty-four years of adolescent rebellion? Would I bond with Charlotte next? Somebody kill me.

"I don't know why you're fighting it, Trace. Your mother would follow you to hell. It's just that she'd claim she was leading."

"If we were going to hell, the Princess of Darkness would be leading," I muttered.

Drew grinned as if to say, *I told you so.*

I spotted the clock. "Drew, look at the time. You've got to go."

He gave his head an emphatic shake. "Mom asked me to wait till she made a phone call."

"Must be calling Taylor." Now real help would arrive. Taylor Eaton, Drew's father, was a corporate lawyer, not a criminal attorney. But he would be a better choice than Drew representing himself.

He shook his head no. "Dad's working in London, and Mom doesn't want him to know about my troubles. She has another idea."

I really didn't like the sound of that. "Drew, maybe you should let me —"

He began pacing between the lilac chaises. "Tracy, I told you that I learned my lesson. The unconventional route doesn't work for me. Mom's right — the safe way is the only choice now."

The safe way, Charlotte's way, was to never make waves. Couldn't he see that was the path to prison?

Charlotte's door flew open. As she marched across the hall, she wiped frantically at her suit sleeves. Despite Drew's problems, I nearly cracked up. The walls of that guestroom were blackboards. Mother had always put artists in there and provided them with pastel chalk. Though nothing had rubbed off on her, I knew that, given her penchant for neatness, she couldn't tolerate being around anything as dusty as chalk. While savoring the sight of her anxiously rubbing at invisible spots, I amused myself with the fantasy that my prissy mother-in-law had the D.T.'s.

When Drew asked her for an update, while Charlotte's lips pinched together in mean-spirited scorn, triumph glinted in her eyes. Vanessa came to stand behind her like some unconventional honor guard. I noticed the kid's expression looked oddly reflective of Charlotte's. Was she mocking Drew's mother? That generally called for more between the ears than Vanessa seemed to carry.

"We fixed it," Charlotte announced, beaming at Vanessa.

Now that was so unfair. I, with my perfectly normal appearance, had always been too much of a maverick for Charlotte. But the pink-haired dunce was okay?

Then Charlotte dropped her bombshell. "I called CeeCee."

The Pain? She was an Assistant District Attorney. I leaped to the only possible conclusion. "You got them to drop the charges?"

Charlotte's nose wrinkled in annoyance at my distraction. "I convinced CeeCee to leave the D.A.'s office. She's agreed to defend Drew."

This day just kept getting better and better.

CHAPTER ELEVEN

I screamed, I pouted, I practically tore my hair out. But nothing I did budged Drew and his mother. They still insisted on hiring CeeCee to defend him. While not equally important, it was equally frustrating that every time I tried talking to him, Drew kept walking away.

"Drew, there are some great defense attorneys in this town. Pick one used to working on the defendant's side of the aisle," I insisted to his back.

"Prosecutors and defense attorneys are used to thinking from the opposing side. She'll be up to speed in no time," Drew said.

I'd prefer someone already up to speed.

"Besides, CeeCee's a great lawyer. She had her pick of top firms when she graduated from law school. Firms are still always trying to recruit her."

"Are you nuts?" I spun him around to face me. "She *lost* the Sullivan trial, after the guy committed the crime on TV. How bad does that make her?"

A flicker of doubt surfaced in Drew's eyes, but it vanished so fast, I wondered if I imagined it. "Juries are unpredictable. Every lawyer has a loss like the Sullivan trial. But CeeCee's record is one of the best."

I couldn't believe this. I thought I was supposed to be the crazy one. "What does this mean for her? It's just a temporary leave, right?"

"No, that's what I suggested, but the D.A. vetoed it," Charlotte said. "Conflict of interest or some such thing."

"She'll never be able to go back?" I asked.

Drew snorted. "Not under this D.A., that's for sure."

The impact on CeeCee's career stunned me as much as their choosing her. Sure, lots of prosecutors did abandon the public sphere for the private side, but CeeCee always seemed rooted there. Maybe she'd already planned to make the move, and Charlotte's request simply provided the springboard. Still, I'd feel better if Drew's wasn't her training case.

Drew took my arm and gently led me away from his mother. He'd never been able to stand up to his parents. No matter how many times I stretched the umbilical cord, it always snapped back.

"Tracy, you always want me to understand how your family operates. Now I need you to see what's right for me and mine. CeeCee is like us. We're already ahead of the curve working with someone who sees things the same way." He shrugged. "It's decided, babe."

My heart contracted.

"Well, at least I can help —" I sputtered

"Tracy, it's better that you leave the decisions to CeeCee, Mom and me."

No! Was I losing him? What was happening here?

I peered around an orange Post-it note stuck to one of the upstairs windows, on which Mother had written, "Wash me," to watch the scene down in the driveway. Garcia charged up the drive. Backing her up were two beefy deputies who wore the beige Sheriff's Department uniforms along with expressions so menacing, if we had a tree out front, they probably would have strung him up right there.

CeeCee arrived shortly thereafter. With her stylish black suit and white blouse mirroring her dark hair and pale skin, she managed to convey the impression that she was both correct and dramatic.

Charlotte couldn't stop hugging CeeCee. You'd think her son had been released from custody, rather than taken into it. Actually, Drew's greeting to CeeCee seemed to go on awfully long, too. Was that why their hiring her bothered me? Did I fear her correctness would appeal to him now?

No, I wasn't threatened. Really. Drew had known my take on life since I rammed his roommate's bumper. And he'd made a commitment to me. There was nothing at all hesitant in the passionate kiss he gave me before he went downstairs to surrender to the cops.

But he had shut me out of his defense team.

CeeCee caught sight of me at the window. She pointed at me, and then at the front door, as if she wanted me to come down. By the time I made it there, she was already in our entry, waiting.

CeeCee lit into me instantly. "I've heard about your little detective games, but you won't be playing them this time. This is *my* case, and we'll do it my way. Understood?"

For Drew's sake, I nodded. For my own, I said, "Sure thing, ClaraClara."

Steam practically pumped from CeeCee's ears. "How many times do I have to tell you? My name is *CeeCee*. Why do you always call me something else?"

That's what I did. I've called her by thousands of names starting with "C," all repeated twice. "Because no one is actually named something as insipid as CeeCee," I insisted. Though it actually was typical of the stupid nicknames the old rich give their debutantes to distinguish them from the hoi polloi.

"I've told you a thousand times, I was named for my grandmother." In anger, The Pain's voice took on the blueblood accent she muted before juries. "Her name was Cee."

"And what? When the hospital asked your mom what she was calling you, she hiccupped?"

CeeCee shrieked in frustration. "You're so obnoxious, Tracy. Have you ever taken anything seriously?"

"My husband is about to be arrested for murder — I'd say that's pretty serious. Some people handle stress with jokes."

"At other people's expense?" The Pain demanded.

Well, yeah. That was the only way it worked.

With no warning, she shoved me against the wall. "Listen, you spoiled little interloper. He needs me this time. *Me* — his life depends on it." With a toss of her black hair, she took a step back. "If the truth be told, he always did."

She turned and went out, slamming the door behind her.

I crept to the faux Frank Lloyd Wright panel next to the door and looked through the clear parts of the colorful geometric design. With a shudder that passed through her trim shoulders, The Pain reached into her black Chanel bag. She extracted a tiny Gucci container that looked like a slim cigarette case. The case actually held a small bottle of hand sanitizer. She squeezed a glop of the stuff into one palm and vigorously rubbed her hands. Who knew I was so catchy?

When Garcia ambled over to her, CeeCee reached into her purse again. After pawing through it, she searched the ground at her feet.

"Anyone see a Louis Vuitton card case?" she called.

Apparently, nobody did. Chanel, Gucci, Vuitton — not too shallow. I thought I was the one from the *nouveau riche* family.

"First my extra keys, and now my card case," I heard her mutter.

"Maybe you got a stalker," one of the deputies joked.

Yeah, and maybe pigs break-dance. Even snotwad stalkers have standards. I continued watching even after a beefy detective dragged a handcuffed Drew to a patrol car down the road, and took him away. And when CeeCee climbed into her slate blue BMW and followed along behind it. I stopped watching when Charlotte and Vanessa continued waving to the departing vehicles, arm-in-arm. What the hell was that all about?

I stomped back to the staircase, where I found Mother seated a few steps from the bottom.

"I might have been wrong about that young woman's intentions," she said. "It's possible that she'll save Drew's life — while destroying yours."

"I can't worry about that now. Drew's all that matters."

"So you're leaving his fate in the hands of woman who could be defeated by — Skippy Sullivan?" She made a disgusted sound. "You know what I've always taught you, Tracy. There are two kinds of people in this world, the ones who follow the rules, and those who break them."

That's what it always came down to, following the herd or cutting your own trail. "No, Mother, I'm not leaving Drew's fate to anyone. *I'm* going to save him."

"Need any help?"

I gave her a sharp look. But I did need someone. That was why I considered the idea of our joining forces. The *only* reason, I swear. Drew was wrong. We weren't — God help me — *bonding.*

"You volunteering?" I asked.

Mother's beautiful face flushed a deeper rose than any I remembered back when she had hot flashes. She thrust her fists into the air in triumph. "Yes! Murder really is my beat now. I'm a detective, just like you, darling."

I must have been demented.

CHAPTER TWELVE

They arraigned Drew the following morning, and he almost had to face it without me. Somehow, as The Pain prepared for it, neither she nor Charlotte thought to tell me.

I'd been alone in my room, planning our investigation, when Mother burst in, waving a note Vanessa left saying she'd be accompanying Charlotte to Drew's court appearance. The time must have also been mentioned, since when Mother looked her watch, she shouted, "Now! It's almost time."

Though I wore the baggy yellow sweats I'd put on when I awoke, there was no time to change. We left the house at a gallop. Mother's a crazy driver, so it only made sense for her to take the wheel. But traffic between my country home and the Malibu Courthouse was brutal, and it was only because she drove on the freeway shoulders that we made it there in good time. The shoulders were totally open. Why doesn't anyone else use them?

Yet for all that rushing, we burst through the courtroom door just as it was decided. No bail, the judge decreed. Drew, in his orange jailhouse jumpsuit, still stood at the defense table with CeeCee, but a deputy came to his side to lead him away.

The noise we made with our chaotic entry drew everyone's attention and brought things to a halt. Vanessa sent off a cheerful wave, and Charlotte hastily looked away. My gaze went to Drew. Though dejection weighed down shoulders, his face took on such a glow at the sight of me, it looked like the sun suddenly found it. Tears stung my eyes.

Then I noticed the frowning judge on the bench. He was an aging man, with a bristly salt-and-pepper comb-over that looked like a raccoon had climbed onto his head and died. He scowled at the interruption to his proceedings and reached for his gavel — until he recognized Mother. With a flush, he sat up straighter.

"Ladies and gentlemen, we have a celebrity in our midst. Martha

Collins, the actress." In a show of vanity, he gave the dead animal a
pat. "Miss Collins, what's brought you to my courtroom today?"

Mother went into an award-caliber performance, simultaneously
conveying touching humility and the subtle idea that she found the
judge hot. "Your Honor, the defendant, Andrew Eaton, is my son-in-
law. An innocent man, I swear to you."

"And who is this young woman with you?" he asked of me.

Mother looked at me, clearly only noticing my clothes for the
first time. She — Chanel Suit; me — saggy sweats. She turned back
to the judge and said, "My maid."

I wasn't even mad. She was trying with all she had to save
Drew.

"Your Honor, can't you find it in your heart to let us take him
home?"

When he issued the bad news, it was in a most courtly manner.
"My dear, not even for you."

Drew sent me one last futile smile before the deputy led him
through the prisoner door. It was only then that I saw the spite on
CeeCee's angry, pinched face.

Once we arrived back home, I did enjoy a bit of revenge when I noticed
both Vanessa's car and the horse trailer were missing. Charlotte and
Vanessa must have decided to go in separate cars, only Charlotte
didn't have one. I bet that pink-haired traitor showed her where we
kept the keys for the junked cars and told her to help herself. But
after shifting the cars around outside, I'd forgotten to remove the
ring with most of the keys from my pocket. All they would have
found was the key for the horse trailer. Still, not even the image of
Charlotte maneuvering that land boat through crowded streets was
enough to lighten my furor. I promised myself, before this case was
over, CeeCee and Charlotte and I were gonna rumble.

Fortunately for Charlotte, I had attained that Zen plateau before
she toddled on back to our waiting arms. Sitting at the table, still in
my yellow sweats, I probably looked like a giant, vindictive banana,
but I didn't care. Charlotte strode into the room and promptly tripped

on one of Harri's fuzzy catnip mice.

Holding it up by the tip of its chewed leather tail, Charlotte regarded the toy as if it were as vile as the real thing. "Does this belong here? I think not."

So...what? The cracker crumbs Buddy had left were going to object? "She's a cat, Charlotte. She doesn't pick up after herself." Since not all those crumbs appeared to be today's, I shrugged. "Hell, neither do I."

"You should, Tracy. Sloppiness is a slippery slope."

The only kind I liked.

Charlotte absently held the filthy mouse, her hand hovering midair, forgotten. Her bearing seemed even more rigid than usual. She wasn't sure what kind of reception she'd find here after what she did.

"Tracy, dear, I don't suppose you know where to find keys to the other cars?" she asked. "That vile horse trailer is quite impossible."

Tell me about it. As if the shaky wheels weren't bad enough, it smelled like a manure plant. Too bad Charlotte had picked such an awful time to ask for my help.

I shook my head and said with a clear lack of sincerity, "You know me, Charlotte. I keep sliding down that sloppy slope. But we're all forgetful now, aren't we?" I held her glance long enough to let her know what I thought about her particular memory lapse.

Charlotte noticed she still held Harri's stinky little mouse, and with a squeak of disgust, she flung it away. She affected a cheerful manner and breezed over to the table, where she took the chair by Mother's abandoned coffee cup.

"As you saw, the arraignment went off without a hitch," she said.

Wouldn't a hitch have been a good thing? With her gaze cast down at the table, Charlotte absently drew Mother's cup and saucer to her and lifted it to her lips. I thought about warning her, but why should I? I had to bite my tongue to keep from laughing when I saw Mother's scarlet lip print over the gold rim on one side of the cup, as Charlotte left her coral lipstick on the other. I waited for Charlotte to notice the coffee was cold, as well as devoid of her usual sugar and cream, but she didn't.

"Tracy, it was wrong of...CeeCee...not to tell you about the arraignment."

Right, it was all The Pain's fault.

"But I'm going to CeeCee's apartment shortly, to discuss defense strategy. Would you like to come?"

I'd sooner lick the cracker crumbs Buddy left on the floor. Besides, Drew made it clear what he thought of my involvement. That still felt like a knife twisting in my heart. I turned it around on CeeCee.

"Why is she working from home? I thought she joined a firm." That much Charlotte had told me last night. One of the many prestigious firms that Drew said kept courting her. I suppose she aligned herself with a firm to have access to a law library, staff and malpractice insurance. Drew might not sue her if she lost his case, but I'd hound her to the grave, by every means possible.

Charlotte frowned. "I don't know, but I'm sure CeeCee has her reasons," she went on, swiftly overriding her own apparent doubts.

Someone ought to remind CeeCee that she was supposed to be trying a capital case, not luxuriating in the Jacuzzi while the maid peeled her a grape.

"Would you like to come?" Charlotte's voice quivered worse than the horse trailer. It was killing her to ask.

If Drew's whole life didn't depend on what I could turn up, I'd have gone, just to see how long she could stand it.

Instead, I said, "I don't think your precious CeeCee likes me too well."

Charlotte choked on a little laugh. "Can you blame her? She was devastated when Drew broke their engagement to marry you."

I said, as I had many times before, "They weren't really engaged. They'd just gone out a few times."

"Yes, dear, they were. CeeCee had set the date."

Charlotte drew in more of the cold coffee. This time it dawned on her what she was drinking. She held it in her mouth, her face twisting with disgust, while she struggled with two impossible options: swallowing the vile sludge, or being thoroughly revolting and spitting it out.

Swallowing finally won out. I watched the repulsive cold coffee move through Charlotte's throat like a mouse through a snake. Then she spoiled her image of grace under pressure by seizing Mother's used paper napkin from the table and giving her lips a vigorous rub. When the napkin finally disappeared into Charlotte's fist, her exquisite poise was restored again. Of course, she'd spread her lipstick from ear-to-ear.

But I couldn't take any pleasure from her predicament. Her contention that Drew and CeeCee had planned to be married left me stunned. She was lying, or at least engaging in wishful thinking. The alternative was that Drew had purposefully deceived me, and I refused to believe that.

"No, you're wrong about that, Charlotte. Drew said —"

Charlotte clicked her tongue. "Tracy, have you learned nothing from your mother? Men lie. Sometimes they just want to protect us, but they do it with lies."

"Not Drew." He was simply incapable of fibbing, despite the fine example I kept setting for him.

"Drew is my son, and I love him. But he has downplayed his relationship with CeeCee." Charlotte sighed. "I'll prove it to you. Let's go to your computer and search *The Times'* archives. I'll show you the write-up on their engagement party."

So, it was true. She wouldn't take the charade this far. It was too easy to disprove. I'd look it up later, to be absolutely certain, but my gut already knew. Her forthright gaze met mine, more kindly than I expected. Yet that kindness did nothing to offset the sense of betrayal that ripped through my heart. It occurred to me to wonder if that was how Drew felt when I lied to him. Nah, he expected it from me.

"CeeCee was quite devastated when Drew broke it off with her," Charlotte repeated.

"And so were you," I said softly. It was just a guess, but that alone explained why she always treated me like road kill. Especially since I was so freakin' loveable.

A stab of disappointment that flashed in her deep blue eyes confirmed my suspicions. Charlotte's shrug attempted to deny it, however. "Oh, we had some plans, CeeCee and I. Since we share the same initial, I hoped to give her most of my monogrammed linen. How else would she be able to have such nice things? But my son's happiness matters more to me than that. It does."

If she said it enough, would it be true?

"Lucky for you, Tracy, you don't need my old things. You have your own mother to provide you with her...treasures." Though surrounding us was the showplace room in the house, other nightmarish settings must have flashed before Charlotte's eyes. She stiffened her neck and shoulders and seemed to be struggling to avoid shuddering.

And I *still* couldn't enjoy the spectacle, dammit, as another awful thought hit me. After a lifetime of fashioning myself into the un-Martha Collins, I had, as had my mother before me so often did, become the other woman. Would I hold my man as well?

Charlotte held the shared cup and saucer at arm's length, as if they were toxic waste. She rose and placed them in the sink, even though the dishwasher was just below it. While Charlotte had elevated neatness to a religion, she obviously thought she should be the general in her cleanliness holy war, and I the foot soldier. Too bad the closest thing we had to a maid here was too stunned by her husband's twisting of the truth to perform her function. Who would have thought equivocation would turn on *me?*

After Charlotte left, with a sigh, I rose and followed her out. I padded barefoot to the base of the stairs to go up and dress. But angry voices echoing against the staircase walls — Mother's and Charlotte's — stopped me. It was inevitable that they would tangle again, staying in the same house. But it surprised me that they met on this set of stairs. Hard as it was to believe, there were two staircases to the second story, because not all the rooms on that floor connected to each other. Mother designed it that way in case she had guests who didn't happen to be on speaking terms. Now what architect would think of that? For Mother to have run into Charlotte there meant she set out to ambush my mother-in-law.

"You decimator of family values," Charlotte shouted, her voice reeking of disdain.

Mother's triumphant laugh echoed loudly. "Hah! It's your child, not mine, who's in the slammer."

"And what put him there if not the effect your daughter's antics have had on him?"

Sure, it was my fault that he punched Ian. Charlotte was pissing me off again.

"You nasty old bitch," Charlotte shrieked. "Don't think I've forgotten I owe you a black eye."

I walked away before I did something I'd regret, like joining the fracas. Mother might be able to get away with tangling with her, but if I did what I felt like doing, I'd destroy whatever future I might have with Drew. However satisfying I'd find knocking Charlotte on her prissy little can.

I decided to kill a few minutes in the room I intend to make into the library. A huge stone fountain filled the center of the room and big fluffy floor pillows substituted for furnishings. When Mother lived in this house, she called that her meditation room. Dad insisted it was actually where she and her friends smoked dope. Not your mother's kind of library maybe, but definitely mine.

I heard the water gurgling through the fountain when I neared it in the hall. Though it operated electrically with a flip of a switch, I never turned it on. Who was in there? I approached the wide double doors at an angle.

Raul, Vanessa's friend, sat erect on one of the pillows. He was a tall man, several inches over Vanessa's own towering height, with a black ponytail that trailed down his back, and dark smoldering eyes. But his unrelenting nervous energy made him far leaner than his girlfriend-wannabe. He always wore '50s retro clothing, but in such an offhanded way, I wondered whether he chose them to be cool, or if they were simply what someone had left in his closet. On his hands were the faint scars made when a dermatologist burned off gang tattoos. He held those hands out before him, film frame style, in two facing Ls.

The water in the fountain sputtered like Mt. Vesuvius, and the shouting in the stairwell blended with the noise from the TV, still blaring in the living room. Despite all the hullabaloo, I thought I heard Vanessa say, "Raul, you can't ask me to wear that."

Raul's deeper voice rose above it all. "Sweetcakes, it's not going to happen if you don't put it on."

Shouldn't that have been the woman's line? What were they talking about — it couldn't have been what I thought. But no wonder Vanessa turned the fountain on. She didn't want anyone overhearing this conversation.

I wanted to inch closer so I didn't miss a thing. Curiosity had always ruled my life, but lately, what else did I have? Only the argument in the stairwell spiked in volume, drawing my attention in that direction. My ears felt like yo-yos.

"You want to do *me* a favor?" Charlotte's voice rose to such a shrill, it should have attracted dogs. "That's a joke."

So why wasn't anyone laughing?

When I turned my head to see whether Mother would finally kick Charlotte down the stairs, I caught sight of a man ducking into the pool house outside.

Damn those reporters. Why did they think I parked those cars around the property, if it wasn't to keep them out? With my frustration so far past the detonation point, I felt myself propelled in the direction of that uninvited guest. I might not be able to be able to hit my mother-in-law, but thankfully, someone else was asking for a pounding.

Chapter Thirteen

The intruder had left the door to the pool house open. I stepped into the doorway, but the interior was too shadowy to see. There was a big picture window in that room, but it hadn't been washed in decades. That dirt blocked more light than blindness. When the maid finished loading the dishwasher, she could get started on those windows.

Once my eyes adjusted, I made out ancient wrought iron furniture stacked against one wall. Piled high on a rotting, white rattan sofa were stacks of faded navy-and-white stripped cushions. This was the first time I'd really looked at those cushions. Apart from the fact that both were striped, the pattern didn't match the hammock the police found here. The cops had to know they couldn't link that hammock to us. What else had they found that proved to be so damaging to Drew?

I didn't see our visitor, but he couldn't have left. "How long do you want to play this stupid game?" I shouted. "Believe me, I won't quit before you do."

Precisely how stubborn I could be must have been clear in my voice. When a man stepped into the light, I saw it was Nick Wickerson.

"Listen to me, Mr. Tabloid Trash — get outta here now, or I'll shoot you for trespassing."

He must have believed it. When I stepped aside to let him pass, he moved pretty quickly. I love it when people consider me a dangerous character. Wickerson's tan corduroy jacket and blue denim shirt were the same as what he'd worn on the screen when he did an update earlier today. Below them he had on jeans and running shoes. And I always imagined anchors delivered the news in their B.V.D.'s.

"Snooping in my pool house was so important, you were willing to climb over all those cars to get to it?" I asked.

Wickerson's flickering grin looked more like a muscle twitch. "I didn't climb anything but a lot of hills. I came in the back way. I grew up out here; I know all these trails. My folks didn't move till I was in law school."

Another lawyer? Didn't anyone but Drew actually want to practice law anymore? Still, it was good to know that when the Bar Association defrocked him, Drew could follow Nick Wick's career path, even if it did mean a long slide down the food chain. And let's face it, most people don't rank lawyers that high.

Wickerson stuffed his hands deep into his pockets and strolled to the side of the pool, where he stared into the water. The set of his thin mouth looked awfully smug. I wondered whether he really knew something I didn't. I remembered my impression that someone was behind the coverage of Drew's arrest, fueling it like a raging inferno.

Taking a wild stab, I said, "What's up, Wick? You couldn't resist returning to the scene of your crime?"

He feigned shock. *"Mine?* Why would I kill Ian Dragger?"

Was he protesting too much? "Ian gave you quite a grilling on the stand."

Pure grandstanding on Ian's part, too. It surprised me that the judge allowed it. By showing how tacky some of the tabloid shows were, how did that change what Skippy and the DOLTs did at the *Scarlet Stories* show?

Wickerson scooped up some gravel that the wind had deposited near the pool. The nervy jerk proceeded to skip those stones over the surface of the water. "I couldn't buy publicity that good," he said. "I should have paid Dragger for it."

Had he? Did they bicker over price? A sound from the living room attracted my attention. I looked through the window into the house. The noise had come from the TV, where Wickerson appeared on the screen, dressed as now, doing another update. The word, *Live,* flashed in the corner.

I pointed at the television. "Look, you have an evil twin."

His steely gray eyes bore into mine. "Don't kid yourself, lady. I am my evil twin."

Yeah, I was getting that idea.

"But that says it's live," I insisted.

With an exaggerated snort, he said, "Do you believe everything you see on TV? I thought you were a show biz brat?"

Embarrassing maybe for a card-carrying cynic like me, but I did believe what I saw on the tube. When I was a kid, I thought we were the only ones not like those sitcom families, and I yearned for that normalcy. But then I met Drew's family and gave thanks for the reprieve.

"Cheesy set," I said to shift the attention away from me. *"News!News!News!* can't do better?"

This time, he kicked a stone into my pool. "It's just a start. I'm headed to the top. I want to go all the way."

"Hey, pal, I want to be called to dinner a dozen times a day, but that doesn't mean it'll happen."

Those shifty gray eyes frisked me. "Funny, you'd never guess that. The difference is — your man's gonna get me what I want."

I put my fists on my hips — which were only five pounds over my smoking weight, I wanted it known. "How 'bout if he's not guilty?"

A smirk stole over his pale, tight lips, which failed to touch his sharp, unsmiling eyes. "What does guilt have to do with it?"

With no more than a nod of dismissal, he started back to the trail that led off the knoll. I stopped him by shouting, "Hey, Wick. Did you leave the law because it had too many rules? Because in television, anything goes?"

"Don't kid yourself. Anything goes anywhere — if you're smart enough to make it stick."

That had always been my motto, too — I just didn't want him sticking it to Drew.

I watched Wickerson leave and kept staring after him until he had disappeared behind another ridge. But a thought occurred to me. I rushed to the spot where he'd left. The ground dropped sharply there, and I could make out the pattern of soles where he had jumped down to the trail. Then I raced to the reverse side of the knoll, where the cops said Ian's killer had made his approach. The soles of patterned sport shoes had made marks there, too. Were the two sets of prints made by the same shoes?

Bummed not only by my lack of progress, but my failure to punch out Wick's lights, I returned to the living room. Vanessa was there now, stretched out on one of the couches before the tube, having pushed so many decorating samples to the floor that it looked like a bad taste minefield. She wore a taupe print granny dress, but she'd added a silly little rose silk flower to her dress's shawl collar.

"Have a nice visit with Raul?" I asked.

Vanessa's empty doll eyes widened more than usual. "Raul wasn't here."

Huh? What was she trying to pull? Man, even dumbbells were leading me around by the nose now.

To get back at her, I pointed at that stupid thing pinned on her dress. "Nice flower," I said. But who was I kidding? Vanessa never picked up on sarcasm.

To my surprise, she flushed an even brighter shade than the flower and covered it with her hand.

What the hell was that about? I heard the sound of heels tapping against the floor, and Charlotte appeared in the doorway. No sign of a shiner; Mother was slipping.

Charlotte glanced at the glass Parson's table at her side, with its dust-dulled surface. Her nose twitched in disgust. She pressed one finger to the dusty surface and held it out to me.

"Charlotte, the cleaning lady comes on Monday." At age seven, I had an imaginary friend, but an imaginary maid seemed more useful now.

Charlotte clamped her coral lips together in disapproval. "Not soon enough, Tracy, dear. I'd love to see this place cleaned before I return this afternoon."

I'd love a belt of Tequila. Something told me we were both about to suffer a grave disappointment.

Charlotte gave her honey-blonde helmet a regal bow in Vanessa's direction. "Are you coming, Vanessa, dear?" she asked.

Vanessa jumped to her feet faster than I'd ever seen her move. "Yes, Charlotte," Vanessa gushed.

I waited until that odd duo left for CeeCee's place before mocking Vanessa's "Yes, Charlotte." Then I dashed upstairs to make a call and to change. Since my encounter with Wick ate up more time than I thought, I just threw on some clothes I'd tossed on one of the bedroom's chaise lounges a couple of days earlier.

To my surprise, since she only had a few hours' head start, Mother beat me downstairs. She'd changed into a ruffled silk dress in a retina-scalding Kelly green. While its flared skirt chastely skimmed her knees, the neckline practically plunged to her waist. No way did her impressive rack stand that high naturally at her age. But there was a reason why, to the plastic surgeons of Beverly Hills, every day was Martha Collins Day. Of course, given the choice, I'd prefer Mother's porn-queen look to Charlotte's neo-nun any time.

She'd coupled the dress with another one of those fedoras, a tan one this time. I expected her to go into another mystery author pose, but she just stared off, distracted.

She finally spotted me. "Good, darling, you're dressed."

Dressed? How could she say that? I was wearing the grubbies I'd worn to the SCREWED party. Those things had nearly given her a stroke at the time. Martha Collins, Fashion Police. Now they didn't trouble her. Who was this imposter?

While hunting for my mislaid purse, I blurted out the truth I'd learned about Drew and CeeCee.

With a martyred sigh, she said, "How could my child be so naïve? Of course, Drew was lying about CeeCee. Anyone could have seen that. Where did I go wrong?"

No, this was my mother, all right — the one who thought it was always about her.

She frowned, with no regard to the wrinkles that would cause. "But we're still going to save Drew, aren't we, darling?"

"You betcha," I snapped. And when I got my hands on him again, that liar was dead meat. It occurred to me to question why his mother wasn't also road kill. "What happened during your staircase brawl, Mother? Did Charlotte duck?" I mimed the jab Mother had used to knock Charlotte flat on her fanny at my wedding.

Mother briskly strode down the tiled hall toward the front door.

"I don't know what you're talking about, Tracy. Charlotte and I just had a little mother-to-mother discussion."

I snorted. "That's not what I heard."

"Then you didn't hear everything."

I stared after her in disbelief. Truly, I was the only sane one in the bunch.

Man, were we in trouble.

CHAPTER FOURTEEN

After parking in Drew's space in the SCREWED parking garage, we rode the elevator to the roach coach on the fifth floor. I'd arranged to meet someone there, but I hoped to run into other Slaughter, Cohen staff members as well.

Trying to look casual, I passed through the line before the salad case and selected a clear container filled with a slimy-looking pasta salad. Nodding at the selections, I said pointedly to Mother, "Don't you want to choose something?"

Squaring her shoulders as she might before a firing squad, she answered, "Not even for Drew." While I paid, she used her cell phone to order a spinach salad from a restaurant up the block. How arrogant was that?

"Give me that phone." I grabbed it from her hands. When a busboy pushed a wheeled trashcan past us, I hurled the cell phone into the garbage.

Mother narrowed her eyes. "You'll wish you dove in after it, when you need that phone, young lady. Tracy, do you ever think before you act?"

Thinking before you act — what a concept.

We snagged a corner table. While Mother drummed her fingers against the tabletop, I dove into my pasta salad. Those rubbery spirals might have looked as greasy as the Gulf of Alaska after the Valdez, but they tasted sharp enough to have been pickled in brine. Eating them would give me a permanent pucker.

I wondered whether I could add something to Mother's order, watching longingly as the busboy pushed the trashcan through a swinging door. But I'd die before I'd give her the satisfaction of admitting I goofed by tossing her phone.

I sensed we were being watched and lowered my head, while waiting for something to happen. I could feel when it did. The predatory creatures triangulated me, like wolves. Circled, like

vultures. But these beasts were hungrier than either of the others —
they were lawyers.

When a deliveryman in a jaunty penguin costume deposited
Mother's lunch, I stole a peek at our stalkers to determine their actual
identities. The two flunkies guarding our flanks, under the guise of
engaging in pointless conversations that wouldn't be billable, were
newer SCREWED associates. But the big gun dead center could be
useful, if I played it right.

John Dafford Duckman — or Daffy Duck, as I thought of him —
had been the chief back-stabber in Drew's class of associates. He was
older than the others, having already failed as an accountant when
he went to law school. Months earlier, he and Drew had both been
in contention for a single senior partner seat. Everyone gave Drew
the nod, until that unfortunate snafu of ours put one of SCREWED's
meal tickets in the slammer.

Beating Drew should have mellowed Daffy. Instead, it fueled
the intensity of his aggression. Since being elevated to the finance
committee, he challenged Drew's expenses relentlessly.

From the corner of my eye, I saw Daffy heading toward me.
Before he reached our table, however, someone swooped ahead of
him, plopping down a cardboard box. Roberta Corson, Ian's assistant.
Behind her back, everyone referred to Roberta as Robotic, since
she had run Ian's life and her own with mechanical precision. Only
the equipment seemed to be misfiring today. Clumps of her frizzy
ginger hair had pulled loose from her neat bun, and her reading
glasses, with their no-nonsense steel frames, had slipped too far
down her slim nose to be of use for anything other than pinching her
nostrils. At least Ian's death seemed to be hitting someone hard.

"Here you are, Tracy. All of Drew's things that I could find."
That had been my excuse for visiting. "There wasn't much left,
though. The police took nearly everything."

She wasn't exaggerating. Considering all the years Drew had
occupied that office, the box was nearly empty. There were some
office supplies, though fewer after Mother confiscated several
packets of sticky notes. Some of the funny desk toys I'd bought
to amuse him were still there, such as the voodoo doll I suggested

he name after Ian. Did the police care that he hadn't stuck a single pin in it? But his Rolodex was gone, dammit — naturally, the cops wouldn't have missed that. His extra suit of clothing was also absent, but the DOLT who'd been wearing Drew's shoes probably helped himself to the whole outfit. Even the photo of Drew wearing those clothes, which I'd snapped outside the courthouse, was missing; only its silver frame remained. The police couldn't possibly care about that picture. Maybe Daffy took it for dart practice.

Without waiting to be asked, Roberta slumped into a chair at our table. "I must tell you, Tracy, I question your hiring CeeCee Payne to defend Drew. Well, she is a senior deputy — I suppose her record is strong. But she rarely won against Ian. Of course, innocence has to be the best defense."

So naïve after that many years working in a law firm.

"I can't believe what they're saying about Drew." She brushed back her loose hair, but she failed to secure it, and it fell forward again. "But then, I can't believe Ian's dead, either. What do I know?"

That was what we were there to learn. "What do they have you doing now, Roberta?" I asked.

"Cleaning up Ian's records. There's so much to do, they've assigned Kenette to help me." Kenette Faulkner was Drew's secretary, the other assistant now lacking a boss. "Then I'll be working for a couple of the newer junior partners." She gave her head a swift shake that sent the clumps of hair swinging before her red-rimmed eyes. "It won't be the same. These young ones waste too much time."

Young ones? Scarcely forty, Roberta wasn't enough of a fossil to take that view. But she must have been born old. The way her shoulders rounded now beneath her black cardigan sweater did convey the impression of advancing years. Too determined to keep her nose pressed to the grindstone? Or had Ian just worn out the women around him?

For a moment, when she straightened her slouching shoulders, Roberta looked Robotic once more. "Ian was all business. He used to call in dictation when he ran on the treadmill at the gym at four-thirty in the morning."

Mother chuckled, before glancing at Roberta through lowered lashes. "Come now, darling. He wasn't *all* business lately."

Two red spots burned briefly on Roberta's flat cheekbones. "I don't know what you mean, Miss Collins."

I snorted. "Get off it, Roberta. Hadn't Ian made some entries in his calendar without your knowledge?" I guessed such a regimented man would even enter his trysts.

"What if he did?" Roberta leaped to her feet. She shoved the cardboard box closer to us. A distancing gesture? Then marched off, snapping over her shoulder, "Whatever Ian did in those times was business."

Yeah, monkey business.

Before Roberta had cleared the door, Daffy Duck dispensed with pretense and zipped to our table. "So *that's* what was going on. Ian's cash for expenses was always excessive, but never like during the Sullivan trial. Drew must have found out Ian had something on the side and was shaking him down." With a greasy grin, he leaned against the chair Roberta had vacated. "Kinda funny, though. You'd think Ian would have knocked off Drew, rather than the other way around. Guess Drew's not such a smart blackmailer."

I stole a glance at Mother. Just in time, too. She'd balanced my salad container on her palm and was no more than an instant away from hurling it at him.

I pinned her arm to the table, but I fired off something of my own. "He's smarter than an accountant who doesn't know when a theory doesn't add up."

"You should have let me throw the salad," Mother complained during our elevator ride to the lobby. "Then he'd have had a reason for sporting that oily grin."

"The concept of the last laugh has no meaning to you, does it?"

She chuckled softly. "I always thought he who laughs last — is simply the final one to get the joke."

"We can't afford to burn *all* the bridges to that firm." However satisfying it might be. Roberta had already told me the partners wouldn't welcome visits from me.

The elevator stopped and a couple of young guys in business suits entered. They seemed indistinguishable to me in their dark pinstripes, but Mother found one interesting enough to bat her eyes at. It never took much. And despite her age, he seemed to appreciate her plunging neckline. While they amused themselves, I thought through what we discovered upstairs.

Ian must have been paying blackmail to someone. How ironic that after chiding Drew with not being enough of a team player, he'd used the firm's funds to do it. It sounded like the hemorrhage had been sizeable, too. If Ian hadn't been the big money earner in the criminal department, the other partners wouldn't have allowed it. As it was, they'd obviously made Daffy Duck their watchdog.

When we reached the lobby, Mother waved good-bye to her new friend. I hooked my arm through hers and dragged her out the door. We were a half-block away before she realized we were headed away from the SCREWED garage, where we'd parked her car.

"Tracy, if you think I'm going to march around the block so you can take off one more ounce —"

I pulled her to a stop before an ice cream shop.

She gave her chin an arrogant lift. "I see — not taking it off, but putting more on. Really, darling."

While I pushed her through the door, she kept protesting she was lactose intolerant — extra pounds intolerant was more like it. Mother didn't shut up until she spied Kenette seated at the table farthest from the door.

Drew's assistant was a pixy of a girl, with red hair worn in a gamin style, huge moss green eyes, and a quick grin that seemed too wide for her little face.

The bigwigs at SCREWED had made noises about firing Kenette Faulkner once they learned she was a moonlighting actress. Knowing she was on borrowed time, Drew begged Mother to help her find acting work. Nothing came of the first audition Mother set up, but the director remembered how talented Kenette was and had recently cast her as the best friend of the star of a new sitcom. The show was scheduled to start shooting in less than three weeks. Kenette had been looking forward to giving her notice when Drew was arrested. Now she was holding off to help us from the inside.

Kenette took my hands in her small fingers and held them tightly. "Tracy, tell Drew how much I miss him. It's no fun there without him."

Drew was the fun guy? Man, that place was duller than I thought.

With her break half over, we quickly filled Kenette in on what we learned from Roberta and Daffy.

"An affair, huh?" she said. "I wouldn't have guessed that. But Kathy has been popping in a lot lately. Prior to the last few months, she and Ian always led such separate lives."

Poor Kathy. I felt rotten about the way I'd always searched for her clay feet.

"What do you need from me?" Kenette asked.

"Roberta said you were helping her to shut down Ian's office. Can you get a look at the entries he wrote in his calendar?" I asked.

"Won't be easy. Roberta guards Ian's calendar like it's a love letter." Kenette noticed the time and jumped to her feet. "But don't worry, Tracy, I'll find a way." With a quick hug for each of us, she sprinted out the door.

I bit my lip. "I hope she can do it. We need that woman's name — the one Ian had been sleeping with. As well as the person who had been bleeding him."

Mother stared through the window of the ice cream shop. When I followed her glance, I saw Roberta shuffling past on the sidewalk, staggering under the weight of three cardboard boxes that looked like the one she'd used to pack Drew's things. A black Lincoln Town Car, of the sort the car services use, double-parked in the street. A driver in a dark suit leaped from the car. While he loaded Roberta's boxes into the trunk, Roberta threw furtive looks back in the direction of the SCREWED building.

With a knowing grin, Mother asked, "What makes you think they're not one-and-the-same?"

CHAPTER FIFTEEN

While we sped away from the SCREWED building toward the freeway, Mother and I argued about her theory.

I gave my head a skeptical shake. "I can't believe you think Roberta was the *femme fatale* in Ian's life."

"Why not? What's more efficient for a workaholic man than boinking his secretary?"

"Not boinking anyone."

With a sneer, Mother said, "Sometimes, Tracy, I wonder how you can possibly be my child."

That made two of us. But I thought about how shattered Roberta seemed. Guilt and grief often look the same.

We were on our way downtown to the jail to visit Drew. By now his spirits had to be at bottom barrel level. My own weren't much higher. I questioned whether I should have dealt myself in on Charlotte's defense strategy meeting, no matter what Drew wanted. Even though I knew her overall win record was outstanding, Robotic's remarks about CeeCee's losses to Ian reinforced my doubts.

And not because Mother brought up the subject of lawyers boinking, I swear.

That CeeCee had been willing to overturn her career for Drew still troubled me. I wondered again whether she'd already planned to leave the D.A.'s office. Prosecutors didn't make much moolah — lots of them were lured by what they could make in private practice. But given CeeCee's Westwood address, which I'd never visited, she was rolling in family dough. How likely was it that money would play any role in her decisions?

With old money broads in mind, I remembered Mother's encounter with Charlotte this morning, which she later denied. I asked her about it again now.

My maternal parent out-grinned the Cheshire cat. "Oh, I suppose I should tell you. It's true, Tracy. Charlotte and I did argue."

No kidding. Their shouting nearly brought the house down.

"You might wonder why one of the staircases has a carpet runner, and the other does not," Mother said.

I had wondered. Both stairs featured hand-painted tiles on the risers. With its red rose pattern, that runner never seemed to conform to the décor.

"It's a special effects carpet. I took it from some movie I made. If you know the right spot and flick it with your shoe, someone standing on the upper steps is thrown forward. I don't know how it works. It's all very scientific."

I stared at her, aghast. "Yeah, it sounds like rocket design. Why didn't you tell me? I could have broken my neck."

"The odds were against it," Mother said airily. "Anyway, I offered Charlotte the chance to even the score, to make up for what I did to her at your wedding."

"Slug you in the eye, you mean? You know, you've never told me. Why did you punch Charlotte?"

Mother stared out the side window. "She said something that... well, something a mother doesn't share with her child." Her decision to protect me probably held for a good second. "She implied that I had loose morals. Can you believe it? Me?"

Like that was the first time anyone had ever made that suggestion. When the freeway traffic slowed to a crawl, I inched my way across to the next exit to try the surface streets.

"She shouted it out, Tracy. Dozens of people must have heard. I had to defend my honor, didn't I? If you weren't trying so hard to be the star of the party, you would have known it, too."

The star of the party? Didn't she mean — the bride? "And you did nothing to provoke her?"

I knew she had. She'd been taking jabs at Charlotte for all the months of our engagement. The trouble was they each represented what the other deplored most in the world. For Mother, it was Charlotte's worship of order; to Charlotte, it was Mother's militant rejection of the rules. No twain existed between those two extremes.

"Provoke her? I was the victim," Mother insisted in a frosty

REVENGE FOR OLD TIMES' SAKE

tone. But after the briefest thawing off period, she added, "Well, maybe I had mentioned to Taylor that he and I should get a room upstairs in the hotel where the reception was held. I might have said if Charlotte was black-and-white, I was Technicolor."

"And you said this where Charlotte could hear?" I asked.

Mother sighed. "Tracy, really — that was the point. I certainly didn't want the old goat. I have one of my own."

And people wonder why I don't have kids. No question about it, this gene pool had to run dry.

"Uh-huh. So what happened this morning? You gave Charlotte a chance to pop one off at you. You don't mean she went for it?"

Clouds were drifting in from the ocean, blocking the sun. We Southern Californians expect our weather to be as perfect as our lives. Since I really couldn't claim the latter half of that equation, I deeply resented the impending loss of the former.

"Charlotte came closer to retaliating than I expected, darling. When she clenched her fingers into a fist, even though her hand never budged from her side, I didn't waste a moment before flicking the carpet. Naturally, I caught her before she fell down the stairs."

Not so natural. I might not have guessed that. Hell, I might not have done it.

"And I offered her another chance to hit me," Mother said.

"Only this time, since she was in your debt, she couldn't do it. That would have been against the rules in Charlotte-land. You conniving old witch," I said with a chuckle.

While basking in my praise, Mother made a pretense of inspecting her perfect manicure. "And then I followed her back to her room, where we really talked."

As a newlywed, while still hoping to achieve family harmony, I begged Mother to find some commonality with Charlotte. But she always insisted none existed. Now that she had finally become mature enough to try, I no longer cared.

"I told her, even if her son is freed, she's going to lose him, if she doesn't loosen up. Admit it, Tracy — we've had an impact on Drew."

I bet that wasn't the way he'd describe it.

"But Charlotte believes if she holds on tightly enough, she can keep him exactly as he was when we found him."

She made Drew sound like a lost wallet.

"I think I might have gotten through to her. And really, how good a mother would she be, if all she wants is to make her child into a copy of herself?"

What kind, indeed? My tongue still hurts where I bit it.

The surface street traffic was worse than the freeway. My frustration with our lack of progress built to irritation as gridlock ground our journey to a halt. Is L.A. the only place where drivers are confirmed lookie-loos? A stalled car by the side of the road is guaranteed to slow travel, as drivers pause to gape. And when there's an accident, they practically set up camp on the median so as not to miss a thing.

Our current slowdown had resulted from the collective fascination with two window washers setting up at the base of a high-rise building ahead.

I commented to Mother on the voyeurs with so little to interest them in their own lives — only she was too busy gawking at the window washers to listen. As the men tugged at the ropes hanging from the top of the building, their wooden platform rose along the mirrored side of the structure.

Mother gestured toward the platform. "Tracy, did I ever tell you about the time I took my own stunt fall from a scaffold even higher than that?"

No more than a thousand times.

Finally, traffic began to move. I hit the accelerator and hugged the bumper of the car ahead. But suddenly, the significance of that scaffolding hit me as hard as a fall from the top of that building would have.

I slammed on the brakes and twisted my neck so I could stare out the windshield at the window washers' equipment. Horns all around me wailed. Oh, like they hadn't been gawking, too.

"Watch how you're driving, Tracy. If you destroy my car, we'll have to fight Charlotte for the horse trailer. And the joy of seeing her behind that wheel is —"

"Mother, look," I said, pointing to where the window washers were raising their platform by working those ropes.

"Darling, I did look. We all looked. But we're over it now."

As cars maneuvered around ours, I said, "Mother, I'm talking about what they're doing."

"They're washing those windows. People do that when they want to see through them. You might consider trying it with your own."

What would be the point? I loved that architectural nightmare we now called our home. But washing its windows was like slapping lipstick on a pig. Anyway you look at it, it's still a pig.

"It's starting to feel like a cave. There's enough mud —"

"Stop with the windows already." How could Drew possibly say we were getting along? "I'm talking about the ropes holding up that scaffolding." I told her about the ropes I saw in Kathy's kitchen.

Mother shrugged. "So she has ropes, Tracy. Do you want to hang the poor woman with them?"

"They were rock climbing ropes. I see climbers using them all the time." The Simi Hills where we lived was one of the most popular rock climbing locations in Southern California. "You know what that means, Mother? Even if Kathy had never been to our house, she could easily have known where it was. And that hobby would have given her the strength to drag Ian there."

"From where, darling?"

"Wherever she might have parted her darling soul mate's hair with a rock."

With the jail towers in sight now, I took a right at the corner. For the rest of the trip, we batted around alternate theories, all featuring Ian and his women.

"You know, Ian had been a good looking man," I said. "But as relentlessly driven as he was, I wouldn't have classified him as a stud-muffin."

"But, darling, don't you think Ian's murder gives off the most delightful aroma of revenge? Men tend to be more direct. I think our killer must be a woman."

I wasn't certain I agreed with her. Splitting Ian's skull was sure
direct. And anyone could have wielded that rock, man or woman.
Still, she was right about one thing. This crime did smack of revenge.
The question was: had Drew just made a convenient scapegoat — or
was the revenge aimed at him, too?

Drew was being housed at the Twin Towers jail downtown. While
often praised as a model correctional facility, I bet it was still the
last place anyone would want to be, especially someone as private
as Drew. Dark clouds had filled the sky behind those towers now,
making the facility look more ominous than ever. While parking the
car, my heart thudded in my chest, in both anticipation and dread.

As Mother and I rushed to the visitors' gate, we saw Skippy
Sullivan coming out. When I felt Mother pulling away, I grasped her
arm and held her beside me.

"Martha! Tracy!" Skippy called, and he spread his arms wide.

At the last instant, Mother freed herself from my grasp and
stepped back. When Skippy's arms came around us, I was the only
one caught in his embrace. Once again his cologne tickled my
nose, but I held my breath to stop from sneezing on his cream linen
shirt.

Though Mother avoided his hug, Skippy had snagged her arm.
With a courtly flair, he leaned over her hand and kissed it. "Martha,
you look lovelier than ever."

I half expected her to wipe her hand against her dress. But she
merely said, "Delighted," in a voice completely devoid of delight,
but chockfull of malice. "You're looking well…Thomas."

Thomas? Who was Thomas? If this bozo wanted to be so all-
fired dignified, why didn't he use his real name, instead of *Skip?* I
expected him to correct Mother, the way he had chided me at the
SCREWED party. Instead, his chocolate eyes flickered away.

Skippy grasped my shoulders and held me at arm's length.
"Tracy, how distraught you must be over Drew."

"I'm absolutely —"

He overrode my response and continued on, as if he were

answering some question I had asked. "Naturally, I had to come to see him. I support my people. Not that Ian gave the boy much responsibility, but they also serve who only serve papers."

Ol' Skip was getting a little full of himself.

A young female voice from somewhere behind me whined, "Skip, can't we leave now?"

I turned to see a young girl reading a copy of *Backstage West,* a show biz trade rag. While her taste in reading material clearly labeled her as an actress, she was fleshier than any one of those petulant beasts I had ever known, especially the one who had given birth to me. Her straight blonde hair fell past her shoulders, and a short, tight skirt displayed lots of her long, tanned and surprisingly slender legs, considering the roll around her waist. She leaned against the latest and largest Mercedes sedan in a gold metallic paint. Evidently tired of waiting for Skippy, her bee-stung lips formed into a pout. Talk about a walking cliché.

"Coming, Bambi," Skippy called.

Bambi? I nearly choked. What do you call a cliché taken to an extreme?

Skippy tossed off a jaunty little wave that the girl ignored. I noticed on the ring finger of her left hand, she wore a rock that dwarfed Gibraltar. Secular televangelists were so much luckier than the religious ones — they didn't have to keep their Twinkies under wraps.

Starting away even as he spoke, Skippy said, "My dears, I really must —"

For once, I was cutting him off. "No problem, Skippy. We're here to see Drew, remember?"

Skippy stopped and frowned at me. "Oh, but you can't. Drew collapsed when he came into the interview room to see me, and they carted him off to the infirmary. Didn't you know? Another prisoner beat him to a pulp."

CHAPTER SIXTEEN

When the jail deputies refused to let me see Drew, I flew back to Mother's car. I took the wheel over her objection that I was in no shape to drive. True, maybe. But I knew I would zero in on my target with the unwavering precision of a missile.

Okay, my mind did drift off once — but that was probably a record for me. I remembered Mother's exchange with Skippy. "Thomas? Skippy Sullivan's name is Thomas?"

With a superior little smirk, Mother said, "It's more accurate to say he *was* Thomased."

I knew she wanted me to question her, but I refused to bite. I reigned in my focus. L.A. County is a sprawling monster, and the Sheriff's Department oversees large, spread-out parts of it. Before leaving the jail, I learned the Homicide Bureau was housed in Commerce, which couldn't have been more than fifteen miles away. I made the guards draw me a map. Despite heavy truck traffic along the 5 Freeway, my relentless weaving delivered us there faster than I would have thought possible.

We raced into the lobby and demanded to see Garcia. She wasn't there, so Mother and I parked ourselves on a wooden bench. Unfortunately, we shared it with a gang member's mother. Since she couldn't find enough people to tell what a good, misunderstood boy her son was, she made up for it by telling us a few dozen times. When Garcia marched through the door, it was not simply my fear for Drew that made me rush to her side.

Mother and I both shouted out our concerns at once.

"Hold it." Garcia held out her hands in the stop position until we both shut up. "Okay, one at a time."

Together, we plunged in again.

With a resigned sigh, Garcia gestured for us to follow her. Mother and I trailed along as she wove her way through rows of desks to her office on the far side. Along the way, I considered my strategy.

When some people learn how desperately you need their help, they extract something in exchange. I had no intention of handing her that leverage. *Never let 'em see you sweat* — that's my motto. I blocked my fears from my face.

Garcia ushered us into her small office and gestured toward two wooden chairs before the avocado metal desk. The desk was piled high with files and notebooks. But she hadn't allowed the necessities of the job to crowd out the personal touches. Dotting the walls were photos of a muscular man and two attractive preteen girls. And wedged into little spaces were champagne corks, with significant dates marked in ink, and interesting stones and seashells.

Garcia's personal effects certainly humanized her — and that was the last thing I wanted. I forced myself to see her as the cop who stood between Drew and me. I calmly related what happened to Drew. Even if that pseudo-serenity did balloon the knot in my gut to soccer ball size. I watched a domino effect of emotions flip through Garcia's expressive hazel eyes, starting with sympathy, but ending with something more reflective.

Yanking off the Dodger cap she wore, she ruffled her chestnut hair. "Sorry about Mr. Eaton. What can I say? Jail's a dangerous place."

Mother gave her head a pensive tilt. "Is that generally true, Detective? I've always understood that attorneys are popular with inmates, since they're a source of free legal advice."

Surprised respect flickered in Garcia's eyes now. Her astonishment represented a mere fraction of what I felt. Mother's knowledge never ceased to amaze me. They must put all kinds of stuff in those movie scripts.

Garcia picked up the phone and asked someone to check on Drew. While waiting for a return call, she said, "Lawyers are in great demand inside, but your husband might have made the mistake of looking cross-eyed at someone." Shrugging, she added, "That's all it takes."

Concrete filled my stomach soccer ball now.

The phone rang. While listening, Garcia grunted a couple of times, then hung up. "It does appear to have been an orchestrated attack," she told us. "Three men were involved."

While Mother went into a swoon that, on film, would have been the clip they showed on the talk shows — I kept my own feelings in check. Remember: Never let 'em see you sweat. I was getting what Drew needed without giving up a thing.

Absently, Garcia said, "Can it, willya, Ms. Collins? There are no casting agents here. It's all right. He's got a mild concussion and some abrasions, but he's going to be okay. He's safe in the infirmary, and they're questioning the men."

I felt giddy with relief. Drew was safe. For now.

The phone rang again, and Garcia snatched it up. As she listened, her eyes hardened to glass and her small jaw became rigid. Yes! Whatever she was hearing was putting her on our side.

She hung up slowly, with deliberation, and she trained those glass-hard eyes on me. "What kind of shit are you pulling, Ms. Eaton?"

Huh?

"A blonde girl visited the wife of one of the men involved in the attack on your husband and paid her to set it up. A slightly pudgy blonde girl — sound like anyone you know?"

Mother's eyes traveled from my shoulder to my hip. Then she said to Garcia, "No one could really describe Tracy as a *girl.*"

"These guys are not that PC, Ms. Collins," Garcia growled.

I muscled my way into their exchange. "Hey," I yelled. "I'm not pudgy."

"So you did set it up." An expression of resigned disgust stole over Garcia's face.

"No! You don't understand," I shouted.

"Sure, I do. You think you're the first person to think of it?" Garcia picked up a pencil from her desk, only to hurl it back to the surface again.

Think of *what?*

"If your man is targeted for an attack, it must mean that someone wants him silenced. Therefore, he has to be innocent."

Was *that* what it meant? "It wasn't me, I swear."

Garcia snorted. "I hear you'll swear to anything."

Whoever thought all the things I'd sworn to would come back to haunt me? "Look, drag that woman in here, the wife who arranged the assault. Put me in a lineup."

"Lucky for you, Ms. Eaton, she took the money and ran, or you and your hubby would be serving time side-by-side."

Lucky for me? Was she kidding?

Garcia threw her hand out in a flip of dismissal. "Get outta here, both of you. Don't make the mistake of thinking your stature gives you any special rights."

Mother drew herself up and said with the dignity that always thrilled audiences, "It seems to have given us less. Someday you'll wish you listened to us."

Sheer bravado, as we all knew. But a good exit line.

Only Garcia trumped it by shouting, "Ms. Eaton, let me give you a tip — a woman whose husband was beaten without her knowledge would have been more upset than you were."

Whoa! Motto backfire. No fair.

I longed to retreat to that place my parents and I had always gone to when things got tough, where real life couldn't reach us. Only I knew Drew would still be trapped behind, in life's very worst part.

This time I didn't object when Mother took the wheel. I was so lost in my own mental gymnastics, trying to make some sense of it, that I didn't notice where we went until Mother turned into our private road. And it was only when I saw how she intended to deal with the car barrier I'd established, that she captured my full attention. She brought the bumper of her car to rest gently against one of the junked cars, and by accelerating, just pushed it out of her way. Then, taking ridiculous care to line it up just so, she parked her car outside the door.

Since the story had shifted to the jail, there weren't any reporters around now. Would Garcia spread her theory about my ordering Drew's beating and make things worse for us in the court of public opinion? The only cheery note to this entire experience was that Vanessa's yellow VW Bug and the horse trailer were gone.

Both Buddy and Harri greeted us at the door. I scooped up the cat, and we marched dejectedly to the living room. I shoved aside a wallpaper sample, a horror in spurts of green that looked like an explosion in an alien blood bank, and slumped on one of the couches. I hugged the cat for comfort, and for once, her rusty motor began to purr. Incapable of leaving well enough alone, I stroked Harri until she became overly excited. The little bugger bit me and ran to Mother.

Mother picked up the cat and allowed the purr to build until it filled the room. "This isn't like us, you know, Tracy. We're usually so good at shaping the world to our needs."

"Reality bites." Worse even than snotty cats.

I walked to the glass wall and stared out into the rocky hills in the distance. Clouds were gathering there now, I noted with the glum objection of a natural sun-worshipper. My eyes drifted down to the pool. I couldn't believe what I saw there. I closed my eyes, and then quickly reopened them. But the vision remained.

"Mother, come here. Do you see what I see?"

She walked to my side and looked out. "I see dead people."

Thus demonstrating that the movies truly were her only frame of reference. But she was right. Once again, a stiff was doing laps in my pool.

CHAPTER SEVENTEEN

Mother and I dashed outside. Without a word, she grabbed the pool-skimming basket, while I reached for the brush. Coordinating our tools, we maneuvered the body to the shallow end. Then we pulled the stiff up the steps and onto the patio, in case there was still time. But time had run out for this poor slob.

With his hair in his face, I didn't recognize him at first. But I finally placed the rust sweater vest.

"It's Riley Something or Something Riley," I said.

Mother and I had been working in such harmony, I expected her to understand. Drew was right — we made better partners than I imagined we would. Why should that have surprised me? Genetics did tell.

While she dried her wet hands on the leg of my jeans, Mother said, "That can't be right, Tracy. What are the odds of two people having such curiously similar names?"

Please, tell me I'm adopted.

But I remembered Mother wasn't there when I met Riley. I filled her in on our floater's identity.

"Skippy's Savior, huh?" She glared at the form slowly melting on the patio. "Someone should have knocked him off before he released that buffoon."

I picked up a silly little fabric flower that I spotted on the patio, which I remembered him wearing at Skippy's acquittal party. This one was yellow, but otherwise, it was a match for Vanessa's rose one. Were they a fad?

I absently brushed the petals against my cheek. "Garcia is gonna bust a gut when she learns about this."

Mother choked. "Tracy, you promised."

"You of all people know how little that means," I said. What did I promise? While I rarely keep them, I usually remember my promises. Before I could question her, my nose began to run. I searched my pockets for a used tissue.

"Tracy, stop stalling," she snapped when I took time to blow my nose. "You swore to me that the next time we found a body in the pool, you wouldn't tell the police. You can't break a promise to your own mother, darling."

Not that she knew about. While I stared at Riley, I listed for myself all the reasons why I couldn't possibly do what she wanted. The idea was crazy. Only someone as out-of-touch with real life as Mother is would suggest such a thing. Besides, you can't hide a body forever. Once it surfaces, don't the cops come down harder on you? It would have been the most foolhardy choice I ever made. Somehow I had to make her understand.

The only trouble was, deep down — I secretly thought she was right.

"Admit it," Mother said with growing excitement. "You're considering stashing him somewhere, aren't you, Tracy?"

"Of course not!" I wasn't considering it...really. But if Garcia had come unglued when she thought I had the stuffing knocked out of my own husband to prove his innocence — what would she do when I produced a corpse?

I bit my lip. "What if Drew finds out?" I hadn't paid much attention to my promise to him, either. Would stashing a body qualify as tweaking?

"We'd be doing it for him."

Ooh! Good one. "It would be for him, wouldn't it?" Besides, it was the kind of maneuver I'd always pulled before I let Drew hamstring me. "Okay, let's do it. Where can we put him on ice?"

Mother giggled. "How about the freezer?"

"*My* freezer?" I demanded, shocked. "Where I keep my food?"

Mother muttered to her dead friend, "Nothing gets between Tracy and her food." With an exaggerated sigh, she added. "If you ever explored this wreck of a house you wanted, you'd know there's a chest freezer in the storage room."

I followed her to the room off the garage. "What if the freezer doesn't work anymore, Mother? It is thirty years old."

"What do you care? Your nose doesn't make it out here." She

took a step into the storage room, before reeling back for a breath of fresh air. "Really, how could anyone tell?"

It was pretty ripe in there. Stacked on one side of the little room was what must have been about a cord of firewood before time had reduced it to chunky sawdust. There was a six-inch hole in the roof that had let in years of rain and enough dried leaves to mulch miles of ground. On the other wall, covered in a blanket of dirt, was the freezer. Its electrical cord had been pulled from the socket.

Mother grasped the plug. "No matter how awful this place is, I really hope we can keep him chilled. The dead do deserve our respect, after all."

Yeah, yeah, stashing ol' Riley in a freezer was tantamount to a memorial service. She shoved the plug into the socket. After only the briefest of pauses, the motor began to hum.

I lifted the lid and peered in. It was empty, apart from two items at the bottom, wrapped in butcher paper and identified with black lettering.

"Ewwww! There's meat down there." I held my breath.

"So?" Mother said. "Look what we're putting in with it."

She was obviously being respectful again.

Mother squinted to read beyond the range of her contact lenses. "That's not meat, it's jewelry. Didn't I teach you anything? Let's see, pork was for pearls, but I can't remember what I considered chicken."

I stretched my arm to the bottom. I felt a little anxious when I poked the first package, but relaxed when its lumpy contents didn't feel a bit like fossilized pork chops. I handed the chicken package to Mother. When she tore through the paper, she uncovered a ruby bracelet and earrings.

"I was wondering what I did with these." Mother held one earring up to her lobe.

For thirty years? "Mother, you give conspicuous consumption a bad name."

She scowled. "Just for that, young lady, I'm giving you the pearls. It wouldn't hurt you to wear jewelry occasionally."

Did pearls go with the free T-shirt from the hardware store? I tore open the package to reveal a long rope of lovely quarter-inch pearls. I wrapped them around my head three times and let them drape over my forehead like an athletic headband.

When we felt the first suggestion of cool air building in the freezer, it was time to transfer our guest to his new room. I spotted a badminton net under some rackets on a metal shelf behind the rotting wood. I worked the net free and shook it out. A few sections had torn, but it seemed remarkably strong after so long. We took the net back to the patio and rolled Riley onto it.

"Pick up your end of the net, Tracy," Mother said.

"Wait," I said. "One of us should check his pockets." Mother stared off as if she were attending a particularly boring party, not holding a corpse in a sling. Naturally, that chore fell to me.

I pulled a black cloth wallet with a Velcro closing from one pocket. The cheap wallet contained no identification at all, but it was stuffed with sodden hundred dollar bills. In his other pocket, I found a Louis Vuitton card case. What a pricey contrast to the soggy wallet. Nothing else in those pockets apart from some change, which I left there. But I noticed the base of that fake boutonniere was still pinned to his sweater. I unpinned that. Attached to the pin was a cylinder that must have been a half-inch across and more than an inch in length. Why did such a flimsy flower require such a sturdy base?

I rested all of Riley's things on his belly, and I finally took hold of the net. He was heavier than he looked. Despite that, naturally, I held my end of the net higher than Mother did.

"Get a better grip on that netting, Mother. If this guy goes splat, I'm not scraping him off the sidewalk."

"Tracy, really — let the poor man retain some dignity."

As if I was the one who suggested letting him dignify the freezer.

With some grunting and swearing from two of us, all three of us made it to the storeroom. Before we wrestled him into the freezer, I stuffed his wallet and card case into my pocket for later disposal. And I wrapped the little flower and its pin in the butcher paper the pearls had been hidden in. I stuffed them below a flattened beach ball on the metal shelves.

We successfully wrestled the body into the freezer. But it really winded us. Mother closed the lid and leaned against the freezer, struggling to catch her breath. I slumped against the wall, staring at the pearls that had slipped over my eyes.

Mother gave the freezer lid a gentle pat. "This will work. No one would think to look for him here."

Not unless their minds worked like ours. There couldn't be too many others that did.

"It was fortunate that we discovered him when we were home alone, Tracy. I sense a change of fortunes here. Now the breaks will all start falling our way."

I shifted the pearl ropes back to my forehead, clearing my vision. Well, maybe not *all* the breaks. "Mother?"

"Yes, darling?"

"Vanessa is eyeballing me."

CHAPTER EIGHTEEN

Even I, with my tremendous gift for denial, couldn't pretend the stricken look Vanessa wore meant she was happy to see us. That she stood rigidly in the storage room doorway, with eyes stretched as wide as serving platters, proved that she had watched us perform Riley Something's unusual burial. Before I could begin my rationalization tap dance, Vanessa turned on her heels and ran toward the house as fast as her tapered granny dress would permit.

"Quick!" I yelled to Mother. "She's getting away."

Though Vanessa was bigger and stronger, our determination not to join Drew in the hoosegow gave us the edge. We overtook her, and with Mother grabbing one of her arms and me the other, we dragged her to the kitchen, where we pushed her into a chair.

"Get the bungee cords, Mother. From around those boxes on the floor. We'll strap her down." I sat on Vanessa, but she bucked like a bronco. It took all my might to hold her there.

"Tracy, this is crazy. Can't we discuss things calmly?" an anything-but-calm Vanessa cried as she struggled to throw me off.

Mother wrapped the bungees around her.

"Martha, *please* — you can't do this," Vanessa said.

"I'll make it up to you, darling," Mother promised, as she secured the third of the cords around Vanessa's thrashing body.

Buddy seemed to regard it all as great fun. He danced in a little circle around us, barking joyously. Harri hissed from her perch on the counter. The phone rang; I had no choice but to let the machine get it. And Vanessa screamed at the top of her lungs, for someone — anyone — to rescue her. Much as I love chaos, this time, it overwhelmed me.

"Tracy, you're going to be sorry you did this," Vanessa cried.

Big deal. You could say that about most of my choices.

Once again, Vanessa began hollering loud enough to bring down the house.

"What are we going to do with her?" Mother asked over Vanessa's screams.

"How do I know?" I shouted. "You're the one who decided to stash Riley." Though Vanessa was strapped across her torso and legs, one of her feet flew out and kicked my shin. "Ouch! I know — let's implicate her in some crime. Then she won't be able to blab."

"Hey!" Vanessa cried.

"Wonderful idea, Tracy. But what can we use?"

"If only we could tie her to Riley's death. Jeez, I can't think." I shook handfuls of my hair in frustration.

Charlotte picked that moment to walk in on us. "Dear God, what are you two lunatics doing?"

She clutched the counter for support. Belatedly, she noticed she'd wiped a jelly glop on the heel of her hand. For a moment, her eyes bounced between the two victims, the tied-up girl and her hand. But once she ripped a piece of paper towel off a roll on the counter and addressed the most critical problem, she was then able to deal with Vanessa's plight.

"Why have you strapped poor Vanessa to that chair?" Charlotte cried.

Mother threw up her arms, so fast I thought her boobs would pop free of that low-cut dress. "We had no choice, Charlotte. She watched us stuff the latest dead man from the pool into the freezer."

Talk about loose lips. I glared at Mother, but it was too late. Charlotte's skin paled to the color of salt.

"Dead man? There was another dead man in the pool? You two didn't —" Charlotte sputtered.

Plunging into damage control, I snapped, "Get with the program, will you, Charlotte? The dead guy is not the problem now. We have to decide what to do with Vanessa."

Vanessa's voice dropped to the soothing level that animal control people use when their tranquilizer darts fail to work on mountain lions. "Release me, Tracy, and I'm sure we can arrive at an equitable solution if we discuss it in a civilized manner."

Finally getting past the jelly, Charlotte slapped her hand on the counter. "Discuss it? Vanessa, dear, you're too kind. What is there to discuss?" She turned to me. "Tracy, release her this instant."

Mother whirled around on Charlotte. "You righteous bitch. To think I defended you to Tracy."

"Hold it," I said.

They ignored me and began screeching at each other, words smashing into words.

"You mantrap," Charlotte cried. "When I need your defense —"

"Mantrap? Hah! If I threaten you that much —"

I whistled to get their attention. "Can we address what's really critical here?"

They all stared at me.

Once calm was restored, I addressed that vital concern. "Am I the only one who's noticed Vanessa's IQ has just *doubled?*"

As our curiosity overtook our tempers, the three of us who were still free to move pulled up chairs and sat facing Vanessa. Even Charlotte seemed intrigued enough by Vanessa's transformation to shelve the problem of Riley Something for now.

I stabbed a finger at Vanessa. "You're not dumb."

"I'm not a publicist, either," she said with a flippant grin.

"I knew you were faking. I bet that hair's not real, either." I took hold of a pink clump — it even felt as silky as a doll's vinyl hair — and I gave it a tug.

"Owwww!" Vanessa shouted.

Charlotte clapped her hands. "Girls, stop playing. Tracy, will you focus on what's important?"

"You're right, Charlotte." With hope fluttering in my chest, I asked Vanessa, "If you're not a publicist, you probably didn't set up the talk show tour, huh?"

Anger flared in those big doll eyes. "Of course, I did. It's done right, too."

Rats! "What are you really?" A connection Mother had been urging me to make finally clicked. "Oh…Eccerly. Any relation to Neal Eccerly, the head of development at Starline Pictures?"

Her cupid's bow lips curled sourly. "He's my father. But we

don't get along. He doesn't understand that I have my own style, and I have no intention of following in his footsteps."

Mother drew her chair closer to Vanessa and patted that pink hair. "It's fine to be your own woman, darling, as long as you keep those lines of communication open and try to make it home for Sunday dinners."

"Mother, you're so easy," I muttered.

 Charlotte purred, "Haven't I always said that?"

"So, Vanessa, what is it you really do?" I asked.

Vanessa gulped. "I'm a journalist."

I looked at Mother. "Could we be any more screwed?"

Let's see if I understood this: During the darkest, most damaging period of any of our lives, my mother brought into my home our own in-house chronicler. Since we were already nose-deep in road apples, I untied Vanessa, and we all took a place at the table. I remembered a carton of Ben & Jerry's Chunky Monkey that I'd hidden in the freezer so Drew wouldn't find it. I stuffed a spoon into it, and we passed around the carton while Vanessa slowly told her story.

"I'm not an actual reporter yet. But Raul has promised to help me with my audition tape for *Scarlet Stories.* He's a segment producer there."

That explained her devotion to *Scarlet Stories.* But it was hard to believe she hadn't found a suitable story here yet. *Scarlet Stories* must have had far stricter standards than I imagined.

But it seemed Vanessa just couldn't choose among all the potential stories we'd presented to her. "See, first I'd heard that Alec was staying here, while Martha was in Beverly Hills. I thought they'd split again," Vanessa said around a delicate taste of ice cream. "Only Martha moved here, too. And let me tell you — their room is next to mine. They spent all night saying good-bye before Alec left, if you know what I mean."

Mother gave her eyes a coy batting, in response to the admiration Charlotte struggled in vain to hide.

Vanessa turned to me. "Tracy, did you know that people their ages —"

I wrinkled my nose. "Jeez, Vanessa. They're my parents."

With a shrug, Vanessa handed off the ice cream carton to Mother, who just passed it along to Charlotte. "When that bombed out, I thought I'd explore how much actual writing Martha did on the book you claim you wrote together. But I finally figured there's no real surprise there, Tracy. You're just a good daughter."

Storm clouds gathered in Mother's deep blue eyes, even if Vanessa's impression was true. But I shot Mother a warning look to remind her how desperately she hadn't wanted the story surrounding that book, and our last little caper, to come out. She took the hint, but with a grudging pursing of her full lips.

"And now you have all the chapters and verses in the book of Drew, and you plan to run with it, huh, Vanessa?" I concluded.

Where the hell was that ice cream? I noticed Charlotte rose and got her own spoon before digging in. Did someone tell her that made the whole carton hers?

Vanessa nodded reluctantly. "I'm sorry, Tracy. I'm really fond of all of you. Even if you weren't very generous when you thought I was a dunce. But what can I do?"

Before I could make my case for keeping her trap shut, we heard the front door open and close. I looked at Charlotte. Though she'd stuffed her mouth with Chunky Monkey, she insisted she'd locked the door when she came in.

"Where is everyone?" my dad's voice called from the hall.

He burst into the kitchen. Unlike Drew, Dad's personal style was anything but sedate, yet he took similar pains with his appearance. Until today. The coffee stain that now graced his ivory silk shirt had to be a first, and I found the sight of his snowy mane standing on end downright scary. Even his trim white moustache drooped.

"How did you get here?" I asked. "You look like —"

Dad gave his head a sharp shake. "The hell with how I look. Doesn't anyone here answer the phone? Or even check messages?"

What a silly question. If I planned to check messages, there would have been no point in avoiding those calls. "Look, Dad, I'm sorry we didn't answer the phone, but it's been crazy here. If you've heard enough to bring you home, you know about Drew's problems. But things are worse than you imagine."

"Honey, things are worse than *you* imagine." Dad's eyes, the color of a tropical sea, clouded as they traveled to Charlotte. "Someone has put a contract out on Drew's life. The boy is going to die if we don't do something about it."

CHAPTER NINETEEN

D ad took my place at the kitchen table, while he related the story. "We ran into Dewey Glover in Flagstaff. He's an old pal of Philly's and an ex-con. Dewey asked Philly, 'Ain't Andrew Eaton your nephew?' And he gave us the scoop. That somebody laid out big money to see Drew doesn't make it to the trial."

"Who would have thought my brother would have such familiarity with ex-cons?" Charlotte spat, her anger directed at her brother's acquaintances, not the message that was the real cause. "Where is Philly, anyway?"

"He stayed on to see if he could learn who put out the hit. He'll be along as soon as he can," Dad said. "But, Charlotte, Dewey's my friend, too."

Charlotte's eyes narrowed on Dad. "Why doesn't that surprise me?"

Pausing in the agitated laps I was doing around the kitchen island, I said, "Charlotte, you better be glad Philly has such friends. That might save your son's life." My kitchen workout progressed. "I don't get it. With Drew facing trial, Ian's killer is in the clear. It was crazy enough to throw doubt on Drew's guilt by bumping off Riley Something. But killing Drew makes even less sense. Why not let the system have its chance with him?"

Dad grabbed Charlotte's spoon and helped himself to a big scoop of ice cream. Hey, I was starving — that five pounds had to be gone by now. When was it my turn?

Mother rose and leaned over Dad's shoulder, smoothing his rumpled hair.

"There's only one reason, baby," Dad concluded, blowing cold Chunky Monkey breath my way. "Drew knows something about the killer. Even if he doesn't know he knows it."

The theory Garcia had advanced — and exploded — was proving to be true. But if Drew knew something that damaging to someone, why wasn't he aware of it? Sloppy thinking wasn't his style. He was up to the ying-yang in order.

"As to this Riley-chap — he might be only peripherally related." Dad tilted his head back and beamed up at Mother. "Remembering your old freezer — that was good thinking, Martha."

And people wonder why I'm so reality-challenged.

I told them we had to try again to convince Garcia that Drew was in danger — the stakes were too high to go it alone. Mother insisted on making the call herself. She still believed her prominence had to buy her a few perks. But when she returned to the kitchen after placing that call from her room, sporting the ruddy glow rage always burned on her fair skin, I knew nothing in her arsenal had budged Detective Patti Garcia one iota.

"It's not good," Mother said. "They've deemed him well enough to return to the general population. And they'll be transporting him to his preliminary hearing tomorrow in a jail bus with other prisoners."

"Noooo," Charlotte moaned.

I whirled around to her. "Charlotte, call CeeCee. She has to arrange something safe for him."

With no more than a swift nod, Charlotte approached the island phone. She got right through to Wonder Girl. But judging by Charlotte's clipped remarks, CeeCee wasn't that thrilled to hear from her.

"CeeCee, yes, I know how busy you are, dear. But this —" She listened for a while, her thin lips growing tighter, before breaking in with the story. Finally, Charlotte said, "Very well. I'll expect to hear from you." When she hung up, she explained that CeeCee had agreed to see what she could arrange.

"She didn't seem too happy about it," Vanessa observed before she shoved the last of the ice cream into her face.

"No, she didn't. She didn't seem to care about Drew or me." Charlotte's honey-blonde head shook with surprised indignation. "But I'm sure she's just distracted by the stress of preparing for the trial."

She was working so hard to free Drew that she couldn't be

bothered keeping him alive? Didn't fit with the woman who mauled me and warned me to stay out of her way.

Since Charlotte had yet to remove her hand from the phone, she snatched it up the instant it rang. "Yes...? Thank you, CeeCee. Of course, I understand...but —"

From where I stood across the island, I could hear that the dial tone had already returned when Charlotte bid her precious CeeCee good-bye.

"She's won him a reprieve," Charlotte reported. "They'll keep him in the infirmary until he has to leave for court in the morning. And they won't transport him in the bus, but in a car with two deputies. But she doesn't think they'll keep up the precautions for long."

"Jiminy Cricket," Dad muttered. "What are we gonna do?"

Charlotte's pretty face stiffened, as she struggled to hold back tears. She whirled around on me and shrieked, "You have to do something, Tracy. You're the one with all the ideas."

"Tracy's ideas are generally a little too out there for you, Charlotte," Dad cautioned.

"I don't care how crazy they are, the crazier the better. That's the only thing that's going to save my son now."

They all turned expectant looks to me. Who made me the chief nut? Oh, right — I did. An idea took shape in my head.

"Mother, how clean are those cars in the driveway?" I asked.

Charlotte shuddered. "Not at all. I can't imagine when the horse trailer last saw soap-and-water. But who cares?"

"Charlotte, darling, I think Tracy wants to know whether the police can trace them." Mother didn't bother to hide her smirk. "I've been told they're not registered, Tracy."

"Not as regular street cars, but the state must maintain some record of discards." I chewed at the inside of my cheek.

Dad popped to his feet. "With a welding torch, I can make short work of those serial numbers. Half of those wrecks out there have been patched together from a few different cars anyway. The police won't know where to look."

Slowly, as I paced in agitated bursts, I outlined for them as much of a plan as I could throw together at such short notice. At the completion, they cheered with excitement. Except for Vanessa, who cleared her throat. Damn, I was slipping — I'd forgotten about her. I had outlined for a tabloid reporter-wannabe a scheme that was sure to put us all in the pokey.

With a decisive nod of her pink head, Vanessa said, "You've only addressed half of it, Tracy. What about your alibis?"

"Yeah," I admitted, "I'm still working on that."

"Maybe I can contribute that part, Raul and me." She sketched an idea of her own, and while the timing would be tricky, it would provide a solid alibi.

"Vanessa, you'd do that? What about your audition tape?" I asked.

"I'm not forgetting it. I expect you and Martha to come up with something good for me." Vanessa looked to both of us.

"Vanessa, darling, you'll get your story if I have to streak through Beverly Hills naked," Mother vowed.

There was a sacrifice. "What about Raul? Are you sure he'll go for it?" I asked.

Vanessa chuckled. "Raul's an ex-gang banger. His whole crew is made up of his old homies. He doesn't have that much love for the police. I'd bet anything he'll agree."

What a great girl she was. I wished I'd known it sooner.

Charlotte thoughtfully tapped her finger against the table. "There's still one potential problem. What about Drew? We can't predict his reaction, since he might not be as...uh...free-thinking as I am."

My breath caught in my throat — never did I think I'd hear those words. But Charlotte was right. Drew's instinctive reaction could doom whatever actions we took to save his life. In the silence that followed, the only sound was my fist striking my own palm as I sought a solution.

"Oh, for Pete's sake," Vanessa snapped. "We'll knock him out. They sell chloroform in some drugstores."

"They do?" I asked.

"What kind of a mystery writer are you, Tracy? You should know these things." Vanessa shoved the empty Chunky Monkey carton at me.

I was liking her less now. "Okay, Vanessa, I said you were smart."

Mother looked to the ceiling. "And people ask why I only had one child."

"Tell me about it," Charlotte muttered. "I have three, remember?"

Once the mother chorus wound down, I said, "Afterwards, you're going to have to stash him, Charlotte." When I told her where and how, she gasped. But to her credit, she agreed.

Then everyone dashed off to prepare for tomorrow. Or simply to stand over the shoulder of those making the preparations, offering unsolicited supervision, as Charlotte did to Dad.

That left me alone in the kitchen with Buddy. I held him close and ruffled his shaggy head. "This has gotta work, boy — or visiting day with Daddy is not gonna be at the jail, but at the cemetery." Just saying it gave me a chill.

While in that position, something in my pocket dug into my hip. Riley's wallet and card case. What kind of business had that clown been in? I eased the saturated cards from the case. You could have knocked me over with a feather when I saw those business cards were CeeCee's. She had been looking for a Louis Vuitton card case when she was here for Drew's arrest. I supposed the case could have slipped from her purse and been carried to the backyard on the wind, where Riley picked it up, before someone pitched him into the pool. Except the winds hadn't been that strong, and for the case to have moved along the chain I'd proposed required a whole lot of coincidence.

The kitchen intercom crackled, and Mother's voice came through. "Tracy, can you help me find those old trunks of clothes I left here?"

"Be right there." I stuffed Riley's wallet into a drawer crammed with dishtowels. But after a moment's hesitation, I returned the card case to my pocket. I'd keep that — until I decided how to make use of it.

CHAPTER TWENTY

The Keystone Kops had nothing on us. Nor The Three Stooges. Nor any group of escaped mental patients. Nor...but you get the idea.

And yet, as crazy as our scheme was, there were so many details that had to be put into play. Mother had contacted Glen Jeffrey, her partner in the junked car business. Glen found us replacements for the cars that currently filled the driveway, so the cops didn't wonder where they went. He trucked the replacements in last night, before leaving on a long vacation to a country without an extradition treaty, paid for by his partner in business and my partner in crime. He even found another horse trailer to fill in for Charlotte's buggy.

Dad contacted an old studio chum to borrow some crash test dummies and the remote control operators they use when conditions are too risky for stuntmen. His friend buried the paper trail on the stuff, though Dad vowed to find some way to pay for it, since the studio wasn't gonna get that equipment back. Us Graingers, we'll break any law on the books, but we're courteous about it.

Mother dug out the old clothes she'd left in my house when she moved out years ago. She even agreed to sacrifice the wigs she'd brought. When she and Vanessa finished painting those dummies, they looked as good as models. To the terminally nearsighted, anyway. Dad worked through the night removing all traceable evidence from those cars and taking out the stall sections from the horse trailer. I borrowed some electrical equipment from Philly's room. Mother and I also conspired with Raul to create what we hoped would become a foolproof alibi.

And while we all labored hour after grueling hour, Charlotte also did her part, by making exactly two phone calls. One was to a car rental company, to acquire some legit wheels for her use and ours. The other call — well, we had yet to see if that would work.

This morning, we put it all in motion. I kept a string of chatter going when we gathered at the house, to bolster the morale of the troops. But my own hands shook as I donned my costume and latex gloves. I wished again that Philly were here. How could I pull off the impossible without him? And my nutty plan *was* impossible; deep down, I knew that.

There were just so many areas where it could go awry, starting with the Eye in the Sky. Helicopters hovered overhead all the time in L.A. Traffic watchers, eager beaver reporters, not to mention police and fire departments. Blue Thunder lives! We just had to hope it didn't live where we were operating.

Another concern was the route the car transporting Drew would take. Raul and his TV crew assured us they had personal knowledge of all the ways the Sheriff's Department prisoner buses traveled to the various courthouses serving the area. But would a patrol car stick to the usual plan? Just to be sure, Raul put extra guys out there, dressed as road workers, to control the traffic flow.

Using Drew's keycard, one of Raul's guys went to the SCREWED building's roof to serve as our lookout. The rest of us assumed our places nearby. As the minutes ticked away, I became so certain my scheme wouldn't work, that when the lookout's voice came through the radio, alerting us the county patrol car was near, I yelled, "Holy crap!" and nearly produced that substance on the spot.

But I pulled it all together as soon as I saw that the traffic flowing to the intersection had slowed, and then stopped. Apart from Drew's transport car, that is, which Raul's guy waved through.

When the black sedan sporting the police radio antennae passed the corner, the lookout sent four of the remote-controlled junked cars crashing into it. Despite having been hit on all sides, the deputies squeezed from their vehicle with their weapons drawn. But the sight of those made-up dummies behind the wheels of the cars that hit them seemed to rattle them. Not for long, but long enough for Vanessa and me, dressed in clown costumes — a shorter stretch for her than me, you had to admit — to jump from the junked car that carried us. One swipe of chloroform — and the deputies hit the blacktop. With bolt-cutters, Vanessa cut the cuffs that held Drew in the rear seat.

She yanked Drew from his jail transport car and threw him into the rear of our clown car. I leaned into the jail vehicle for one instant and pulled something from the baggy, multicolored clown pants I wore. I hesitated before dropping it on the floor. Should I? I'd regret it, I knew, if I did. But I feared I'd regret it more if I didn't. With no further deliberation, I tossed CeeCee's ritzy card case on the floor.

Then I hopped behind the wheel of our little car and gave it all the juice it had. Dad had promised a turbo-charged engine in that wreck, and he wasn't kidding. We lit away from the scene mere seconds after we arrived.

Several blocks away, Dad lowered the ramp on the rear of the horse trailer. Once our little clown car zipped inside, he pulled the ramp up behind it. A kerosene lamp in the corner was the only illumination in the shadowy interior, which smelled worse than usual. Vanessa and I jumped out. Drew tentatively followed.

I watched as Drew's head whipped between the larger and smaller clown, Vanessa and me. He inched closer, studying my features through the white makeup, before pulling me to him.

I clutched him back, my arms locking so tightly around him I thought they would fuse in that position. Only in relief did I acknowledge how much I had feared for his life. Holy Jailbird, Batman! I pressed my face into his chest and just breathed in his scent from the soft gray wool of his suit.

"Thank God. Tracy, if you had any idea what I've been dodging in jail," Drew muttered into my bright orange wig. "But I knew you'd find some way to free me."

Strong hands suddenly ripped me away from Drew. An instant later the only sign that he had ever held me was the white makeup I left on his jacket. Someone had muscled me aside, stealing my place in his embrace.

"Not me, Jack-o," I said and gestured to the interloper who clutched him now.

"Mom?" Drew squeaked.

Charlotte continued to hold her son in a fierce hug. "What did you expect me to do? Let them kill my child? Besides, Tracy assured me her insane plan would work."

And we knew who she'd blame if it didn't.

Dad checked his stopwatch. "Tracy, honey, you and Vanessa don't have time to talk. Get going, girls."

Dad was right. I finished wiping off the last of my garish makeup and changed from my clown suit to a sedate blue linen suit.

Dad extended a couple of items to Drew. "Son, you've got to slip into these things. Vanessa was kind enough to Dumpster dive for them." He held up for Drew's inspection a sagging, shiny navy suit, the repository of all the various forms of garbage that must have been thrown in that Dumpster, as well as an inky black man's wig, which looked more like a particularly loathsome hairball that some cat had coughed up.

Drew's brown eyes bulged. "You expect me to wear some bum's clothes? No way."

Incredible. *That* was where he drew the line. He hadn't winced at a jailbreak.

Vanessa reached into the car for her bottle of chloroform.

But Dad held up a hand to stop her. "No time, Vanessa." He made a fist. "Hope you understand, Andrew, my boy, that this is for your own good." Who would have thought there'd be so many punches thrown in this caper? At least Drew was finally learning from the master.

Dad caught Drew before he fell and gently lowered him to the floor. "You'll dress him and get him there, Dad?" I asked.

He nodded.

Dad was taking Drew to the Norman Club, the old money bastion with locations in many large cities, including Los Angeles, which Drew's family had belonged to since...well, since the Norman Conquest. That was the weakest part of the plan. Only members could reserve rooms, so the room had been booked in Charlotte's name. If the cops thought to look there, we were screwed. But we were counting on their merely combing sleazy hotels.

Dad nodded. "Don't worry, baby. I promise I'll get him there safely, and they'll believe he's Monsieur Chien, the eccentric, reclusive French star, who needs some private time."

Dad can sell a con almost as well as Philly, only he calls it acting.

"Now get going, Tracy," Dad snapped, "or the ball's gonna drop on your end."

Charlotte, Vanessa, and I climbed into the cab of the horse trailer. Then we slipped out the passenger door and raced down the street to where Charlotte's rented silver Taurus was parked. We heard the engine of the trailer start up, as Dad drove off to where he had another car stashed for the last part of his and Drew's journey.

We piled into Charlotte's rental, and she sped off for the *Scarlet Stories* studios. Sirens wailed all around us. But nothing happened to impede our progress. We counted on the chaos we left behind creating a smokescreen, and it did.

At the Hollywood studio where *Scarlet Stories* taped, Charlotte screeched into the lot. As expected, since this wasn't a scheduled taping, the only cars parked there belonged to Raul and his guys. No cop cars yet, but we hadn't a minute to waste.

The security door had been wedged ajar with a rock. I yanked it open and raced through. I could hear Charlotte's and Vanessa's heels tapping rapidly against the floor behind me. We ran all the way to the studio.

"Tracy!" Mother cried, when I burst into the studio. "What kept you?"

I wanted to tell her that next time she got to bust the jailbird out, only I was too winded to talk. On the monitors, the feed going out over the air, in place of the usual *Scarlet Stories* rerun, showed Mother and me being interviewed by Raul. On the screen display we wore the same garments as we did now, and the word *Live* flashed in the corner, even though we'd taped it last night. Thank you, Nick Wick, for that lesson in TV honesty.

The small *Scarlet Stories* interview set, with its blonde faux-wood desk and burnt orange side chairs, was arranged precisely as it had been when we taped the first part of this show the evening before. Mother and I climbed back into those chairs now, and Raul took his place behind the desk.

"Raul, you're sure the network won't fire you for airing this?" I asked, still catching my breath. If they wanted him to anchor, and to create shows totally on his own, wouldn't they have asked?

With a wink, he said, "Trust me, *chiquita*. I know where all the bodies are buried around here. Lots o' leverage. Besides, my bosses wouldn't care if I blew away a class of kindergartners if it brought in ratings. And the ratings for this show are going to be outta this world, once people learn it was your alibi during Drew's jailbreak." He flashed me what I could only describe as an evil grin. Good thing he was on our side. I gave that grin a second look — he *was* on our side, right?

As Raul took us through the interview, Mother and I built a case for Drew's innocence, though she did most of the talking. I wasn't confident I could capture the exact tenor of my speech and mannerisms of the night before. But she'd been shooting scenes shot out-of-sequence for her entire professional life.

The cops burst into the studio moments before the broadcast ended. I had to hand to it to Charlotte — when she angrily shushed them from her offstage position, she sounded as genuinely righteous as Mother had on the air.

By the time the show finished, Garcia was already scrutinizing the tape the engineer had made. But he had seamlessly married the pre-taped version to the live half of the broadcast. Fuming with frustration, she placed several calls to friends of her own. To Garcia's surprise, her own contacts verified that we had been speaking live from that studio at the precise time when Drew was abducted.

Mother had coached us all on how to behave when Garcia told us about Drew's abduction. We acted surprised, but not too much; we'd warned her something would happen. But it made no difference. No matter how good we were, she didn't buy our performance.

With the golden glints in her hazel eyes flashing, Garcia grabbed my arm and yanked me away from the others. In a hoarse whisper, she said, "I don't know how you did it, but I'm gonna find out. And when I do, I'm gonna nail your old man." She threw my arm away in disgust. "And then I'm going to nail you." She marched off.

I should have let her go, but I couldn't help myself. "I thought you were different. Freer somehow, adventurous."

She turned back to me. More fatigue than fury showed in her

weary eyes now. "Maybe once, but not anymore, thanks to people like you. Don't ever make the mistake of thinking we'll find ourselves on the same side."

I wouldn't. But a little part of me couldn't help but regret it.

CHAPTER TWENTY-ONE

I hovered behind Charlotte at the front window of my house. "Is that cop still out there?"

"Yesss," Charlotte hissed.

There was such anger in the sibilant sound, but I wasn't sure whether she was mad at the cop ordered to guard my driveway, or me. Me, undoubtedly, given her track record in the blame arena. Though I had to admit that, since we heard about the contract taken out on Drew's life, she had handled everything with uncharacteristic aplomb.

"Man, that chaps my hide. How do I work with a cop dogging my steps?" I banged the wall with my fist; that shook a cloud of dust off the inside of the window. The outside, too, judging by the clean spot I found myself looking through. Bang enough walls and I wouldn't have to wash those windows at all.

Mother called from the hall, "It's only natural that Garcia wouldn't want to let you out of her sight now. What did you expect, Tracy?"

This, from the woman who taught me from birth to deny the concept of consequence? But that was why I avoided the real world at all costs — I didn't get it. I'd expect the law enforcement types to want the same thing as I did, to see right prevail by any means possible. But I was guessing it was the "any means possible" that would always prove to be the stumbling block to togetherness between them that stick to the letter of the law and those of us who float in its spirit.

"At least that awful Mr. Wickerson has left," Charlotte sniffed.

I knew that from the relative quiet. For a solid hour, Nick Wick kept ringing the doorbell, causing Dean Martin to start the song, "Ain't That a Kick in the Head?" so many times, I almost applied Dean's advice to Wick. Later, he took to pounding on the door, shouting, "I know you have Drew in there. Let me see him, or I'll destroy you all on my show."

If only I were as sure about Drew's whereabouts. Dad still hadn't reported in after leaving to deposit Drew in the Norman Club. Was he laying low because a deputy had been posted to watch us? Or had Dad and Drew been caught? No, Garcia would have delivered that news herself. I should have worked out a code, something Dad could say over a phone line that could be tapped. Vanessa was right — for a mystery writer, I left I lot to be desired when it came to True Crime.

We hadn't heard from Philly, either. Had he learned anything we could take to the police, which would end this nightmare? Was he on the trail of a lead, or on his way home? I knew Dad would have left him with travel money. But I also knew Philly could easily have squandered it. Was he thumbing his way here now, harboring information we desperately needed?

On the upside, the presence of the fuzz did put a damper on the full-fledged media assault I expected. Wick had been the only one ballsy enough to pierce the invisible barrier. Though the rest of the crew couldn't be far away. And they wouldn't make my movement any easier, either.

Frustration built in me to the point that I had to take some action. I stormed toward the back of the house.

When I passed the kitchen, Mother called, "Tracy, where are you going? Kenette left a message with those dates of Ian's, the ones he entered into his calendar."

"Write 'em down," I growled. Did I have to tell her everything?

I threw the sliding door open and stepped outside. Buddy slipped out with me. Since it was too much trouble to put him back inside, with my dog dancing at my heels, I made my way to the rear of our property. There I jumped down to the trail and followed the reverse of the path Ian must have taken in his final hammock ride.

But unlike everyone else who had hiked there recently, I wasn't wearing sport shoes. After we came home from the *Scarlet Stories* studio, I changed from the suit I'd worn for the interview into jeans and a T-shirt, and slipped my feet into a comfy pair of worn black flats. The first time those leather soles slipped on a rock sticking through the sandy trail, I considered going back to the house for sneakers. But the fear I felt spurred me on.

Off in the distance, I spotted a pair of rock climbers setting up their rappelling gear on a cliff. Another face of the same ridge brought a half-dozen more climbers into focus. With a strong pair of binoculars, I realized, they all had a good view of my home. We weren't keeping many secrets from anyone who wanted them.

I stopped to dump sand from my shoes. One downside to living on a sandstone mountain range was that the soil was nearly as sandy in places as the beach. It didn't retain footprints well, either. Though some marks did remain. I noticed someone had dragged an object that looked like a roller suitcase. Indentations wheel-distance apart stood out from the faint footprints in the trail.

But while Buddy kept urging me forward, to the extent of nipping my bare heels, my thoughts were still with Drew, somewhere across town. No matter how many times I tried out alternate theories, I still couldn't understand the attacks on him. Maybe Mother was right, that *revenge* was the operative word here. Against Drew? Who hated him that much?

When a second trail split off from the main one, on impulse I followed it higher into the hills. It wove around a rocky hill and led into a paved road. At the far end of the road I came upon a couple of structures within a tall chain-link fence. The high transmission tower shooting up from the stout cinderblock building at the rear of the fenced property told me this was the scene of Skippy's crime. The studio that he and the DOLTs had overtaken to achieve their moment of loony infamy.

The place was abandoned now. While the tower did transmit the signal for the KLR radio station, the studio in the cinderblock building below it was only used in emergencies — and when certain well-known comics decided to crash the place.

In a different part of the property, fenced off from the radio facility, was the more high-tech former studio of *Scarlet Stories* and other cable shows. Alongside the studio, several large satellite dishes still turned their faces to the sky. But the property was idle these days, and even for sale, according to a sign hanging from the front fence.

While pacing the perimeter, I came upon a piece of yellow crime scene tape tied to the fence. Several feet in from the barrier, a dark patch stained the sandy soil, which someone had ringed with chalk. That had to be where Ian had been struck.

Obviously, the cops knew that. I saw all kinds of chalked areas now. As the defense counsel, CeeCee must know, too. But no one had told me. What was it they thought? That Drew and Ian met out here, climbed a high fence, and argued — until Drew grabbed a rock and knocked Ian out? Why would they have met here when our house was only a couple of miles away? And with all this open acreage, where it would be easy to stash a body, why would Drew dump it into his own pool?

A weathered redwood deck, with some webbed lawn chairs scattered about, jutted out from the rear of the TV studio. On the ground beside it, a number of cigarette butts had been crushed into the dirt. The employee break area. Beyond the deck two aluminum poles rose from the ground about eight feet apart. Thick ropes tied around each of those poles draped onto the ground. The cops had ringed the poles with chalk, too.

The significance of those poles hit me. They'd held a hammock. *That* hammock — not ours — brought Ian to our yard. The cops sure weren't keeping me abreast of things.

But I only saw space for one hammock. I remembered what I thought were suitcase wheel scuffs in the trail. How dumb was I? Why would someone pull a suitcase on a hike? Those tracks hadn't been made by wheels — but by *shoes*. Riley must have been killed out here, too, and lacking a hammock, the killer dragged his body back to my house.

It was pretty clear neither murder had been planned. Unless the killer was as spontaneous a dunce as I was. But what was so special about this place? Sure, it was isolated, but just as visible to hikers and climbers as my home.

I saw the signs of struggles now, both in the dirt within the studio complex and outside the fence. Of course, these hills were dotted with signs warning hikers of the mountain lions and bears, as well as rattlers and other forms of wildlife. The scuffling of the dirt didn't have to be related to either murder. I cast a nervous glance over my shoulder in case any of those animals happened to be hanging around now, eyeing their next meal. But I didn't look too hard. As usual, the two-legged predators were proving to be far more dangerous.

Nothing tweaked Buddy's antennae, either. He had become so bored with our outing, he'd stretched out on the road to take a nap. I whistled for him now. After a slow stretch, he loped to my side. We started back down the trail together. Only a tiny lizard cut across our path, and Buddy dove for it. I tried to get out of his way, but he was too fast for me. He plowed into my leg and knocked me off balance. I grabbed for a dried bush at the side of the trail, but my aim was off. I fell flat on my face.

While the miserable mutt chased the elusive reptile, I lifted my face from the dirt. But having had the wind knocked out of me, I only found the strength to prop my chin on a rock sticking up from the trail. While I stared out in that dazed state, a small buff-colored rectangle slowly came into focus. I stretched my arm out and plucked the little rectangle from where it had caught in tumbleweed.

It was CeeCee's business card.

I jumped up, faster than I would have thought possible. Thoughts whizzed through my mind equally fast, though none stayed long enough to form useful connections. That I found the card there shouldn't have struck me as strange. I'd already surmised Riley had been killed at the studio and dragged back to our place, and he had CeeCee's card case in his pocket.

But seeing the card there, so far from CeeCee's orbit, gave me the creeps. All at once, there were too many totally different worlds colliding. And I had to find out why.

I burst into the house. "I'm back," I shouted. Buddy barked to indicate his return as well.

Charlotte stepped from the kitchen, drying her hands on a

dishtowel. Jeez, another sight I never expected to see. Had my imaginary maid come to life?

"Any calls?" I asked her.

"Lots. There was —"

I cut her off. "Did CeeCee call?"

"No," was her clipped response. Charlotte's pale lips formed a taut line.

Why not? Her client had been broken out of custody. Shouldn't she have accused me of the dirty deed?

Charlotte absently wrung the towel. "It's just as well, Tracy, dear. I do hate lying, and the thought of fibbing to CeeCee —"

"Get over it, Charlotte," I snapped as I headed for the stairs. "Call her. Find out what she knows. And don't spill a thing to get it." From halfway up the stairs, I shouted, "Mother, where are you?"

Mother started down the staircase. "Darling, what's wrong?"

I turned back toward the hall. "Get your car keys."

Mother scurried behind me. "Where are we going?"

"We're going to investigate this murder, exactly as we planned." I headed for the door.

"Tracy, have you forgotten? There's a police officer out there, who's sure to follow us when we leave."

"Good," I shouted over my shoulder. "Let him see how it's done."

CHAPTER TWENTY-TWO

The cop patrolling our driveway must have decided to catch a snooze under the gnarly olive tree that grows where the drive meets our private road. He'd parked his patrol car in plain sight. But I didn't see him when we first approached. Then I noticed him sitting cross-legged on the ground, with his tan uniform shirt pressed against the tree's bark.

When the Mercedes rolled past, I tooted the horn. Scrambling to rise, he slipped on some olive pits. Apparently, he kept slipping all the way to the patrol car. I knew that even after we drove past, since Mother watched the action in the visor mirror and gave me a running commentary. That woman never could resist a man in uniform.

When the show ended, she said, "Charlotte seemed a mite peeved with you. You can't keep from upsetting her, can you, darling?"

That was rich, coming from her. "Too bad. She can take it out on her rightful daughter-in-law."

I sped down the dirt road, sending up a cloud of dust behind me. I noticed a cluster of media vans had gathered where our private street met the county road. I foolishly hoped they wouldn't find anything interesting in my speeding away. Sure, with a cop in pursuit. Dream on. In a flash, they formed an instant caravan.

"Where are we going?" Mother whispered, as if one of those people back there could hear her.

"To give Toby Newton the third degree." I flexed my fists around the steering wheel covered in black leather. When I was jazzed, I felt so dangerous. Reality better not burst my bubble.

Watching our long tail now in the passenger side mirror, she said, "Toby Newton? Isn't that some kind of cookie?"

No one should ever say "cookie" to a starving woman. I explained that Toby was the witness who lied to the police when he said Drew had been stalking Ian.

"How did you find him?" Mother asked.

"He's in the book."

At a stop sign, I rolled on through to test the orders the cop had been given. He didn't pull me over — hell, he slowed at the sign less than I had. So Garcia had ordered me watched, but not harassed. Good to know. The media conga line didn't hesitate at all.

"You mean the *telephone* book?" Mother asked with sardonic irritation.

What was her problem?

"That reminds me, Tracy. I jotted down Kenette's message, *as you ordered.*" Now she produced a full-blown frown. "Do you think you're the only one who knows anything?"

Duh. "Just tell me what Kenette said, Mother."

Her frown shifted into a more perplexed mode. "It's not good, Tracy. Ian's personal entries in his calendar were in numerical codes."

At Topanga Canyon Boulevard, I headed south. "Sure, that's how law firms trace their billings."

Mother gave her ash blonde waves a shake. "Kenette eliminated the SCREWED client codes. Apparently, Ian had established his own system. Kenette found a code file in his computer, but it's password protected. Roberta caught her trying to break it, and now she'll have no more access to Ian's office."

"Man, that scorches my stew." I fumed in silence. "Mother, give me your cell phone."

"What phone?" she asked coldly.

"Oh, yeah." I hated it when she was right. I would crawl into the trashcan for her phone at the SCREWED roach coach now if I could.

An expression of pure ecstasy stole over her face. "Does this mean you're admitting it was stupid to throw my phone away? Be still my heart."

And people wonder why *I'm* sarcastic. But I'd die before I'd admit it to her. Besides, there's always another way. I remembered a particular pedestrian we'd passed a few blocks back. Without waiting till I reached the corner, I went into a sudden left. Sure, it meant going over the center median, but it wasn't *too* bumpy.

Mother, who gripped the armrest, might have felt differently.

The pedestrian quickly came into view up ahead on the sidewalk. He hadn't made much progress, but he was still chattering away on his cell phone. Those gizmos really are so distracting.

I yanked the car onto the sidewalk and popped from the door. Though he kept the phone pressed to his ear, the man's jaw dropped at the sight of a car blocking his way. With his hiking boots and plaid flannel shirt, he seemed more the survivalist type than a cell phone user. His scrawny beard, one of those chin warmers *sans* moustache, further reinforced the loner lumberjack image. I always thought those beards made their wearers look so very earnest, but hopelessly misguided. All the better for my purposes.

"Is that call for me?" I asked breathlessly.

"Uh...no. That is —" he sputtered.

I snatched the phone from him and listened for an instant. "No, it sure isn't." I ended his call. "You don't mind if I make a call, do you?" I punched in SCREWED's number.

Mother stepped from the car.

The poor guy looked to Mother for support. "Did you see what she did?" he said, more stunned than outraged.

"What are you, the Phone Police?" Mother asked.

What a team we made. When the SCREWED receptionist answered, I asked for Roberta Corson, only to be told she'd called in sick. And I had no idea where she lived.

When I returned the guy's phone, I noticed the cop and the news crews were headed our way. Making legal U-turns had slowed them down — my way was better. Mother and I returned to her car, and I pulled into traffic. Another thought occurred to me, and once again, we took another sudden turn as if the car was in direct communication with my brain. In the rearview mirror, I saw the patrol car cut off a few drivers in an attempt to follow, before the press vans copied him. Man, we were more connected than a freight train.

At the sound of screeching tires behind us, Mother turned down her visor to watch. "They must think you're evading them."

"And that's my fault?" I snorted in disbelief.

"Darling, you are driving. Be fair, it's an easy mistake to think you might know where you're going." Mother stared serenely out the window, while muttering under her breath, "Who would have thought I'd become the sensible one?"

In her dreams. Where does she get these delusions?

Turning back to me, she asked casually, *"Do* you know where you're going?"

"Yes — to Kathy Right's. And we better hope Ian's little widow has neither fallen apart, nor become more entrenched in her belief in Drew's guilt. Right now, she's all we have."

The widow proved to be *both* shattered and entrenched. We found her seated alone at a patio table in her large backyard. A full pitcher of martinis sat on the smoky glass tabletop, apparently untouched, alongside an empty martini glass. But her eyes were so glazed the pitcher should have been empty. Was that her second batch? Nope, the eyes that suddenly zeroed in on us as we approached looked stone cold sober.

"Stop right there," Kathy snapped. "The D.A. said I'm not supposed to talk with you."

Prosecutors were so anal about separating everyone into different camps. Was that divisiveness really necessary?

Kathy started to rise, slowly and with apparent reluctance. I dropped to my knees before her. I took hold of her hand and eased her back into her seat.

"Kathy, just hear me out," I said. "Drew didn't kill Ian."

With a sigh, Kathy directed a kinder expression my way. "It's natural for you to think that, Tracy. You simply don't want to believe you could have been involved with a murderer."

I tightened my grip on her hand. "I don't *think* so, Kathy, I *know* he didn't do it. Look, you of all people should understand. You and Ian didn't match, any more than Drew and I do. But you know what it's like to connect to the inner person that you alone can see." I reached for her other hand. She didn't resist, but her fingers just rested lifelessly in mine. "I'm telling you from my intimate knowledge of him that Drew didn't kill Ian."

I held my breath. Her flat brown eyes gave no clue to her thoughts. Then, slowly, with no change in the rigid posture of her face, her fingers began tightening around mine.

"You understand, Tracy. That's precisely how I knew Ian. And that's why, no matter what anyone says, I *know* Ian wasn't having an affair. He might have been involved in something with another woman, but it wasn't sexual. You believe that, don't you?"

I believed it, all right — about as much as I believed in the Easter Bunny. Roberta's embarrassed reaction was proof enough. And Mother was never wrong about these things. Ian was clearly flicking his Bic at the wrong Virginia Slim. But somehow I needed to convince Kathy I believed in her husband as strongly as she did. Not merely to pry information from her, but because Kathy needed my conviction to bolster her own. I pushed all doubt from my mind and kept nothing there but my belief in Drew.

Kathy misread my expression as I'd hoped. "You do understand."

She pinched her eyes closed and the mottling of imminent tears rose to the surface of her fair skin. I waited for the teardrops to fall, but instead, her lids flew open and hardened with accusation. "I told you Ian was involved in something shady. That's what you want, isn't it, Tracy? Why should I help you uncover it? You'll use it to destroy his reputation."

I felt a stab of disappointment. It was ironic, really. I'd spent years hunting for proof of Kathy's hypocrisy, and now that I had it, it saddened me.

With a sigh, I dropped her hands and rose to my feet. "Why should you help me? So an innocent man doesn't spend his life in prison. I'll find the truth anyway. But I'll get there faster with your help." When she didn't respond, I snapped, "Kathy, you've spent your whole life fighting for what you believe in, sometimes at considerable sacrifice. Are you really going to turn your back on the truth now?"

With a jut of her chin, she said, "I am not. What do you need?"

"For you to make Roberta open Ian's private files to me."

"Done." She leaped to her feet and strode to the house.

Damn, I'm good. Still, I wasn't letting the compassion I felt for her scramble my brains. Kathy wasn't off the hook as a suspect, despite her obvious grief. Some killers regret it later. But the only motive I could ascribe to her was anger over Ian's affair. If she believed he hadn't been having one, what reason would she have had to kill him?

The maid wasn't in the kitchen today; no sound of children upstairs, either. It made the place feel so empty, despite the sounds Kathy created rummaging through her purse for her Blackberry. The climbing ropes were still bunched on the table.

"Do you climb rocks?" I asked, fingering the fat ropes.

Given the arch of Kathy's wide brown brow, she seemed to think the answer to my question should have been self-evident. Jeez, maybe I had squandered all my marbles. To redeem myself I plunged into a recitation of the quality of rock formations in my neighborhood.

Kathy cut me off with an impatient toss of her hair. "I climbed that rock face behind your house a couple of weeks ago. We laughed about how easy it would be to spy on you."

Just because you're paranoid doesn't mean they're *not* out to get you. "You and Ian?" I asked, feeling creepy.

She searched the phone's address book. "No, me and CeeCee."

"CeeCee *Payne?* You're friends?"

"Have you ever heard of anyone else named CeeCee?"

So she didn't buy CeeCee's lame story about her name, either.

"We were friends." Kathy swiftly corrected herself with an emphatic, "We *are* friends. It's just that Ian never liked me being close to CeeCee."

"Sure, he often opposed her in court," I said.

Kathy tilted her head thoughtfully. "No, that's not it. Ian was social with a number of prosecutors. He thought it gave him an edge when negotiating deals for his clients. But...not CeeCee. He avoided her, and I sensed he wished I would, too."

"But your friendship was too strong?"

"Not really. But how many other women climb even better than I do?"

We flew out the door of Kathy's house, only to find the caravan that had followed us there now filled every parking space on Kathy's hillside street. But the media types weren't waiting patiently in their vans. They rushed at us *en masse,* shouting so many questions they made me dizzy. A lifetime of creating tabloid headlines gave Mother better avoidance skills. With her in the lead, we slipped through the gauntlet. Before I climbed into the Mercedes, I noticed the deputy was the only one who hadn't left his vehicle. I gave him a big silly wave. He jerked his head away. Did that mean I couldn't see him? Jeez, my cat was smarter than that.

I eased the car into the street. The other vehicles followed instantly. Connected again, we zipped down the hill together. But I ran a red light and broke the chain. I snagged the last parking space outside of Roberta's address.

Roberta's apartment building was a typical California structure, especially for the south of Wilshire, south of Brentwood area. It was a U-shaped building in peach stucco, whose courtyard had been filled with the requisite kidney-shaped pool. It might have been the epitome of gracious living on a budget at one time, but now the dusty stucco needed a paintjob. It didn't look like Ian had kept all his women in style.

Mother and I climbed the outdoor concrete staircase to Roberta's apartment. She must have been watching for us through the peephole, because the faded rust-colored door flew open before we knocked. Without a word, Roberta flung her arm toward the interior of the apartment, which I took to be a graceless gesture of welcome. Equally silent, I stepped past our sour hostess.

But Mother paused beside her, and with a patently insincere smile said, "So glad you're feeling better, dear."

The veiled reminder that she'd played hooky was all it took to pierce Robotic's armor. She lowered her head, like she'd been caught by the hall monitor. "I was tired today."

Tired of going to the office when Mr. Mighty wasn't there.

Ornate antiques in muted brocade fabrics and dark woods filled the living room. Navy velvet drapes were drawn across the room's lone window. The only illumination in the funereal room came from a pair of Tiffany-style lamps at either side of the sofa.

Roberta led us down a short hall to her home office. Eggshell lace curtains hung at the window, allowing the sun's rays to stream through, and making this a brighter setting. But if the living room was a mortuary, this room was a shrine. Covering the walls were framed photos of Roberta and Ian; at the office; at various Christmas parties; in some of the SCREWED conference rooms. The only other decorations were copies of Ian's degrees and other commendations. Stacked in the corner were the empty cardboard boxes we'd seen her carrying.

So that was why she'd looked guilty — she was stealing Ian's keepsakes. The furtive glance she'd thrown over her shoulder probably meant she'd called the firm's car service to take her home. Nothing we saw supported Mother's theory that Roberta had either been bleeding Ian or servicing him.

Besides, the pattern of taking his castoffs appeared well established. The large mahogany desk, which crowded the short wall below the lace curtain, was the desk Ian had used before he became elevated to the highest level within SCREWED, a place where status was measured by the size of a man's — desk.

Businesslike now, Roberta sat rigidly erect in the desk chair before the computer monitor centered on the desk. The monitor was blank, but with one decisive shake of the mouse, Roberta awakened the sleeping keeper of truth. No prissy screensavers for this baby.

"Tracy, I strenuously object to your picking through the ruins of Ian's life. But Kathy insisted," Roberta said through her tightly clamped jaw.

Mother placed her hands on Roberta's shoulders. "Object all you want, darling, but you'll be able to access those ruins from here, won't you?"

"Of course," Robotic said, bristling. "I often worked at home on weekends when Ian asked."

Naturally, she did.

While Roberta called up Ian's files, Mother took a slip of paper from her purse and held it out to me. There were a list of dates and times at the top of the sheet, which Mother had taken from Kenette's message. At the bottom, she tapped a scarlet nail against the filename, *personal_codes.doc.*

Roberta demanded that we turn away while she entered the password. But when we turned back after the completion of that secret entry, I saw that, despite her objections, she seemed as anxious for a peek into that file as we were. Her shoulders rounded more than usual as she eagerly bent toward the monitor. I bet that even though she possessed his password, she had too much respect for Ian's privacy to violate it. But since we were forcing her hand, she couldn't wait to learn the identity of Kathy's rival, and hers.

Ian thought he was clever by entering his secret meetings into his calendar in code. But now we would break it. When the file opened, I peered over Roberta's shoulder. Mother stood a few feet behind, alternately squinting and widening her eyes. Robotic gave off a very human groan when she saw what the file held.

"Arrgh," I cried in frustration. "Ian, you secretive bastard!"

"Tell me what it says." Mother demanded.

"He set up a code within a code. He didn't identify the codes in his calendar by names or locations — he used telephone numbers. The number for all those occasions he entered into the calendar himself was: 818-555-6969. Now how the hell are we gonna break *that* code?"

CHAPTER TWENTY-THREE

As we walked dejectedly past the parking area for Roberta's building, Mother pointed to a shit-brown Buick Regal, at least ten years old. Its license plate read: SEC2IAN.

"Secretary to Ian?" Mother asked. "A bit much, wouldn't you say?"

"Roberta sure has a terminal case of hero worship. Too bad the object of her desire was no hero." Why else would Ian have worked so hard hiding his little meetings unless they were of a nature that had to be hidden?

I spied the patrol car double-parked up the block, but we'd finally lost the press. Progress. I raised my arm to signal with my thumb the direction we'd be heading in now — only at the last second, I might have switched to another finger.

Whatever.

I made a wild U-turn in front of the patrol car, reveling in the fact that the cop wasn't going to ticket me. Only then did I remember that we were in L.A. city and he was a county deputy. The other guys could still give me a ticket. Man, I thought I had a Get Out of Jail Free card. Of course, if I had, I'd have given it to Drew.

On Wilshire, I headed toward the freeway so we could zip back to the Valley and finally see Toby Newton.

While stopped at a light, Mother looked off to the side and snapped, "That Thomas, always grandstanding."

Thomas? I followed her glance to an appliance store. Its window display featured about a dozen TV screens, all flashing the image of Skippy Sullivan behind a podium. A press conference? Why did that surprise her? Ian's murder and Drew's arrest had short-circuited the attention Skippy expected after the trial. He wasn't one to suffer in silence.

Just as the traffic light turned, the image on those TV sets changed. Plastered across them now, in living color that was downright ironic, was a photograph of a man. He looked more dignified in the picture than he had when I'd met him — and especially more than when we pulled him from my pool.

Though horns honked behind me, I didn't budge. "Mother, quick. Look at the screens."

"It's Riley."

Though his dark hair was swept back in the photo, instead of center-parted, and his gap-toothed grin had been transformed into pensively pursed lips — that was our freezer tenant.

I double-parked and threw on the flashers. The guy behind the patrol car practically honked a symphony, but I ignored it. "Mother, scoot over into the driver's seat."

"Why should I?"

"Because I'm going to run into that store to learn what this story is all about, and I'm double-parked. A cop won't ticket us if he thinks the great Martha Collins is driving the car."

"Tracy, really — have you learned nothing from all your years with me? They won't ticket me even if I'm the passenger."

For that it might be worth keeping her around more. Nah, I'd enter the degree program in traffic school first.

I threw the door open, causing even more drivers to hate me. Get over it, already — I was in crisis mode. I sprinted to the sidewalk. The store had attached a small speaker to the window display, so I only needed to stand there for a few moments to learn what I needed to know.

I dashed back to the car. "The press conference wasn't to spin out Skippy's legal victory, but to announce that his dear Savior is missing. Riley didn't turn up for a dinner appointment with Skippy, and they haven't seen him where he lives. Mother, we're in deep doo-doo."

"Of course, he hasn't turned up at those places. He's in your freezer. Honestly, Tracy, what were you thinking?"

I glared at her. "Maybe that my advisor would show a bit more loyalty."

She grunted, a sound that could have meant anything — *but* an acceptance of responsibility. I threw the car in gear, though it drove strictly on autopilot. I directed all my attention to finding a way out of the Riley Something mess. If there was a solution on the horizon, however, I sure didn't see it.

Toby Newton's shabby duplex, on a dead-end street on the eastern end of Studio City, made Roberta's slightly worn complex look like a palace. Cardboard sheets, covered with aluminum foil, substituted for glass in the upper unit's window frames, and a rope held the door of the lower apartment closed. A rusted car, propped up on blocks, kept the cracked driveway well oiled.

While we waited at the door for our host to untie the lock, I thought it wasn't too surprising that Drew sensed a shakedown from a guy who seemed this down on his luck. But Toby Newton had a good job as a radio station engineer. From outside his duplex, I questioned what he did with his money.

Once the rope fell away, the door drifted open by itself. We stood on the step, staring in. A naked man, apart from the faded aqua towel he'd wrapped around his sagging fortyish gut, had wandered off, more interested in his cell phone conversation than his visitors.

Even before taking a step into the place, I grasped where a fair amount of his money went. To cigarettes and booze. So much smoke had built up in that dump, the air was blue. And ol' Toby was positively rich with bourbon and beer empties.

But I was also guessing a fair amount went to the ponies — since yellowing racing forms doubled as carpet in this joint, and after eavesdropping on his conversation, it was pretty clear he wasn't talking with his parish priest, unless the priest moonlighted as a bookie.

He wasn't wasting his money on furniture, though. He'd outfitted the place with milk crates and soiled mattresses stacked on a worn vinyl floor. When I sat on one mattress, a spring bit me in the butt. Mother was smarter; she stood. How I wished I'd brought Charlotte. She wouldn't consider my place so bad after seeing this.

Now that I'd seen him, I really hoped Garcia considered Toby Newton a big part of her case. Unless he cleaned up really good, he wouldn't make much of a witness against Drew. Learning that alone was worth the visit. If I could shake his stalking story, it would be even sweeter.

To my surprise, when we finally talked, Toby clung to his account with unexpected tenacity. "Hey, I didn't stand your old man up that first time he asked to meet. I was late getting to the coffee shop, that's all. I seen him leaving, driving outta the lot right behind that guy the cops said he killed."

"How would you even know Ian Dragger?" Mother asked.

"He had his name on his license plate. 'Something-2-IAN,' it said."

So Ian had used Roberta's car. I knew Drew met with Toby during breaks in the Sullivan trial. Why wasn't Ian at the courthouse then? What brought him to a Studio City motel coffee shop in Roberta's car?

Toby flopped on the mattress across from me. The towel parted. Whoa! Information overload.

He gave his hairless chest a few lazy scratches with his dirty, cracked nails. "I watched 'em for a while. This Ian-guy kept looking into the mirror to see if anyone was behind him. And your old man drove careful-like, so the guy didn't shake him."

Drew always drove carefully. I'd say he was an old lady behind the wheel, but that insulted old women drivers everywhere. Still, I doubted that Drew had noticed that was Ian ahead of him. He certainly wouldn't have identified that car as Roberta's. The SCREWED secretaries, who didn't rate building parking spots, mostly took buses to work. That would have made it easy for Ian to stop by her place and borrow her car. But why was the status-conscious Ian willing to be seen in anything but his pricey Range Rover?

I continued questioning Toby. But while his answers grew more disinterested, they never varied. So much for my theory that Toby was a paid member of the construction crew that built the frame around Drew. He was telling the truth as he saw it. By sheer coincidence, Drew and Ian happened to be at the same unexpected place, at the same time, during the trial. Why would Ian have cared if Drew saw him there?

And what about Toby? Drew believed he had leaked advance word of Skippy's intended assault on the *Scarlet Stories* studio to Nick Wick in exchange for a little coin. That convinced Drew that Toby expected a bribe from him. But Drew's impression didn't jibe with the guy flashing me. While I doubted Toby would refuse a bribe if it came his way, he didn't strike me as industrious enough to solicit one.

"Drew said your companion in the radio studio the night Skippy Sullivan took over the place was none other than Nick Wick. Mind telling me how Nick knew to be there?"

Toby chuckled. "You won't believe it, but Skip himself alerted Nick."

"So he really is a hypocrite," Mother said, giving her hair a toss.

"How do you figure that?" Toby absently reached across his mattress to where a wrinkled Hawaiian shirt had been tossed on a milk crate.

I snorted. "Skippy had been almost as vocal in his denunciation of *Nick Wick's Sin City* as he had of *Scarlet Stories*. What would you call that?"

From the shirt's breast pocket, he pulled a pack of cigarettes and lit one with a match from a matchbook stuffed into the cellophane wrapper. "You got it all wrong. Skip was smart, see. He said he'd use the enemy's tactics to defeat him. He figured *Sin City's* coverage of the DOLT assault would give him more ammunition, you know? That Skip really believes in his cause. It's like he's starting a whole new religion, only he's the god."

Mother leaned over and made a puking sound into my ear. "Enough to turn the Pope into an atheist."

Toby took a deep drag on his butt. He exhaled that thick cloud straight into my face. As if the stale stuff in the air wasn't bad enough. When I quit smoking, I promised myself I wouldn't turn into one of those fanatical nonsmokers, but this guy was making me rethink that decision. Hell, you'd think the weight I'd gained would have done that.

I struggled to rise from the mattress, but not before taking a moment to glare at our scruffy host. He seemed unaffected when he tossed the pack and matches onto the milk crate between us. Mother alone had the sense to look at that matchbook.

She grabbed it and shook it in Toby's face. "What is this place?" She held it out to me. In hot pink lettering on a black background, the words *Hideaway Motel* jumped out at me.

Toby chuckled. "That's a dump down the block, where married people do the nasty with folks they're not married to."

"Mother, why do you care?" While she had plenty of experience with nasty-making, the Hideaway wasn't her kind of place.

She thrust it into my face. "Read the telephone number, Tracy."

818-555-6969. "That was Ian's number — the one in his code file," I sputtered. "His tryst appointment."

"That'd be the place for it," Toby said with a knowing yellowed grin.

"And how does it happen you have it?" Mother asked.

Jeez, staring down her nose at Toby, she looked as moralistic as a nun. What a twist.

"The coffee shop where I met her old man..." He thrust his thumb in my direction. "...gives 'em out. It's attached to the Hideaway."

What had Drew stumbled into?

CHAPTER TWENTY-FOUR

After we left Toby Newton's place, I swung through a fast food drive-through to pick up some fries to hold me until we made it home. And all I had to endure was a snide comment from Mother about super-sizing myself. Since the cop still dogged us, I told the kid at the window to give him a burger. What a sport.

While I kept myself from wasting away during the drive home, Mother and I brainstormed what we learned from Toby Newton.

"Tracy, you keep saying Drew knew something damaging to someone, which he didn't realize was important. That's it. Ian scheduled a quickie with his paramour, and when he spotted Drew, he thought our boy had unearthed his secret."

I rolled that theory around in my head as I munched a fry. "That would explain why Ian started riding Drew during the trial. But your theory would only work if Drew were the victim and Ian the suspect. The other way around, it doesn't hang together." It also didn't explain why Ian became more aggressive after the verdict came down.

"Don't I keep saying it? *Cherchez la femme.* The woman had some issue with Ian, and she killed him. But she feared Drew knew about her, so she had to silence him, too. We find the woman, and we have our killer."

Yup, it was that easy.

Mother snorted in disbelief. "Imagine killing someone over an affair. As if it's that serious."

"Some people would do anything to keep it from those it might hurt." The wide blue eyes that met mine looked so baffled, I considered trying to explain. Only I figured neither of us would live that long.

"Anyway, that still doesn't explain Riley. How does he fit in this *ménage a trois?*"

"Darling, must *I* figure out everything? I'll leave that part of the puzzle to you."

Lucky me.

Our personal media stalkers had gathered again where we first encountered them. And their numbers had grown. I waved as we passed. I couldn't say whether the cop was as friendly.

In the rearview mirror, I watched the patrol car stop where our private road met the driveway. I parked beside Charlotte's silver Taurus and Vanessa's yellow Beetle.

I felt so defeated that I didn't walk half as fast as Mother once we were inside. It was only when I heard her joyous, "Alec!" that I rushed to the living room. Mother and Dad were already clasped together in a passionate lip-lock. But I found Charlotte sitting primly before the *Who Wants to Look Dumb on National TV?* game show, with Vanessa slouched at her side.

Despite his present activity, I threw a host of questions at Dad. "Where were you? Is Drew all right? Why didn't you come home?"

With Mother still wrapped in his arms, Dad said, "Whoa, honey. One question at a time. How could I come home, when you had the law stationed at the gate?"

Me. Now everyone was blaming me.

"Remember, Tracy, your Dad is supposed to be driving on Route 66," Vanessa reminded me. "If the police know he's here, they're gonna look closer at everyone's alibi for the time when we busted Drew out."

I'd really had enough of Vanessa's showing off.

By then Dad and Mother had come up for air. Dad said, "Relax, Tracy. Monsieur Chien is safely ensconced in the Norman Club, though Drew wasn't happy that I put him in that suit."

Charlotte bit her lip, chewing off some of her lipstick. "They could tell he was really a person of quality, couldn't they? Despite his garments."

The rest of us just looked at each other. That was a question we kept avoiding answering. The Norman Club prided itself on officially buying its members' little fictions. Behind the scenes, though, the employees must be having some fun at Charlotte's expense. She thought they regarded her as a kindly society matron caring for someone down on his luck, not some old witch getting it on with a homeless guy.

Charlotte, who continued to stare vacantly at the TV, didn't seem to notice that nobody answered. "I hope you told him to follow the club's rules, Alec. Our family has a position to uphold there."

Yeah, Drew would uphold it as a bewigged bum with a shiner. I had to change the subject before I gave Charlotte the Darwin Award. I asked Dad what he did with the horse trailer we'd used to stage Drew's jailbreak.

"Gave it to a street person, who promised to hide it where the cops wouldn't find it. He and his buddies will make good use of it."

At least somebody was happy. Someone had lit a fire in the living room's huge Arizona Flagstone fireplace. I drew a black leather chair closer and stared into the flickering flames. Weary and defeated, I must have drifted off to sleep.

Until I heard Charlotte snap, "Get a room, you two."

I clenched my eyes closed. After being flashed by Toby Newton, I couldn't take much more emotional scarring.

"Loosen up, Charlotte," Vanessa said. "I think they're kinda cute."

"Really, Charlotte," Mother sniffed. "Just because you're not getting —"

"Enough!" I shouted.

"Exactly," Mother said.

When my eyes popped opened, I saw Mother and Dad were now twisted together on one of the living room's couches. But it was not like they only had eyes for each other. From their pretzel clench, they glared at Charlotte, while hurling scornful epithets, which she threw right back at them. Dad and Mother were awfully lovey-dovey lately. That stage usually preceded an outright breakup. It might have happened already, only Mother had Charlotte to ride the love-hate swing with these days.

"Stop this bickering," I shouted. No fair. They were older — where did they get off forcing me to act like a grownup? Having had my fill of the squabbling seniors, I went upstairs to my study. There, I sat at my desk, staring out the window to where the sun was setting. Another day gone. And I was no closer to understanding anything.

Early the next morning, I returned to the same spot, slouching in my desk chair. This time I stared at the blackened screen of the laptop monitor, rather than out the window. When I absently tapped a key, CeeCee's name still stretched across the screen. I wanted to shoot someone — I just couldn't narrow it down.

Vanessa popped into the doorway, providing me with the perfect target. "I'm bored, Tracy. When are we going to work on my audition tape for *Scarlet Stories?"*

"One dilemma at a time, sweetie."

"At least let me see Raul. I'll be careful," she whined.

After the alibi scam we pulled with *Scarlet Stories,* we agreed Vanessa and Raul should sever their personal connection until we cleared Drew. Who would have thought I'd become the most consistent one in this bunch?

"Vanessa, you let Garcia see you with Raul, and you're gonna make that audition tape from the Big House."

Vanessa gave me a slow, accepting nod. Despite the pink hair, it looked quite sage. "Are we making any progress?"

Before I could answer, that weird synchronicity that surfaces only on rare occasions in life — and which I considered reality's only redeeming quality — exploded. Dad shouted through the crackling intercom, "Tracy, baby, get down here. *Now.* You have to see this."

Vanessa and I competed to see who would make it down the spiral staircase first. Despite her weight advantage, I won. I found them all riveted to Nick Wick's update on the TV.

"...high-ranking insider confirms the Ian Dragger murder has taken an unusual twist. Detectives want to question L.A. County prosecutor-turned-defense attorney, CeeCee Payne, in connection with her client's breakout."

"CeeCee?" Charlotte said in a hushed whisper. "Why would they suspect her?"

Because I dropped her card case in the car that transported Drew. Oh, boy.

While the parental units argued over whether elevating CeeCee to sainthood was still warranted, I staggered to the kitchen to be alone. Naturally, that was impossible. Harri stood on the counter, squawking at the top of her scratchy feline voice. Every cat owner knows the "feed me" cry, and there was such outrage in her posture, I expected to find her bowl empty. More guilt, exactly what I needed. But Harri's bowl was filled with kibble. She just liked getting fed.

Don't we all? Get in line, baby. If I hadn't been so agitated, I'd have collapsed from hunger. But I'm a total coward when it comes to that cat. I took the kibble from the pantry and tried to fake her out by shaking the bag over the bowl. While I made a fool of myself in that way, Dad walked into the kitchen.

"Honey, are you okay?"

"Dad, tell me the truth — did you know about CeeCee?"

"Not till I heard it on the tube, I swear." He held up his right hand.

"CeeCee and Drew," I snapped. "Had you guessed they were engaged?"

He tossed his longish white hair back. "Well…sure, sweetheart. Everybody knew."

"*I* didn't." For about the thousandth time, I reiterated Drew's lie.

We sat across from each other at the table. Absently, I reached into the cat kibble bag and pulled out a piece, which I started to bring to my lips, as if it were some tiny dark potato chip. But Harri's outraged shriek alerted me before I bit it. I flung the bag onto the counter.

Dad's congenial face grew stern. "You're not telling me everything, are you, young lady?"

With a sigh, I spilled that I dropped CeeCee's card case in the car when we busted Drew out.

Dad blew out a deep breath. "Gee, honey, that doesn't sound like you. It's petty enough for Charlotte."

I slapped the tabletop. "Okay, Dad, it's now official: I feel lower than whale shit."

But he wouldn't let it go. "I mean, *really* petty, Trace."

"Enough!" *Always take the high road* — that's my motto — *you meet fewer people there.*

On the counter, Harri tore the kibble bag to shreds. At least someone was happy.

"Unless...honey, is there any chance you were acting unconsciously? You found her suspicious, and you used that method to get the cops to notice her. I know I always found her shifty."

How I longed to cling to that lifeline. CeeCee's behavior *was* suspicious. But that wasn't why I dropped her cards, and I knew it. Dammit. I hate it when my honest streak surfaces. The next thing you knew I'd stop taking conning lessons from Philly. Where would it end?

I pushed myself to my feet. "Thanks, Dad. But I made this mess, and I have to fix it."

I went to the living room, with my father in my wake. Vanessa was gone now, but Charlotte still occupied the couch before the TV. I noticed Dad took Mother's hand and led her toward the stairs.

I waited till they were away before I said, "Charlotte, you're coming with me."

Without moving her eyes from that stupid game show, Charlotte asked indifferently, "Where, dear?"

"We're going to clear CeeCee, so she can do the job you hired her to do for Drew."

From the staircase, Mother shouted, "No — me. Tracy, you have to take me." She rushed down the stairs, with Dad following behind her. The neckline of her wrap-around cherry print dress had loosened. "I'll be just a minute, Tracy. Then we can go."

"A minute?" Dad demanded.

"I don't have a minute, Mother. CeeCee doesn't."

Mother said, "Darling, simply because I have needs, that's no reason to turn your back on me."

Why does she persist in saying things like that?

"A minute!" Dad shouted.

I shook my head. "Mother, this time it has to be Charlotte."

Charlotte approached behind me. "Why?"

Because CeeCee wouldn't hit her.

Mother flew down the stairs, "That settles it, I'm coming with you. Alec, please understand, our beloved child needs my help."

Right. She figured there was going to be a cat fight and wanted to be on hand to strike a blow. And when I thought about how mad CeeCee must be, I considered that a great idea.

CHAPTER TWENTY-FIVE

The two mothers squabbled over which car we would take.

"Charlotte, you don't know the area," Mother said, marching past Charlotte's rental toward her own Mercedes.

Charlotte held firm. "But I am the only one who has visited CeeCee's place, and I'm a safer driver." She glared at the darkening sky. "It looks like rain."

The clouds did look threatening now. But safety was such a concern to Mother and me, that we addressed that suggestion with a chorus of belly laughs. Charlotte, poor fool, didn't grasp that the matter had been settled. She plunged into the next round of verbal sparring, while Mother slipped behind the wheel of her Teutonic tank. I called shotgun, leaving Charlotte to climb into the rear seat with what scant dignity she had left.

Over the next couple of miles, as the cop tucked in behind us, and the press behind him, the only sounds in Mother's car were rumblings about the backseat's limited legroom.

As it turned out, it was just as well we didn't allow Charlotte to drive, since she proved to be a lousy navigator. I knew CeeCee lived somewhere along the glitzy high-rise corridor that ran down Wilshire Boulevard in Westwood Village. Naturally, it would have been out of character for me to check the address first. But I did expect to have along the only one of us to have visited it. Lotta good that did.

"Charlotte, make up your mind," Mother snapped with thinly veiled anger.

Charlotte pounded the back of Mother's seat. "Don't you yell at me, you...uh...I mean, Martha." Yeah, the veils were virtually transparent now. "It's along here somewhere. It's a small building, I remember that."

That surprised me. Given CeeCee's opulent taste, I figured she'd have one of the showiest penthouses. Doorman, parking attendant, red carpet you could sink into up to your knees. The units in the only small buildings around there tended to be relative bargains, not what I'd associate with CeeCee.

"We've visited each small building twice, and you can't remember which one it is," Mother said. "Why did we bring you?"

I brought both of them so someone could shield me from CeeCee's punches. But who would protect me when those two started swinging at each other?

In one of Mother's close sweeps near the sides of the cars parked along the curb, a newspaper vending machine caught my eye. "Mother, pull over there. Quickly." I pointed to a driveway.

"Before the green building, darling? Charlotte, was CeeCee's building green?"

Charlotte shrugged. "It might have been."

"Forget about CeeCee," I said. "It's the newspaper I wanna see. Did either of you read it today?" I only caught a glimpse of the headline when we cruised past, but that was enough to increase the tidal wave of acid in my gut.

"At home I always read it first thing," Charlotte said. "But you probably don't take *The New York Times*. Is there another newspaper here?"

"Yeah, newspaper, indoor plumbing — the works," I muttered.

"I normally never fail to read the newspaper, either," Mother said. "I need to feel informed."

That meant she read the show biz gossip column *and* her horoscope. I yanked open the car's ashtray. Empty. I slipped a hand down the back of my seat. No dice there, either.

"Tracy, what are you looking for?" Charlotte asked.

"Change, of course." Where did she keep hers?

With a martyred sigh, Charlotte reached into her wallet for some silver, which she deposited in my palm. I zipped from the car. Even before I popped a coin into the slot of the newspaper rack, Riley Something's face screamed out at me, from an article that dealt with his disappearance. What had I been thinking, agreeing to stash him as I did?

Once I began reading the piece, I discovered Riley Something's name was really Riley Jacks. Back in the car, the mothers read over my shoulder.

"I don't get it," I said, shaking my head.

"Why he was killed? Yes, dear, you keep saying that," Charlotte said.

"No, why someone with cool name like Riley Jacks went out of his way not to use it."

"Mark my words," Mother said, waving her finger in my face. "He had something to hide."

Sure — how he ended up in our pool.

By now Charlotte convinced herself that the small building we'd pulled up before really was CeeCee's. I studied the tasteful little structure with new eyes. It was painted a creamy dark green and surrounded by a fawn-colored stone fence. Impeccably maintained, but it was no match in luxury for the towers soaring up beside it. And unlike the neighboring buildings, there wasn't a driveway where we could leave the car. An electric gate crossed the parking entrance, making it off limits to guests.

Since Mother's car still blocked that driveway, a car in the center turning lane tapped his horn to attract her attention. Without so much as a glance into the rearview mirror, Mother backed into traffic to allow that man access to his driveway. She's nothing if not considerate. The squeal of brakes behind us made me cringe. I turned and tossed off an apologetic wave to the driver who almost plowed into us. I noticed then that the cop who had shadowed us all the way to Wilshire Boulevard was nowhere around.

As the car from the center strip went into its turn, the building's electric gate slid open. Mother positioned the nose of the Mercedes to follow that driver through.

Charlotte shrieked, "Martha, how dare you. That parking lot is only for residents."

Mother twisted around to argue, "Who'll know?" But by then the gate had closed. "Satisfied, Charlotte? Now we'll have to park blocks away."

"So we'll walk. Civilized people do," Charlotte said.

Civilized people — she meant New Yorkers. As far as us

uncivilized Angelenos were concerned, if we were meant to walk outdoors — why would gyms come equipped with treadmills?

True to Mother's prediction, we did end up blocks away. I tried to read the Riley article as we walked. Even though I was anxious to get to CeeCee's, I also needed to know if the article shared anything new on Riley's whereabouts. The mothers kept hounding me to keep up, but I couldn't read while walking fast.

When I approached CeeCee's building, Mother and Charlotte were on their way through the security gate. CeeCee probably buzzed them in. Good — let them soften her up. Only I noticed that pair of witches held the gate for me. Cowards.

With the newspaper spread before my face, I went back to reading. Cars went by in the street, a pair of kids slid past on skateboards, but I didn't pay much attention. Until someone grabbed hold of my arm and threw me against the stone fence. Since the action tossed the newspaper over my head, it took a moment to learn the identity of my assailant.

Nick Wick, I discovered, when he ripped the paper away. "Think you can avoid me? Think again, sweetheart," he snapped. "You're gonna take me to your girlfriend upstairs, and she's gonna lead me to Drew."

"I'm not taking you anywhere, Wickerson." I grabbed my crumpled newspaper from him. "Except to jail, if you don't quit bugging me."

"Lady, one of us needs a reality check."

One of us? I avoided reality like I owed it money, and he was a tabloid reporter. I'd say neither of us would recognize the real world if it bit us on the fanny.

The miserable bastard pressed his hand against my throat, pinning me against the wall. And he was strong, dammit. I flailed at his brush-cut hair with the newspaper and croaked out a feeble cry for help. But this was L.A., where nobody walked, remember? Where were Mother and Charlotte? Green dots danced across Wick's smarmy face as I went into oxygen debt.

"Let her go," some woman shouted.

A pair of hands yanked Wick away from me. Another pair seemed to be checking me over, though in parts of my body where he hadn't hurt me. I yelped when I saw who was connected to those hands. Garcia. Talk about jumping from the frying plan into a full-fledged inferno. She wasn't checking me over — she was frisking me. When she finished with my body, she pawed through the brown leather tote that hung from my shoulder.

"Hey, that's illegal," I shouted.

"So call a cop."

Only when she determined that I carried nothing of interest to her, did she step away. I noticed that my driveway deputy had joined us again, and was holding Wickerson. He must have met with Garcia somewhere. Standing off to the side, stood a dumpy LAPD officer. His turf, their case.

"Beat it, Wickerson," Garcia said, "before I convince Ms. Eaton to file charges against you."

Wick glared at me. "This isn't over," he said.

No shit. My bum-dressing husband was hiding out in some old money dive on the lam from the law. Another man, slightly past his prime, had taken up residency in my freezer. And I hadn't any idea how to set things right.

Once Wick was out of earshot, Garcia asked, "Where are your cohorts?"

Never one to miss a cue, Mother rushed to my side. "Tracy, darling, are you all right?"

"No thanks to you, Mother. Where were you when Nick Wick was beating the crap outta me?"

"Fighting Charlotte, of course. I knew I couldn't take him on by myself, and Charlotte refused to release the gate."

"I didn't want to inconvenience CeeCee by making her buzz us in again," Charlotte called from behind the gate she held open.

Readjusting my clothes after my frisking, I said, "Sure, who cares if Wick kills me, as long as we don't inconvenience CeeCee."

"Nah, let's inconvenience her," Garcia said. Once again those eyes twinkled, but the accompanying smile looked tight and hard, "It's time we found out what everyone knows."

Not everyone, I hoped.

Garcia left the cops downstairs, while she ushered the rest of us into the building. We four rode the small elevator in silence. Until Mother brushed against Charlotte, and Charlotte shoved her.

"Don't you push me, Charlotte," Mother snapped.

"I have a right to my space," Charlotte spat.

Within moments, they were slapping each other.

Garcia looked my way. "Close to your family, are you?"

I could only groan.

The elevator doors opened outside CeeCee's door. When Wonder Girl yanked the door open, her pale face looked rigid with fury. Without a word, CeeCee turned, leaving us to follow her.

While the building's exterior was restrained, the luxury that began at CeeCee's door rivaled anyone's. Yet the décor was hard and cold. The floors were a dove gray marble. There were no area rugs, nothing to relieve the severe contrast of dark gray leather furniture and smoked glass tables on the pale gray floors.

The whole place was as flawless as the photo spreads in the decorating mags. Even neater than Charlotte kept her home. I'd never been so proud to be a slob. A temporary legal shop had been set up on a slate table in the dining room, with laptop computers, as well as files and law books. But they had been placed in rigid stacks, and there were no messy associates around to detract from the order.

CeeCee led us through those sterile rooms, to an equally cold kitchen with gray granite counters under white cabinets. No doodads or cooking gadgets spoiled the unrelieved expanse of those surfaces, beyond CeeCee's Chanel purse, which rested on one counter.

CeeCee herself relieved the gray theme by wearing black crepe pants and a white silk blouse. Was that what she considered at-home clothes? When did she let her hair down? Not now, certainly — she didn't even invite us to sit. We all stood in different parts of the spacious kitchen, while Garcia paced among us, firing questions.

After CeeCee denied playing any role in Drew's escape, even though I'd gone there to clear her, I muttered, "Prove it."

CeeCee let out a shriek of frustration. She reached into her purse for her Day Planner, knocking the purse off the counter. She ignored the contents that spilled onto the floor, slapping the Day Planner open on the island between us. As she flipped through it, she jabbed a finger in my direction and asked Garcia, "What about her?"

"Ms. Eaton is…accounted for at that time." Garcia's questioning eyes held mine.

Apparently, CeeCee found nothing in her calendar to alibi her for the time of Drew's escape. She explained that she must have been working alone at the time. With the Day Planner left open, I started flipping through it, more from perversity than genuine nosiness. I stopped when I hit an entry that shocked me.

"You — *you're* the woman Ian had been involved with," I sputtered, pointing to an entry. "You used telephone number codes, just as Ian did. This one's for the Hideaway Motel. During the breaks in the Sullivan trial, you rode the wild turkey with the opposing counsel in an hourly motel."

CeeCee's milky white skin reddened, but her voice sounded steady when she said, "I don't know what you're talking about."

Mother picked up something that had fallen from CeeCee's purse when it hit the floor. "Really, darling? Then why do you have this?"

She held up one of SCREWED's electronic employee keycards. And this one sported Ian's photo.

CHAPTER TWENTY-SIX

If Chaos held a presence in that kitchen before the shocking revelation about CeeCee's private life, afterwards it positively ruled. Worse yet, it really greased Mother's tongue.

"Haven't I said it, Tracy?" she said. *"Cherchez la femme."*

Jeez, give the French a rest already.

Mother would not be robbed of her triumph. She whirled around on CeeCee and asked in a gravelly voice, "What's the matter, sister? Did Ian decide to return to Kathy, and you couldn't stand that?"

Sister? Who did she think she was portraying? Al Capone?

Garcia clapped her hands. "Cut the chatter."

CeeCee turned away. "Kathy? Kathy's his wife. Why would you imagine I'd want what she had?"

Mother always believed things had to be about sex. What if CeeCee had simply tired of losing cases to Ian? He spoiled her otherwise outstanding record.

"Sell that to someone who knows nothing about the world," Mother said from her bed's eye view. "Like Charlotte."

Charlotte might be as naïve as Mother believed, but even she seemed to be following the thread. I noticed Charlotte's warm skin had taken on an ashen tone. And that wasn't because a gray granite counter seemed to be holding her up.

"Hey, *can it,*" Garcia shouted. We all clamped our mouths shut — except for Mother, who opened hers to plunge in again. Garcia's hazel eyes narrowed in on her. "Keep talking, Ms. Collins, and you'll spend the night in lockup."

With no more response than a lifting of one of her fair brows, Mother finally shut her trap. Wow, was Garcia good or what? I'd probably want to keep her around for her ability to control Mother, were it not for my freezer guest.

Garcia now directed her steely look at CeeCee. CeeCee was too cool to let that rattle her. But when Garcia approached her, though the detective was a good head shorter, CeeCee took a step back.

"You were conducting an intimate relationship with Ian Dragger, the defense attorney, during the Sullivan trial?" Garcia asked, with a skeptical lift of her own thick brownish brow. How do people manage to lift only one?

"It's not illegal. Believe me, we weren't discussing the trial." Another step pressed CeeCee against the counter. Finding herself on the ropes seemed to snap her out of that defensive posture. She began picking up the objects that had fallen from her purse. "The Bar Association might object, but you'd be surprised how often it happens."

Not me, I wouldn't be surprised. Nothing that happened between lawyers could possibly top what I'd seen on movie sets. I was shock-proof for life.

Garcia pursued CeeCee. "It is suspicious, especially since you didn't see fit to disclose this relationship earlier."

It fit, too. Drew had told me the woman who called to say Ian was on the way to our house sounded familiar to him. Could CeeCee have made that call?

CeeCee rose to her full height. "I was protecting Kathy and her kids. What Ian and I had was just…athletic."

Athletic, huh? That reminded me of something Kathy had said — CeeCee climbed rocks in our neighborhood. Which made her strong enough to drag Ian there. But why involve Drew? Was Mother right, was revenge against the men who rejected her at the root of it?

Despite a skin tone that looked more green than gray now, Charlotte seemed to be reading my mind. Creepy thought. "You're full of conflicts, CeeCee. First with Mr. Dragger, and now Drew. You had an obligation to tell me that you had a relationship with the man Drew was accused of killing."

But where did Riley fit in?

"Charlotte, you begged me, remember? I completely altered my career to protect Drew."

I remembered that Daffy Duck, one of the senior partners at SCREWED, surmised Ian had been paying blackmail to someone. Had the enterprising juror followed them to the Hideaway and learned their secret? While Ian might have chosen to pay Riley off, CeeCee could have found another way to rid herself of a liability.

"*Protecting* Drew, CeeCee — or railroading him?" Charlotte demanded.

If she really wanted to frame Drew, would she have dumped Riley's body there at a time when Drew couldn't have killed him? Maybe she was implicating me, too. Or were there two killers, the second of which copied the first? The questions were starting to hurt my throbbing brain. But one thing was clear: I no longer wondered why she set up shop in her condo, away from the firm that had hired her. CeeCee's cards couldn't get any closer to her vest.

Charlotte let out a little cry. "Oh, God! The attack on Drew in jail — did you engineer it?"

I'd forgotten about that. Great, now Charlotte could out-detect me. But that attack made more sense. If Ian had believed Drew knew about his relationship with CeeCee, she must think so, too.

"To think I planned to give you my linen. I'm going to be sick." Charlotte clamped her hand over her mouth.

Garcia ordered me to take Charlotte to the bathroom. I guided her away, as CeeCee shouted directions to the powder room.

But when we approached the darkened powder room, I kept Charlotte moving. "Suck it up, Charlotte. We're going to find another bathroom."

I dragged her down the hall, past a guestroom, a TV room and a tidy home gym. I paused before the gym for a moment. In the center was one of those multipurpose pieces of exercise equipment, and on the floor, a few free weights. Hanging from hooks next to a mirrored wall were colorful climbing ropes such as the ones I'd seen in Kathy's house.

I pushed Charlotte until we came to the large master bedroom. I pointed to the adjoining bathroom. "If you have to hurl, do it in there."

The gray theme ended in the bedroom. The king-sized bed rested on a platform of pale birch. Underfoot was a stone-colored wall-to-wall carpet in a thick plush. But the minimized-to-the-max style still ruled. A taupe comforter had been tucked tightly enough around the mattress to pass a Marine inspection, and no pillows marred the expanse of the headboard. Mother had waved enough decorating magazines before my nose for me to say with certainty that the bedroom's furnishings had cost several times the budget for my whole house. Or what would have been the budget before my husband took up employment in the clink.

Charlotte perched on the edge of the bed. "No thanks, dear. I don't think I'll be sick now, I just need to sit."

Not good news. I counted on having some time alone in this room outside of Charlotte's inhibiting presence. But she hadn't objected much lately. What the hell. I threw open the door of the walk-in closet and began pawing through the built-in drawers.

"I can't believe what CeeCee did. To think for years I would have preferred —" Charlotte stopped and glanced my way. Good thing she broke that thought off; there was far too much killing around here lately. "Maybe having been rejected by Drew was what changed poor dear CeeCee."

Sure, it was *still* my fault. I continued digging through CeeCee's drawers. Since time was short, I didn't pay much attention to her stuff, other than to note she really wasn't into frilly undies. Ian's jollies must have been set off by strictly utilitarian white bras.

I checked the pockets of her many conservative designer suits. But there weren't even any dirty tissues in those pockets. What kind of woman was she? I reached into the pocket of my jeans, where there was always a used tissue — especially when I tossed them into the wash — and I stuffed my Kleenex into the pocket of one of her chi-chi suits just to know it would gross her out when she found it. Given recent revelations about CeeCee, I feared I'd abandoned pettiness too cavalierly.

I paused before a shoe rack Imelda Marcos would have envied, which covered the entire rear wall of the closet. The shoes were mostly conservative, too. But CeeCee had big feet; I could practically stick my whole forearm into those shoes.

I left the closet and surveyed the room. It was large, but mostly empty. Apart from the bed, the room's sole contents were two black side chairs at the window. I stretched out on the carpet and felt their undersides.

"Tracy, dear, what are you doing?" Charlotte asked.

And I worried about Charlotte's inhibiting presence? She was barely conscious. "I'm searching for anything that might be hidden here, which could clear Drew."

"Detective Garcia —"

"Garcia plays by the rules." Except for frisking me. "You saw where that got Drew." Would Charlotte tattle on me now to her poor misguided CeeCee?

But she surprised me. With a toss of her head, she indicated the bathroom. "There's still another room here."

Charlotte sure was loosening up. And it only took her son's imminent murder to do it. But I noticed she didn't offer to help.

The bathroom was as opulent as I expected, with a pearl gray Jacuzzi tub and one of those stall showers that contain enough water nozzles to hose down an army. But there weren't a lot of hiding places. I found a medicine chest behind the mirror over the gray pedestal sink. Beyond a few French skin lotions, all she had in plentiful supply were some bottles of that hand sanitizing goo.

Then I spotted a closet tucked behind the bathroom door. It was a linen closet. Faultlessly neat, but more overstuffed than anyplace else in the apartment. Charcoal bath towels and sheets in muted tones filled two shelves. Toiletries covered another shelf. Two pillows in taupe pillowcases occupied the space at the top, and pushed between the bottom shelf and the floor were two uncased pillows.

I pressed my hands into and around everything, but I found absolutely nothing. Those extra pillows were squeezed in so tightly, they bulged from the inadequate space. It seemed unlikely that she'd stuffed anything else in there, but I'd checked everywhere else. I reached my arm along the gray marble floor. My hand bumped into something, but the pillows fit too snugly into the space for me to pull it out. I yanked the pillows free and tossed them onto the floor.

I reached in again for the object. A scale. Could it be the lean CeeCee found the nasty thing as offensive as I did? I shoved it back. But the scale bumped into something else. I stuck my head into the space — and nearly swallowed my tongue when I saw what was hidden there. A pair of shoes — men's shoes. With dress uppers and sport soles.

I snatched those shoes and ran from the bathroom. Pausing only long enough to wave them at Charlotte, I flew back to the kitchen.

I shook the shoes before Garcia. "Do you know what these are? They're Drew's shoes."

Charlotte came up behind me. "Tracy, dear, I'm sure there's an innocent explanation. Maybe Drew...uh...changed here."

I spun around to her, aghast. "Charlotte, what are you saying? Drew didn't *sleep* with CeeCee, if that's what you mean."

Charlotte pressed her hand to her chest, as if I'd suggested the unthinkable — when it sure sounded to me like that was precisely what she had been thinking. I turned back to CeeCee. "But I would like to know how they got here."

Garcia stepped between us, her head turning back-and-forth as if she were watching a slow moving Ping-Pong game. "So would I. We've been looking everywhere for them." She directed a searching look at CeeCee. "Ian Dragger's killer wore those shoes."

How did she know that?

"I've never seen those shoes before. *She* brought them in," CeeCee insisted, pointing at me.

Though Garcia spoke to CeeCee, she looked at me. "No, Ms. Eaton carried nothing in here." The tiniest spark of laughter surfaced in her eyes, an acknowledgement of having searched me before I entered this place.

Garcia approached CeeCee. "Ms. Payne, I think it's time we continue this conversation at the Homicide Bureau."

CHAPTER TWENTY-SEVEN

Garcia's threat made CeeCee's fair face go so pale that, compared to her, the dead look ruddy. "I'll have your job for this," CeeCee said in a hushed whisper. Her hooded eyes narrowed to slits.

A shrug was Garcia's only response.

CeeCee declined Garcia's offer to call a lawyer. "They don't come any better than me," she snapped. Shock might have registered on her face, but CeeCee's ego remained as robust as ever.

CeeCee did insist on changing into one of her lawyer suits. Considering the tears she'd be shedding where she was going, my having put a used tissue in her pocket now seemed more like an act of charity.

"Okay, folks, show's over," Garcia said. "Everybody out."

I resisted her efforts to shoo me toward the door. "No, wait. Please, Detective, tell me about those shoes. How do you know Ian's killer wore them?"

With a reluctant toss of her short chestnut hair, Garcia relented. Though I'd already carried the shoes in there from the linen closet, she donned a pair of latex gloves she pulled from the pocket of her blazer, before turning them over.

"These are custom made shoes. They sell them through ads in various executive journals. See that code?" She pointed to some numbers stamped into the shoe's arch. "The manufacturer confirms these were made for your husband, and we have a photo of him wearing them. We also know that whoever brought Ian Dragger to your yard wore these shoes. We've had everything but the shoes themselves."

Jeez, and they weren't even Bruno Magli shoes. Who knew they would tell such a tale? The imprint of that code must have been the evidence that the cops insisted implicated Drew. It didn't escape my notice that Garcia no longer seemed so sure Drew had been wearing those shoes when the murder took place.

To my surprise, honesty reared its pinhead again, and just when CeeCee was hip deep in crap. "At a party Drew's firm threw to celebrate the Sullivan verdict, I saw one of Skippy Sullivan's followers wearing those shoes." Jeez, what was happening to me? If I couldn't short-circuit this truthful jag soon, I'd have to enter a convent. I tried to think of a lie I could tell, any lie, to reverse the streak — but my mind went blank.

Garcia nodded. "That's already been reported. The man in question claims Skip Sullivan made him leave the shoes there, which Mr. Sullivan confirms."

So the shoes were left in Drew's office. But Ian's killer used them later that night. And CeeCee had Ian's keycard badge. As a senior partner, Ian's badge opened all the offices in the SCREWED suite, including Drew's. And now those shoes were hidden here, in CeeCee's home.

The obvious conclusion flabbergasted me.

And I wasn't the only one. Once we returned to Mother's car, Charlotte climbed into the backseat without protest. For miles the only sound we heard from back there was an occasional murmured, "CeeCee — oh, my."

Too bad the other mother in that car wouldn't shut up. "Didn't I tell you, Tracy? I said it felt like a woman's crime, that it smacked of revenge. In one swoop, CeeCee retaliated against the two men who had rejected her. Didn't I say it was all about sex?"

"Yeah? Then how do you explain Riley?" I demanded.

"What about him? He bragged about being the juror who convinced the others to vote for acquittal. Why shouldn't CeeCee kill him? He denied her a guilty verdict. Really, Tracy, it's so obvious, I'm surprised you can't see it."

"Oh, I can see it, Mother. Just not how it relates to sex."

"Trust me, darling, when you get right down to it, everything is sex." As good as that exit line was, Mother refused to let the conversation die. "Tracy, I can't tell you how good it feels to know I was right all along. I said, *cherchez* —"

"That's it, Mother," I exploded. "No more French — or I promise you, I'll be an orphan before we reach home."

My shouting roused Charlotte. "No more French? Honestly, Tracy, you'd think you'd be used to Martha's swearing by now."

Man, I needed to get another life.

Vanessa flew at us the instant we returned to the house. "Do you know what they're saying on TV? That CeeCee was taken into custody." Vanessa's large arms gestured so wildly in the air around her, she looked like she was trying to smack a bug. "That should have been my story, Tracy. You didn't even tell me you were leaving."

True. But I couldn't have foreseen the events that unfurled at CeeCee's.

"Hang in there, Vanessa. You'll get your story," I said.

While the mothers went to the living room, Vanessa blocked my path. "When?"

"When I know, you'll know." I slipped around her.

I found Dad playing solitaire at the kitchen table. With no more than a grunt of greeting, I went straight to the freezer. Pushing aside packages, I hunted for the second stash I'd hidden there, now that the ice cream was gone.

"If you're looking for your chocolate, I ate it," Dad said.

Feeling betrayed, I just stared at him.

"Why don't you eat a carrot, sweetheart?" Dad said. "You know how happy it will make your mother if you lose that baby fat."

Boy, when the blows start coming your way, they don't let up. Now even my father hadn't noticed how much weight I'd lost. That he considered it baby fat, at my age, didn't begin to soften the blow.

"And you know how I live to make Mother happy," I said, but my delivery lacked its usual zing.

I wandered to the pantry and stared at empty shelves. There weren't even any crackers left anymore. Nothing to eat, nothing to mouth-catch — before long, we were going to turn into the Donner party.

But I knew what I needed, and it had nothing to do with food. There was something I had to do. Too bad I had no idea how to pull it off.

"You ate my chocolate, Dad. Now you owe me."

"Sure thing, baby. I'll do anything. Except give you back your chocolate."

"Then you're going to have to do the next best thing." Scattering the cards, I leaned across the table said in a harsh whisper, "I *must* see Drew."

CHAPTER TWENTY-EIGHT

"Come on, Dad," I repeated. "You've got to help me. I *have* to see Drew."

I kept it to a low whisper because I knew if I shared my desire with everyone, Charlotte would want to go, too. Then Mother would attach herself to the train. Once Vanessa learned I was meeting Drew, she would insist on seeing Raul. Not to mention demanding the story for her audition tape. And that would unravel the whole ball of twine. I knew my dad wouldn't blow my cover, but what I hadn't anticipated was how easily he could accomplish it.

"No problem, baby," he said. "I figured you would. After I set up Monsieur Chien downtown, I arranged with my friend Louie, who owns his own cab, to take you."

"No kidding? But how can you alert him that we need him now? The cops have to be monitoring our calls."

Dad's white hair quivered with indignation. "Tracy, give me a little credit. I worked out a code with him, of course."

Jeez, now everyone was out-thinking me.

The code worked, though it still wasn't easy. The cab came for me way up the hill. I hiked all the way there, wearing my rattiest jeans and sneakers. But at my side, I carried a paper bag filled with the kind of smart clothes I assumed the Norman Club expected its visitors to wear. The forest green suit and ivory turtleneck stuffed in that bag were the best garments I owned. They were also precisely what Mother would kill to see me wear — so, naturally, for the good of society, I could never allow that to happen.

Louie spirited me away from that spot without being tailed. But there was a price for it — the trip took forever. Our route to downtown L.A. detoured through Simi Valley in Ventura County, Agoura Hills, Malibu, the Westside and Hollywood. Which was the *really* long way. But it was worth it to get there without a cop in tow.

A few miles away from the Norman Club, Louie pulled into a gas station mini-market, where I slipped into the ladies room to change my clothes. But in my haste, I transferred all the dust I'd picked up on my grubbies to my good suit. That pushed me even further into a funk that I could only reverse by stopping at the register for a couple of candy bars. Who cared if the suit didn't fit me tomorrow? So that Louie didn't think I was wasting valuable time on a chocolate break, I also picked up a newspaper. But Riley's face, which still dominated the front page, put me off reading it.

Louie deposited me at the sedate entrance to the Norman Club. The voluminous main room, awash in rich wood paneling and fine chintz, struck me as a cross between a British men's club and some prissy old lady's house. Fortunately, the unifying dowdiness saved it from outright schizophrenia.

Striding across a lobby as long as a football field, I tried to affect the bored indifference only the most obnoxiously entitled would exhibit. Right, Charlotte at her most imperious. But I continued rapping a newspaper section against my suit to knock off the dirt I'd deposited there. I really must have been raised in a barn — a big, posh Beverly Hills-style barn, but a barn nonetheless.

Knowing how ridiculously stuffy their standards had to be, I feared I wouldn't succeed in worming Monsieur Chien's room number from the front desk attendant unless I assumed the rich-bitch part. Before I reached the desk, however, I spotted a sign announcing a speech to be given that very night by the head DOLT, Skippy Sullivan. The sight of Skippy's dippy face exorcised any anxiety I felt. Jeez, if they'd really let anyone in, they probably wanted me there.

After all my preparation, the young blonde girl working the front desk looked worse than I normally did. A roll of fat bubbled over the waistband of her short black skirt, stretching the fabric of her silvery knit top. Though I had to admit the long legs displayed by her mini were outstanding, and her fuck-me silver sandals added such a delightfully slutty touch. When the bored attendant took the trouble to look my way, I thought she looked familiar. I must have seen her in something on TV — there were far too many actors in

L.A. to all wait tables.

Now I worried I looked too good for that dump. I leaned my dusty sleeve on the counter and asked the girl for the room number without a trace of artifice. I was glad when she rattled it off, but all the fun had already gone out of the game.

The thick burgundy carpet covering the fifth floor corridor reduced the sound of my steps to a hush. I knocked at the highly varnished door at the end of the hall.

"Qu'est-ce que c'est?" demanded a gravelly voice.

Having been told by the girl at the desk that this was the only occupied guestroom on the floor, I threw what little caution I'd already exhibited into the gale forces coming my way. "Can it, Sir Dog, and let me in."

"Tracy?" Drew yelped. He opened the door a crack and yanked me inside.

Though he'd lost the wig, Drew still took the precaution of smearing something that looked like dirt on his face, and he hadn't shaved today. He still wore that awful smelly suit, which, in one of its lifetimes, had clearly belonged to a taller, heavier man, since Drew had to cinch the waist with rope and roll up the sleeves and pant legs.

I framed the image with my hands. "It's the shiner that pulls the whole look together. What an artistic touch."

He pulled me into his arms. I gagged from the suit's stench.

Just as I was overcoming that, Drew pushed me away and held me at arm's length. "Trace, how did you get here?"

I shook my head. He didn't need to hear the story of my journey there. But I didn't know how to start the tale that did need telling.

I tossed the newspaper section onto the bed, an antique sleigh bed covered with a shantung bedspread in a dusty blue. I plopped next to it, and from there, I checked out the room, which was surprisingly large, considering the Norman Club wasn't in the hotel biz. Well-polished mahogany furnishings and a pair of comfy looking blue velvet chairs highlighted the décor. I noticed Sir Dog had requested some books from the Club's library, which were stacked on the nightstand next to the bed. But the room did not have a television, a computer, or even a radio. And that meant, despite the insane speed with which information had been moving, Drew hadn't heard what had happened since we busted him out of custody.

Drew stood before me. The longer I took, the more wary his golden brown eyes became. Finally, I broke the news that CeeCee was being questioned for Ian's murder.

True to his profession even now, he didn't give much away. He didn't sputter any of the pointless protestations that would have flowed from my mouth. But not even the five o'clock shadow and the smudges on his face could hide his obvious sadness.

"Why?" he asked at last.

"It seems they couldn't keep their hands off each other." I explained about the quickie motel, and the secret he had stumbled upon. "You really didn't know?"

With a slow shake of his head, he indicated he hadn't. "Knowing them both so well, I wouldn't have predicted it. They're so much alike."

It gave me some small pleasure to note, that while he appeared baffled by CeeCee's choice, he didn't seem to care about the games she and Ian had played.

Drew sank onto the bed next to me. "Trace, are you sure? I can't imagine two less passionate people. Nor less impulsive."

"Drew, the cops are sure." Well, pretty sure.

Drew shrugged. "I had wondered why she agreed to mom's request, but I felt so desperate, I grasped at the lifeline. I felt so safe having her in my corner." A hint of bitterness crept into his voice. "Now it fits. Protecting herself while giving the shaft to the patsy — that CeeCee always was efficient."

Drew's gaze drifted to the newspaper between us on the bed. "So that's who he was. I should have recognized him."

"Who? Riley? Where did you see him?"

"At the coffee shop, next to the Hideaway Motel. I noticed he looked familiar. I should have recognized him at once, having stared at him in the jury box for weeks, but he changed his appearance."

Drew shook the paper. "He looked like this at the motel — hair swept back, serious expression. While in court he looked —"

"I know — as he had at the party." So Riley really had been there, spying on Ian and CeeCee no doubt. And he'd changed his look.

"It's rare when such subtle changes make a difference in someone's appearance, but on him they did," Drew said.

He should see the difference death made.

Drew continued reading. "Riley's missing, huh? They don't think CeeCee…"

Now we'd come to the tricky part. Our household was the only one to jump to that conclusion, since we alone knew Riley's whereabouts. But Drew didn't need to hear the unabridged version. I told him the police were looking into that possibility.

All at once, Drew lost it. He leaned over and buried his face in his hands. A shudder rippled through his shoulders. Despite the smell, I pulled him into my arms.

"You know what really pisses me off, Trace?" Drew muttered into my chest. "CeeCee always made me feel a little guilty."

Yes! He was going to tell me about the engagement. I prepared myself to forgive him, now that he was coming clean.

But the conversation went in a different direction when Drew pulled from my arms. "Not guilty, exactly. More that I didn't live up to her standards. You know, because I worked in a law firm and made pretty decent money, while CeeCee gave up all that to do The People's business."

"You were doing the business of the people who wanted to keep their inheritances."

"Nice try, babe." He traced my jaw with his finger. "And now we've both lost the law, CeeCee and me. I was good at it, too. You know, people make lawyers the butt of jokes, but I always thought there was such a nobility to the profession."

Nobility, sure. But way too picky.

He walked to the window, where he stared through the sheers behind the blue shantung drapes to the street below. "You want to hear the craziest thing? Throughout the trial, when Ian was always putting me down, I kept thinking I could be as good a trial lawyer as he was. That you were right all these years when you said I should be in criminal work."

Hallelujah! My prayers had been answered. I always knew my life would be more fun if I had Drew's criminal cases to pick through.

"And now, when I finally realize how my life should go, it's over." Drew's sigh sounded like a slow leak from an old tire.

"Why?"

He threw out his arms. "Because I'm AWOL from jail. When you're an officer of the court, they frown on that."

I understood that he really did love the law — but it was *awfully* judgmental. "Not so fast, mister. We broke you out to save your life, not to ruin it. Have a little faith."

"Tracy, you're terribly naïve." He smiled at me, in a sad, distant way. "Who cares? All I want now is to forget everything."

He grabbed me into a passionate kiss. His hands roamed over my body in a familiar, though unusually demanding, way. To my surprise, I did something I never thought I'd do — I shoved him away. Hard too. By the time he stopped backing up, he stood a few feet from me, looking stunned.

"Sorry, Drew." I gestured to his clothing. "This just doesn't work for me. You have to draw the line somewhere."

Drew's hand drifted toward me. "Not like you, babe. I didn't think you drew any lines."

I slapped his hand away. "Accept it — this is not gonna happen today, Dog-Boy."

Drew crossed his arms across his chest, which wasn't nearly as hunky looking in those duds. Who knew? Clothes really do make the man.

I crossed my own arms. "Rather the other way around. Were you ever planning to tell me you had once asked CeeCee Payne to marry you?"

"Shit. I knew that would come out one day." He collapsed into one of the side chairs and propped his feet on the other. The shoes had also come from someone's discards. There was a hole in the sole of one of them. "Trace, believe me, I never intended —"

"To hide it from me?" I asked with undisguised eagerness.

"No, I intended that," he said with a knowing chuckle. "Technically, you'd have to say I cheated on my fiancée when I started seeing you. I didn't think you could handle knowing that. Besides, you're so possessive. I knew you'd obsess over it, especially after CeeCee moved out here."

Me? Possessive? Where did he get these ideas?

"But you gotta believe me, babe. I never really asked her to marry me. We just drifted into it. You know how it is...we came from the same social circle, our moms were friends. Eventually, an understanding emerged. I didn't create it, I swear." He hesitated, before shrugging. "But I didn't question it, either. My life seemed so orderly with CeeCee, and you know how my family venerates order. I never admitted to myself how unhappy it made me."

I shoved his feet off the second chair and parked my behind on it. "Not even when you bolted to Stanford Law School?"

"Not even then. I told myself I needed a change. Mom and Dad didn't like it, and it made CeeCee furious to know I was going so far. But the understanding survived. Only as I was finishing law school did I acknowledge that I regarded returning to her as putting my head in a noose."

His description made me feel so warm and cozy. CeeCee, a death sentence — I liked that.

He closed his eyes. "Only then you burst into my life, Tracy." For a moment, the strain vanished from his face. "You were so different from anyone I'd ever met. Like a fresh breeze in the tomb I'd been living in."

I tapped his shin with my foot. "So you liked that, huh? Then how come you're always fighting me?"

"I said I liked the breeze, Trace — I didn't know it was actually a cyclonic force." When he finally opened his eyes, they glowed with amusement. "Besides, change is hard, especially when you've worshipped regimentation all your life. And admit it — you don't let people do things by stages."

"All or nothing — that's my motto." And *nothing* really wasn't

an option.

He leaned forward and took my hand. "You've never really understood how totally bonkers-for-life I am with you, babe."

I felt a lump form in my throat, and I gestured toward the bed. "Do you still want to…?"

Drew sank back in his chair. "Nah, I'm not in the mood anymore."

Now I was. Men, so fickle. What a waste of sexy undies.

With a sigh, Drew said, "I just wanted to escape from the idea of my bleak future for a while. But I better get used to it."

I jumped up. "Stop saying that. Trust me, Drew, to save your life and your career."

Drew went to the dresser, where he kept the hairball wig. "I trust you, Tracy." He plopped it crookedly on his head. "Look at me — would I wear Adolf Hitler's wig if I didn't? I'll even admit that your daffiness stymies the laws of logic. But not the penal code, babe. I'm enough of a realist to know that."

"Reality is the last thing you should be facing now, Drew. It's a self-fulfilling trap. Don't you know that by now?" I grabbed his arms. "Trust *me,* and my way."

With fragile hope, he asked. "You have a plan?"

I gave my head a vigorous shake. "Not in the least. But you know how I work. I just throw a lot of things out there, trusting they'll come together in the end."

"And do they? Always?"

"Always. Well…except when they don't. But then I keep throwing stuff, and eventually it works out. I call it Chaos Theory."

"Chaos Theory, huh? I think the physicists define it a little differently."

"That just shows how chaotic things are. It's my philosophy of life."

"You don't have a philosophy, Trace, just a lot of mottoes and goofy expletives."

"This is deeper than all of them." I kept the sincerity from my voice, so as not to scare him. "Believe it, Drew."

"If you could give me some idea —"

"No time now," I said in a rush. "Just be prepared to pick up your life where it left off."

I threw the door open and marched out with confidence. Having a goal in sight always jazzed me. That strong emotion stayed with me during the time it took for the door to close behind me. Only then did I sag against the gray-and-burgundy striped wallpaper in the hall. While I really did believe in the logic of disorder, I feared, for the first time, that my problems were beyond it.

CHAPTER TWENTY-NINE

After a less circuitous route, Dad's cabby, Louie, dropped me off up the hill from my house. I'd been so distracted when we left the Norman Club, I didn't remind him to drop me off somewhere to change. So now I was about to hike down a mountain in my best duds. I did slip my sneakers on again before setting out — I wasn't so nuts as to hike downhill in heels. But forget about the suit. Before I'd gone only a quarter of the distance, I looked like I'd lived the last week in a dust storm.

I detoured to the empty TV facility. With my fingers curled through the openings in the chain link fence, I willed the structures beyond it to give up their secrets. But all I learned was that they were in escrow, according to the *sold* strip that had been pasted across the real estate agent's sign. Notice of a termite extermination was also attached. Bummed that I learned nothing useful, I turned to go home.

When I reached my yard, I looked as if I'd rolled in the dirt. In that condition, I threw open the sliding door and stepped inside. Mother, Charlotte and Vanessa rushed me at once.

"There you are," Vanessa shouted.

"Tracy, my darling, we were so worried." Mother kept patting me down, as if in search of broken bones. "You didn't tell anyone where you were going."

I threw a quick glance to a corner chair, where Dad sat in uncharacteristic isolation, listening to music on an iPod. When I glanced at him, he kept his eyes directed at the ceiling. I knew he wouldn't rat me out. But if anyone there had half a brain, they'd have realized Dad went off by himself only when a secret was eating a hole through his tongue.

"Gee, I'm sorry," I said with the pseudo-sincerity I learned from Mother while still in the cradle. "I went for a walk. It didn't occur to me anyone would notice I was gone." For four hours?

Gingerly, Charlotte grasped both of my sleeves and held them out. "You're filthy. Where were you walking? In a ditch being dug?"

By drawing my arms to the side, Charlotte gave Mother a chance to study my suit. Despite its present condition, her eyes narrowed in suspicion. "Tracy, why haven't I seen that suit before?"

Pulling free of Charlotte's grasp, I gestured to the TV. "Anything new here?" I asked, to sidestep the clothing issue.

"No, but we're monitoring," Vanessa assured me.

"Glad that you're on that."

I noticed someone had cleared all the decorating samples from the room. No wallpaper patterns remained, no tiles. But there were little white squares all over the walls, where the old paint chipped away when someone tore off the paint color samples Mother had taped to those spots. Charlotte, I assumed — I hoped she hid them somewhere I'd never look. I'd forgotten how spacious the room could feel without that stuff. The only additions now were some eight-by-ten photos scattered on the glass-and-brass coffee table, to which Post-it captions had been stuck.

Gesturing to the photos, I asked, "What's all this?"

Mother's blue-violet eyes flared with excitement. "Those are the photos Daniel dropped off."

"Daniel? Who's Daniel?" I asked.

With a sigh, Vanessa said, "The photographer from *Starz*. The one we brought along to the SCREWED party."

"Oh, Pierre," I said.

"Who's Pierre?" Mother asked.

Vanessa's pink Dutch girl hair shook with laughter. "I'm actually starting to understand the two of you."

"I'm not," Charlotte insisted humorlessly.

I glanced at the photos. But there were far more of Drew and Ian in all their bloody glory than I remembered. Considering where that fight had led us, I couldn't bear to relive it.

Mother tried to get me to look at the pictures Pierre had taken of us earlier in the day. But I insisted I need to change from my dusty suit, and I escaped upstairs to my room.

While I changed my clothes, the things Drew said about CeeCee kept popping back into my mind. I didn't give too much weight to his belief that she wouldn't have fallen for Ian because they were too much alike. Presumably, CeeCee had also loved Drew, and while he was not her exact male doppelgänger, he was close enough. Harder to discount was his contention that she wasn't an impulsive person — when killing Ian demanded that quality.

There was something else I should remember, too. Something incongruous that someone else told me about CeeCee. But I couldn't recall what it was.

Shouting from downstairs short-circuited my thoughts. I raced down there to find them all huddled before the TV. Nick Wick was back on the tube with one of his heart-stopping reports. Now he also had one of those silk flowers on his lapel. Was there nothing people wouldn't wear today to be in style? I was about to make a crack, something about hoping his evil twin had better taste in accessories, when his words hit me.

"Former deputy D.A., CeeCee Payne, the prosecutor on the Sullivan trial, has been charged with the murder of the Skip Sullivan's defense attorney, Ian Dragger. At this hour, Ms. Payne has been released on her own recognizance."

Mother seized the remote from Vanessa and snapped it off. "I like that. Drew doesn't even get bail, but they let that man-eater out to kill again."

The report so stunned me, I couldn't even make a joke about Mother's intimate knowledge of man-eaters.

Charlotte seemed even more shocked. "So it's true, it's really true," she said in a breathless hush.

From behind the sofa, I wrapped my arm across Charlotte's chest in a show of support. Her only acknowledgement was to brush my forearm with her icy fingertips. Though it was a safe bet that none of us had thought of much other than CeeCee's role in Ian's murder since she was taken in for questioning, now that her guilt was all-but confirmed, it shocked us. Especially me, since my own doubts throbbed in my head like corns on pinky-toes. It was such a showy, irrational crime — and that didn't describe CeeCee. Jeez, Mother would have been more likely to commit it.

A thought flashed in my mind: *Charlotte* was the person who made the remark about CeeCee, the one that I realized was significant. I delved into my memory for what she had said.

But that was the moment Vanessa picked to tap me on the shoulder. "Okay, Tracy, it's time to bring Drew home. And for me to see Raul."

"Not yet," I said absently. Dammit, Vanessa drove away the thought I'd been chasing.

"Why not?" Charlotte asked.

Because I didn't know *how* to bring him home. Not so the cops wouldn't know we had Drew all the while. *Trust chaos,* I told myself — it had never failed me yet.

To distract Vanessa, I said, "What's with those silk flowers everyone's wearing?" I glanced at her long tangerine dress, but she wasn't wearing her flower now, nor had she for a while. "How come you don't wear yours anymore? Are they out of style already?"

While an embarrassed flush rose in Vanessa's porcelain cheeks, her wide blue eyes flashed in annoyance at my persistent stupidity. "Tracy, those aren't flowers, they're *cameras.* You buy them in those spy stores that are flourishing everywhere. Raul insisted I wear it when I was working on my story here."

Mother's manicured hand drifted to her face. "How perfectly naughty of you, darling. You might have caught someone's bad side."

Yeah, that would have been a tragedy. "Did you take any pictures of us while you wore it?" I asked.

Vanessa gulped. "Just of Charlotte."

Charlotte pressed her finger to her breastbone, as if she were pointing at herself. "Of me, Vanessa, dear? Why ever —"

A thought burst into my mind. "Twist my knickers in a knot!" I shouted.

I bolted out the sliding glass door and ran toward the storage room. Buddy must have been able to smell when there was fun to be had. Hell, *I* could — why shouldn't he? But I wasn't having such a blast when Buddy wove himself between my legs and nearly pitched me into the pool. I could easily have become its third dead swimmer.

I caught my balance and kept going till I reached the storage room. I stopped in the doorway, unsure of where I had put it. Then the brightly colored sections of the deflated beach ball jumped out at me from the metal shelves. I hurled everything else aside until I found the silk flower Riley had worn on his sweater vest. Clutching it in my hot little hand, I ran back to the house.

Breathlessly, I held it out to Vanessa. "How...do...we...develop it?"

"You need special equipment. But Raul can do it."

I took a big gulp of air, but I still felt too winded to get out the words I needed.

"Call him?" Vanessa offered helpfully, to which I nodded. She danced to the phone.

Great, now people were doing my talking for me. Just as well. Charlotte's chance remark — the one I couldn't remember earlier — had finally returned to me. What a dunce I was not to have noticed the significance before.

I opened my hand, where the little flower and film canister sat in my palm like a tarantula set to sting. I wouldn't say anything to anyone until we saw the photos. But I felt sure I now knew the ugly story they would tell.

CHAPTER THIRTY

W hen Raul came back with the developed photos, I foolishly hoped to study them alone. I shoved him into the fountain room, and I reached for the manila envelope he held. Only Vanessa pushed through the double doors behind me. Raul's black eyes brightened when he saw her, and he absently clutched the envelope to his chest.

"You're looking fine today, Vanessa," Raul said, awkwardly shuffling his feet. "I sure have missed you, sweetheart."

An elated grin began forming on Vanessa's face. I reached for the photo envelope once more.

But Mother came in then, and she cut between that envelope and me, to give Vanessa a nudge. She had been providing the girl with hard-to-get lessons and now viewed their romance as her personal project.

Vanessa offered Raul a cooler smile. "How nice, Raul. But I know we all want to see the photos."

"Not me," Charlotte announced when she entered behind Mother. Despite her slim gray skirt, Charlotte collapsed onto one of the tie-dyed floor pillows, her legs awkwardly splayed. "I'll simply gauge reactions. I can't handle any more real information."

Charlotte had obviously engaged in considerable denial since suspicion of CeeCee arose, probably to the extent of negating the possibility of Dream Girl's guilt. News of CeeCee's arrest now put her over the top. I wasn't sure she should be here at all, but if my suspicions were right, I would need her help.

Giving up all hope of viewing those photos alone, I huddled with the others under the recessed ceiling light in the center of the room. Raul passed the eight-by-ten inch photos to the three of us.

"But they're not —" Mother started to say. Scowling in frustration, she tried to grasp something that made no sense from her narrow perspective.

Confusion also darkened Vanessa's wide blue eyes. "What does this mean, Tracy?"

I knew, of course. But one glance at Charlotte, awkwardly seated on the pillow, told me I had to be absolutely positive before breaking it to her.

"I don't know," I lied. "I have to talk to someone from New York before I can say."

I looked to the person I was trying to protect, but Charlotte's coral lips just pursed in annoyance. "I'm from New York, and you've been talking to me. What more do you need?"

I was starting to understand why Mother popped her one at my wedding. To keep myself from carrying on the family tradition, I looked to the ceiling while counting to ten. But I found no respite there, where the other mother's legacy screamed out at me. Painted across the ceiling was a recreation of Michelangelo's Sistine Chapel artistry — only in the rendition Mother had commissioned, God and Moses wore hippie clothes. And Moses was a woman. And they weren't so much reaching for each other, as grasping.

"This is all so unfair to me," I cried.

Vanessa giggled, as I scooped up the photos. "Charlotte," I said, "tell me about CeeCee's ex-husband."

Charlotte smoothed down her skirt. "Are you feeling well, Tracy? You're starting to make less sense than Martha."

While Charlotte was bent over, Mother flexed her fist before my face. I jumped between them. "Charlotte, I mean it. What do you know about him?"

With a martyred sigh, Charlotte said, "His name is Dallas Hunter. Well-off boy, good family. He worked for the Manhattan D.A.'s office, where he and CeeCee met." With a shrug, she added, "I presume he still does, but naturally, since their divorce I've had no contact with him."

"I want you to call CeeCee's mother and find out how I can reach him," I said.

"Tracy, I can't do that. Ronnie Payne is one of my oldest friends. You can't expect me to grill her for you."

"You do it — or I do it, Charlotte. And I think it'd go down a lot sweeter coming from you." We exchanged really mean glares. "It's for Drew," I reminded her. "I have a good reason."

With a sulky nod, Charlotte relented. But she apparently retained her right to snap a sarcastic, "Anything else?"

I slipped my arm through hers. "Actually, yes. I want you to tell me why, when CeeCee was engaged to Drew, she *needed* your monogrammed linens."

Across the continent, a harried Dallas Hunter picked up his phone on the first ring and answered with a brusque, "Hunter."

Sensing I wouldn't have much time, I spit out my name, and without pausing, promised to only take a moment of his time.

My request produced an unexpected silence at the other end. Finally, he said, "Tracy Eaton, huh?"

"I'm —"

"I know who you are." His voice had taken on an unhurried quality. And through the phone, I thought I heard his chair creak and the thud of shoes being deposited on the desk. If I didn't know better, I'd swear that busy man was settling back for a chat.

After I told Dallas what I wanted, he asked, "Why should I tell you anything? I blame Drew for the breakup of my marriage. I always came up short compared to him."

I felt a stab of other-woman guilt. "Perhaps you signed on too soon. When someone loves another person —"

"Love? Who said anything about love? This is CeeCee Payne we're talking about." Dallas ended with a bitter chuckle.

"If you feel that way, why won't you tell me what I want to know?" I coaxed.

"Can't. According to the terms of our divorce, neither of us can discuss it."

Talk about the unexpected. I tapped my fingers against my desk. "What did you do that you had to agree to such a bizarre condition?"

"Not me — that was CeeCee's idea. She wanted it so much, she agreed to a lower settlement to get it. So tell me, Tracy, why should

I risk overturning that for Drew?"

Never known for my patience, my fuse ignited. "Because you're supposed to be one of the good guys. In your job, you're supposed to hate seeing an innocent man railroaded. Even if your ex-wife did like him better."

When he didn't speak, I thought I'd lost him. But after a thoughtful silence, he asked. "What exactly do you need?"

I didn't think I'd be surprised by what I learned — but when I finally heard it, it was worse than I expected.

CHAPTER THIRTY-ONE

CeeCee opened the door of her apartment to Charlotte and me, wearing a sneer. "I only buzzed you up here because Charlotte was with you," she said to me.

She actually wore more than a sneer; she wore a black velour outfit that looked like upscale sweats. Some Important Person's logo was stitched along the hem of the top in shiny black thread. And there wasn't a bit of cat fur on it; my black things were always covered with it. This woman couldn't survive a day in my world.

"Then we're even," I said. "I only came here to give you the heads-up on something out of deference to Charlotte."

Charlotte beamed at the dueling daughters-in-law. Good thing she got to enjoy it while she could. Her relationship with one of us was about to head south. Which of her loyalties would prove strongest?

My hint to CeeCee did nothing to pique her curiosity. She turned away and walked to her gray-on-gray living room. I became so entranced with studying her retreating form in light of the photos in the envelope I carried, that I only remembered to follow when Charlotte gave me a nudge.

The singular sign that CeeCee's life might not be in a total hurrah state was that she slouched on one of the leather sofas with something less than her usual elegance. Charlotte started to sit beside her, but stopped and took the chair on the other side of the smoked glass coffee table.

"Make it quick," CeeCee said with apparent indifference. "I have a murder defense to plan, remember."

A laptop computer rested on the coffee table before her. But all the work that had been gathered on the dining table during the preparation for Drew's trial had now vanished. CeeCee must have been keeping her whole defense in her head. I hoped she had room there for a lot more.

"Then we arrived just in time to save you work," I said.

One at a time, I pulled the photos from the manila envelope. I handed them to Charlotte, with a nod that she pass them onto CeeCee. The pictures from Riley's secret camera were all in grainy black-and-white. But they were plenty clear enough to show what had really gone down in the Hideaway Motel. And what didn't.

Despite the motel's pandering to the quickie trade, the room in those photos looked like what a family or businessperson might take when traveling on a budget. It held two double beds, covered with lumpy flowered bedspreads, whose dark headboards were placed below a ground floor window that looked out on the Dumpsters in the rear of the motel. In the wide-angle photos, Ian sat near the foot of one bed, facing his secret chronicler — Riley, who was there in the room, not outside of it as I'd expected. Rather than being locked in a passionate embrace with Ian, CeeCee was perched near the pillow on the opposite bed. She'd tossed her briefcase beside her. And beyond it, closer to where Riley sat, a portion of her purse was visible.

The first photo captured Ian reaching into his breast pocket. With his dark jacket open, his SCREWED keycard could be seen clipped to one of his belt loops. In the second, he extended a wad of cash toward the camera. A hand reached into the third shot to accept it. In all three photos, CeeCee stared out the window as if none of it concerned her.

Charlotte hadn't asked me much during the drive there; she probably still didn't want to know. Now I saw that my mother-in-law's elegant, manicured hands had begun to shake. She was a lawyer's wife, after all. She obviously added together one and one — and came up with something really dirty, and not the Hideaway's usual kind.

CeeCee's shiny black hair hung over the photos, robbing me of the chance to read her face.

The next picture I passed along was shot from *outside* the window. CeeCee hadn't moved from her place near the pillow of the bed on the right. Though her purse was open now, and it hadn't been in earlier pictures. Ian sat across from her on the opposite bed. From that perch, he passed her an envelope. In the next picture, CeeCee was seen stuffing that envelope into her briefcase.

"You and Ian weren't lovers." So Kathy Right was — right. If I had only listened, instead of trying to put one over on her, I might have hit on the true nature of her husband's relationship with CeeCee. Honesty — what a concept. "You and Ian conspired to bribe a juror and fix a trial. You took a dive for money." At least that explained the polish of the SCREWED party — it wasn't as if they had to wait for the jury to come back to plan it.

When CeeCee raised her face to mine, it looked as blank as a mask. "You can't prove what was in that envelope," she said in a voice tight with control.

What a feeble effort. I could prove that she, the prosecutor, met alone with the defense attorney and a juror. That she was present when that juror was paid. I didn't need to prove any more. But I knew others would anyway.

"When the cops check your bank accounts, we both know they'll find too much income that can't be explained."

I did wonder why Ian had put CeeCee's payoff in an envelope, when he handed Riley his cash directly. Did that make them feel less shameful?

"I wondered why you always lost cases to Ian, when you beat most other defense attorneys. I thought you were so hung up on him, you couldn't bear to defeat him," I said.

"Hardly that," she snapped.

CeeCee rose and walked across to the modern gray marble mantle. From a black Lucite box, she pulled a cigarette and lit it with a gold table lighter. Back in the Hollywood glamour heyday, I remembered my parents as always having had a cigarette box. But they were known for their outrageous excesses — what was her excuse?

After a drag, she made a face. "Stale. No matter how you try, you can never quit these things."

Don't tell me that — not while I still struggled with the quitting weight gain. No matter. Where she was headed, she'd need a hobby. One that threatened to shorten her life seemed a better choice than many.

"Did you kill Ian?" I asked.

"No, I didn't. And I could have beaten a murder charge." Though her hooded eyelids hid more than usual, I heard grudging honestly in her answer. Besides, she had no reason to lie to us, not after what had already come out.

Charlotte picked up the photos that slipped off CeeCee's lap when she went for a smoke. "Oh, CeeCee." Her words were only barely distinguishable above her groan. "What a mistake you made."

I whirled around on Charlotte. "It isn't a mistake, it's a pattern. That's why she left the D.A.'s office in New York. She had the same deal going with a defense attorney there. But when he feared the authorities were catching on, he took off for parts unknown. CeeCee was allowed to quit with her record intact."

Though a cloud of smoke, CeeCee's dark eyes narrowed. "Only two people knew that, my boss and my ex. And they swore —"

I jabbed a finger at her. "Hey, you swore to uphold the law."

Something exploded in CeeCee, something strong enough to make her crush her butt out against her own stark white wall. "Men have been letting me down for as long as I remember. First my darling father," she spat.

Charlotte had explained about CeeCee's father when she told me why she planned to give her linen to her future daughter-in-law. Though CeeCee's family moved in the same blueblood circle as the Eatons, her old man had run up huge debts. When they threatened to overwhelm him, his ticker gave out, leaving it to his wife and teenage daughter to clean up his mess. They struggled through on the charitable impulses of their affluent friends.

"Then Drew. I thought I had finally achieved the life I was born to." She gestured to the elegant, but sterile, room. "Until this *nouveau riche* brat destroyed it."

I was betting she meant me.

Charlotte came around the couch. "But, CeeCee, Drew doesn't have any wealth. He and Tracy live on what they make. They take nothing from us."

CeeCee flashed her a contemptuous look that said if *she* had become Charlotte's daughter-in-law, that situation would have been different. I wondered if she'd ever really loved Drew, or just loved the position and wealth she thought he'd make possible for her. No question, if he'd stayed with her, he probably wouldn't be jobless now, and he wouldn't live in a crazy house. But he wouldn't be happy, either.

Charlotte didn't seem to notice CeeCee's expression as she prattled on. "Martha is the only one who gives them things. And honestly, I don't think she's done them any favors."

For once, CeeCee and I seemed in agreement — we both looked as if we wanted to put Charlotte out of *our* misery.

"I deserve all this." CeeCee rubbed at the soot she'd left on the wall. "I've sacrificed a lot to work for the people. I could have made more in private practice, you know."

Charlotte stood before her. "So you sell out the people you serve? What stopped you from working in the private sphere? Taylor does."

"I...plead out...some cases that don't matter anyway. What was the Sullivan trial? A media circus. Skip Sullivan wanted his glory, and I provided it. Ian built his reputation. And I was able to live in more comfort. A win-win-win situation."

I noticed CeeCee didn't answer Charlotte's question about why she chose the public sphere in the first place. But I thought I knew. CeeCee needed to create the illusion that she possessed independent wealth. Working in the D.A.'s office helped to provide that fiction. I could imagine her savoring the remarks that would be made behind her back. "CeeCee's a natural prosecutor, but then, she doesn't need the money." The lengths people will go to delude themselves never ceased to amaze me, even after a lifetime with my parents.

Yet I also understood why she quit to defend Drew. She couldn't afford to let anyone look too closely at her relationship with Ian, so she needed to control what came out at Drew's trial. It might derail her career, but it would save her life. Mother was wrong — this wasn't about revenge. Still, CeeCee would have callously condemned Drew to a life behind bars to save herself.

"Now I've lost it all, thanks to her." With an exaggerated nod, she indicated me.

"Tracy isn't responsible for your loss — you've done this yourself, CeeCee. And you've lost more than just..." Charlotte's lip curled as she looked around that bloodless apartment. "...things."

I was betting it was their relationship that Charlotte meant. And despite my own bumpy history with my mother-in-law, I thought CeeCee had kissed off something valuable there, too.

CHAPTER THIRTY-TWO

Charlotte didn't argue when I took the wheel of her rental. We both knew she was in no shape to drive, under the best of conditions. Now the rain was starting to hit, with fat drops that plopped on the windshield. While I navigated the slick roadway, a silent Charlotte stared at the photo-filled envelope resting on her lap.

After several quiet miles, I noticed her right hand had formed into a fist. When she saw me looking, she flushed. But her eyes met mine in a forthright manner.

"To think I worshipped that girl," Charlotte said. "It's been a long time since anyone has made me as angry as CeeCee."

Maybe not since my wedding reception, when Mother gave Charlotte her very own black eye. The first is always special.

"From the time I learned Drew had hit that man, I've wondered what it would feel like to have that release. I've always thought people like us don't —" She broke off that thought with a shallow sigh. While still flexing her right hand, Charlotte held up her other hand in the stop position. Talk about a contradiction in terms. "Not that I believe violence is the way to settle anything. The world needs order. We're no better than the animals without it."

Why should the animals have all the fun? The most important lesson my parents taught me was that life is messy — once you accept that, life fits more comfortably.

A smile softened Charlotte's lips. "However, relinquishing my hope to pay your mother back in kind — is nothing less than the loss of a dream."

"For both of us," I said with feeling.

We shared a short chuckle before falling into silence.

After some time, Charlotte finally noticed we were on the 405 Freeway headed north. "Where are we going, dear? Aren't we taking these pictures to Detective Garcia?"

"Not yet."

"Why ever not, Tracy?"

"Look, Charlotte, I believed CeeCee when she said she didn't kill Ian. Nothing would have made her eliminate the gold-egg-laying goose. Garcia is smart enough to see that."

"So?"

"That means Garcia needs a killer again, and they still have too tight a case against Drew." I banged one hand against the gray plastic steering wheel in frustration; the tires slipped to the side, hitting the reflective lane markers. "We're still no closer to solving these murders."

Back at the house, Mother and Dad sported the robust glow that meant they'd either just experienced a vigorous scrub, or they'd gone off together upstairs for a while. Out in the yard, Vanessa and Raul ran hand-in-hand between the raindrops. Great, everyone was getting some but Dog-Boy and me.

Still, Mother wasn't so drenched in afterglow that she'd lost sight of what mattered to her. "Tracy, be a dear and look at the *Starz* photos. We'll need to have copies of our favorites made before we leave for our tour, and we don't have much time."

My jaw dropped. "Mother, how many times do I have to tell you? My husband is on the lam, while a dead guy lies in state in my freezer — I'm not going on any tour. You might as well cancel it."

She smoothed some stray hairs on my head. "Nonsense, darling, you'll pull it off. After all my help, you should have done it already. You simply need to think harder."

"If I think any harder, my brain will burst," I muttered. But to shut her up, I took the photos to the kitchen.

Dad joined me across the table. "Baby, don't let your mom upset you. She's as worried about Andrew as any of us. She just handles it differently."

Yeah, like a boil on my butt. I ripped off all the Post-it captions Mother had applied to the pictures and tossed them into a crumpled pile. I hadn't realized the *Starz* guy had taken so many pictures at the party, nor of Skippy. Pierre must have thought he'd died and sailed past the Pearly Gates to have fallen into an audience with the Great DOLT.

Those photos of Skippy tweaked an old question. "Dad, what did Skippy Sullivan do to get Mother so mad at him?"

"Oh, that," Dad said with a chuckle, while idly glancing at my discarded pictures. "Martha had starred in a play, in which Skippy had a small part. His first maybe — he was very young then. Anyhoo, the female cast members noticed that someone was stealing their... uh...delicates."

Since Dad always thought of me as a nine-year-old, he tried to protect me from the seamier side of life. It might have been touching, if the seamier side wasn't our part of town.

Dad cleared his throat and rose above his discomfort. "The women set a trap for the thief, and the trail led back to young Skippy. They cut a peephole in his dressing room and ran a camera in. Then they showed the unedited film at the cast party."

What was it Mother had said? That Skippy had been *Thomased*. Of course! They pulled a Peeping Tom act on him.

Dad snickered so heartily, he nearly fell off his chair. "The gals thought he was collecting their lingerie because he was so attracted to them, but in the film, he was *wearing* your mom's."

We laughed so hard, we never heard Mother enter the room. "Alec, you swore you'd never tell that story." Her blue-violet eyes had turned to black ice.

"Wow. He actually fit in your skivvies?" I asked.

In a frosty tone, she said, "Skippy was skeletal then. These days, he'd need something your size."

Ouch. And not true. I'd lost weight — couldn't *anyone* see that? But I'd already garnered a form of revenge against Mother. I didn't find Skippy's behavior so odd; we all have our kinks. But every aspect of Mother's life contributed to her sex goddess mystique. It destroyed her self-image to acknowledge a guy had found her unmentionables more desirable than her. She needed to believe all men would rather throw themselves over a cliff if they couldn't have her.

Chuckling softly under my breath, I glanced again at the photos of

Skippy. While taking a new look at him, I found myself seeing other elements captured in those photos differently as well. A possibility unexpectedly surfaced. I tossed all the pictures not related to the party aside, and I put those that remained in chronological order.

While sorting them, I said, "Mother, get me Riley's photos, willya? The ones from his flower cam."

Mother rushed back to the living room. An instant later, she returned with the manila envelope. I worked those into my collection as well. Then, holding my breath, I went through them all, one more time.

"Holy solution, Batman!" I cried.

Charlotte, Vanessa and Raul rushed in from other parts of the house.

"Tracy, are you okay?" Raul asked.

Vanessa gasped. "Raul, look at her face. She *knows.*" She turned to me. "You do, don't you, Tracy? You know who killed them."

Charlotte stood at my side. "Have you really figured it out, Tracy, dear? Was it CeeCee, after all?"

"No," Mother insisted. "Kathy — it's Kathy Right, right?"

Even Raul jumped into the game. "Nah, it's gotta be that dowdy bitch, Roberta."

I threw my head back and laughed. "Cold!" I shouted. "You're all cold. None of you are the least bit close."

CHAPTER THIRTY-THREE

I made them all gather in the dining room. Everyone but me sat around the huge stone table. Mother had that thing designed to look like Stonehenge; no one could figure how it stayed together. I didn't worry about it collapsing now, however. A lot of heavy stuff had been piled on it over the years. Though maybe never anything as heavy as the truth it would hold today.

When they filed into the room, they all scrambled for their favorite chairs. None of those chairs matched; Mother merely collected an interesting assortment when she put that room together. But they were all of the usual size — except for the one at the head of the table. That was an honest-to-God, gilt and red velvet throne. Guess which chair Mother grabbed?

I suppressed a small chuckle as I paced around the table, clutching my stack of photos and listening to the sounds of the mounting storm outside. The wind howled like some mythical beast swooping down on us; the rain fell in sheets. While I'd resented the dark clouds that had blocked the sun earlier, I now reveled in the appropriately gloomy background the storm lent to my performance.

"Tracy, you're making me dizzy," Mother snapped. "Stop playing Hercule Poirot and sit down."

Not after she snagged my seat. Besides, I was the one who had deduced the identity of the killer. I intended to milk it.

Mother was not so easily deterred. "Tell me this much: Was the killer a woman?"

"Nope."

She frowned. "Was a woman involved at least?"

With a silly grin, I said, "Sure was. The target of the revenge, actually."

"Haven't I said it? *Cherchez la femme.*"

Man, had she said it. "The only thing wrong with that, Mother, is that we didn't need to *find* her — we always had her."

I rushed on before she could question me. "Let's start at the beginning," I said in the great tradition of drawing room mysteries, even if I had gathered together, not the suspects, but my fellow detectives. I slapped a photo on the table. It was the first of the shots Riley's hidden camera had recorded. The one in which CeeCee had sat near the headboard of one bed, while Ian, at the foot of the other bed, was just putting a hand into his pocket.

All the heads at the table bent toward the photo. Charlotte's was the first to look away. "Yes, Tracy, that was the start of CeeCee's fall."

I didn't dispute that bit of revisionist history. "Forget about CeeCee for now. Watch her purse."

That intrigued them all enough to turn their heads to the photo again. The purse, barely visible at the side of what had been Riley's spot on the bed, was the black Chanel we'd all seen her carry.

I put the second photo on the table, the first of the ones shot from outside the window. "Okay, now Riley has left the room. Look at her purse in this one."

"It's open now, and CeeCee's wallet is just peeking out," Mother said. "Wasn't a bribe enough for that slimy man? Did he steal her cash, too?"

I paused at the foot of the table. "My guess is the wallet was shifted in his hasty search. With Ian across from him, Riley wouldn't have had time to open the wallet. But he must have wanted some proof, beyond the photos, that they had all met. Remember when CeeCee came here for Drew's arrest? She'd reached into her purse for her card case, only it wasn't there. And she said something about her extra keys having been missing, too. The case and the keys were what Riley took."

I showed them another photo. Also shot from outside the window, this one captured Ian passing an envelope to CeeCee. He'd put his other hand, the one closest to the window, on his hip, which held his jacket open. His keycard wasn't attached to the belt loop now. Quickhands Riley had snagged something from each of them to support the pictures.

"Enough, Tracy. You've established that The Popsicle stole their things. Who killed those men?" Mother demanded.

Is it any wonder why *I'm* impatient? "Not so fast, Mother. Let's turn to the SCREWED party." I now handed them the photo Pierre had shot over my shoulder at the conference room door. "Follow CeeCee's floating card case." I pressed my finger to the spot on the photo that displayed a bit of brown leather stamped with the Louis Vuitton logo. "You see, Riley's just taking it from his pocket."

I placed the next shot before them, one Pierre had snapped after I left the conference room. "Here Riley's handing the case to Skippy." And then the next photograph. "And now, Skippy's accepting it." Though I kept their attention strictly on the card case, I noticed the scowl darkening Skippy's face.

The following picture I placed on the table showed Skippy crossing the SCREWED suite. I actually remembered that, though I hadn't paid much attention. I pointed out that Skippy was slipping the case into his jacket pocket as he approached Ian's office.

The last one, taken just before we left the party, caught Skippy leaving Ian's office. The frown had been replaced by an expression of intense concentration. And the card case was clasped in the hand that hung at his side.

"How is that possible?" Mother asked. "We found that case on Riley. Did Skippy give it back to him?"

I wagged my finger at Mother, to show that she'd have to wait. Mother made an angry grimace; Charlotte pursed her lips; Vanessa rolled her eyes. Man, I was enjoying this.

"Darling, I'm tired of your silly game. Forget about the rest and tell us." Mother's eyes suddenly widened with shock. "Tracy, are you trying to say the killer is — Skippy Sullivan?"

I made a finger gun and fired it at her. "Bingo."

CHAPTER THIRTY-FOUR

My confirmation created such pandemonium, the troops threatened to short-circuit my ace detective performance.

Fortunately, Dad jumped into the fray. "Now quiet down, you women, and let Tracy go on."

His aqua eyes brightened when he directed them at me, his smart little girl. Though I noticed the lines between Raul's black eyebrows deepened when Dad addressed the gathering as "you women." Once Dad quieted the sulky brood, he nodded for me to go on.

"Think about it. Ian wanted to be known as the best mouthpiece in the land, and CeeCee wanted to live like Madame Rich-Bitch," I said. "Naturally, they would use their little scheme in a trial that commanded such intense press coverage. They'd done it with lots of crooked jurors. Only this time they encountered Riley, who was more enterprising than most."

I snatched the photo of Skippy and Riley together in the SCREWED conference room and waved it at them. "Riley must have decided to squeeze a little extra gratitude from Skippy. Maybe Skippy wouldn't believe the case was rigged. Riley couldn't show him the photos, since they hadn't been developed yet. But he had CeeCee's card case and keys, and Ian's keycard as proof." I dropped that photo and picked up the one of a glowering Skippy on his way to Ian's office. "Only Skippy really saw himself as some kind of secular prophet. How mad do you think he became when he discovered Ian had so little confidence in his cause that he rigged the game to be sure of securing the right outcome?"

Dad snorted. "Skippy Sullivan always was an idiot."

"To be fair to Skippy, I think he gave Ian another chance to explain why he did it. They obviously met at the cable TV studio, the site of Skippy's triumph. The fact that Skippy used a rock as a weapon and dragged him here on a hammock he found there, shows he hadn't thought the murder through."

"Did Mr. Sullivan know Ian planned to see Drew afterwards?" Charlotte asked.

"Good question, Charlotte." I stroked my chin thoughtfully. "I don't know if that call was legit. Maybe Ian planned to fire Drew, and had his housekeeper call. But it's just as likely that Skippy got someone to fake that message. Anyone who knew Drew could have guessed that, as agitated as he was, he would have taken a walk, denying him an alibi. That's why he kept walking shoes at work. And Skippy had been in that office often enough to know it. If that's what happened, Skippy had murder on his mind even then."

If Skippy had faked the call, the fat child fiancée probably made it. Something about that girl drifted in my head — but Mother interrupted, driving it away.

"So where does *la femme* come in? Who was the object of his revenge?" Mother asked. Suddenly, her full scarlet lips formed into a circle. "Oh...me?"

"*Cherchez la femme,*" I shouted.

"Do you mean to say Skippy has harbored resentment against me all these years?" In a heartbeat she became the noble martyred heroine she'd played on the screen dozens of times.

Charlotte slapped her hand against the stone table. "Here goes the Drama Queen. It's always about you, isn't it, Martha?"

"Mother, I doubt he's kept an active hatred going against you all this time. You both played nasty tricks on each other in that theater. But since neither of you wanted to talk about it, the story died. I doubt if Skippy has thought of it often."

Mother nodded thoughtfully. "A narcissist like Skippy wouldn't keep memories that cast his self-image in a negative light."

Now that was expert testimony. "But you threw a party when you lived in this house. My guess was it was *the* party of the season, and Skippy let it be known through others that he wanted to attend. Yet you snubbed him, huh?"

Mother's indifferent shrug seemed to say, *Who wouldn't?*

"Then you showed up at his victory party. But you wouldn't acknowledge him. You even gathered the reporters who came to interview him around you. What a perfect crime Skippy committed

— he eliminated the man who had insulted him. And though he couldn't implicate you personally, Mother, he stuck it to your son-in-law."

I should have known it was Skippy as soon as I discovered Ian's body. The scent in the air that made my nose twitch, as it always did — had to be Skippy's spicy cologne.

I took them through the last of it. How Skippy must have seen the DOLT wearing Drew's shoes. How he used Ian's keycard to obtain those shoes after the party, and, with the keys Riley stole from CeeCee, put the shoes in her linen closet and the keycard in her purse. Since she always carried her purse, he must have performed that operation when she was at home and asleep. Really risky, but it fit with the impulsive, emotional nature of the crimes.

At the conclusion, Vanessa clapped. "Bravo, Tracy!"

I took a stagy little bow.

"Yeah, Trace, you really done good," Raul agreed. "You've worked out everything."

"Not quite. There's still one little hitch," I admitted.

"What's that, dear?" Charlotte asked.

I collapsed into the empty chair at Dad's side. "I haven't the foggiest idea how to prove any of it."

While the wind and rain roared outside, conditions weren't much more hospitable inside. Angry stares faced me around the table. As if I had tricked them.

"What do you mean?" Raul sputtered. "You showed us how it happened."

"No, I demonstrated how it *could* have happened. I'm sure it's true, mind you. But I can't prove it. Besides, there's the little matter of Riley. We can't show that the card case ended up in his pocket — without producing him and his pocket. And they're both a little stiff right now."

Elsewhere in the house, Buddy barked with excitement. Frowning at the distraction, Charlotte demanded, "Then how are we going to prove *he's* the killer, not Drew?"

Now I was sorry I'd grandstanded. My head was as empty as a church during the SuperBowl. And Buddy's barking was becoming too frantic for me to think. "I don't know. Maybe we could trap Skippy somehow. You know, force him to implicate himself."

The expressions on the faces of my audience ranged from disappointment to outright disgust. Man, what a tough crowd.

Buddy's claws tapped against the floor, announcing his arrival in the dining room. With a contented doggie sigh, he collapsed against the flagstone floor. Only then did I hear the sound of shoes in the hall. Squishing…?

Drew's Uncle Philly stepped into the doorway. He was a smallish, lumpy man who was never well dressed in the best of times — and his present state looked light-years past his best. A green plastic garbage bag had been tied over his shoulders like a cape, though the suit below it, his favorite brown tweed, had been soaked, anyway. His pant legs were rolled up above his short brown socks, displaying a couple of inches of his hairy, milky-white legs, and his socks were wet. Under his arm, Philly held a black motorcycle helmet, one of the flared hooded ones that Darth Vader always wore when he went out to do wheelies. His coarse graying hair stuck out more than usual, and Philly looked too tired to have slept in the last few days. But his blue-green eyes absolutely sparkled above his ruddy cheeks.

He flashed us a grin. "It sounds like you need to run a con on someone. Looks like I came home just in time."

CHAPTER THIRTY-FIVE

Philly and I joined the others at the stone table. While his suit dripped on the flagstone floor, and Buddy licked up those drops, Philly recapped what he'd done since Dad returned home.

"I tried to find out who put the hit on our boy, tapped everybody I knew. But I couldn't scare up anything beyond what Dewey told us." Philly's bright eyes landed on me. "It sounds like our Trace pulled it together, though."

Not quite. I didn't know why Skippy wanted Drew dead. But it didn't surprise me that there wasn't much talk to pick up. While I wouldn't follow Skippy to an exit in a fire, the DOLTs were slavishly devoted. There couldn't be many loose lips among them.

Philly finished by amusing us with the tale of his using the travel money Dad had left him on a vintage Harley, picked up at a steal of a price. It wasn't his fault it rained, though that was typical of Philly's luck. Then we filled him in on things at our end. Well, everyone but Charlotte, who glared at her brother across the table. We ended up back with my idea of tricking Skippy somehow.

Philly blotted his wet face with his dingy hanky. "Okay, kid, I get it — you wanna send Skippy a message, only you don't want him to know it came from you. Who'd you plan on using as the messenger?"

I remembered that I'd felt someone had been fueling the media storm swirling around Drew. Now I understood the source had to be Skippy. Putting his part of the equation together with what Toby Newton told Mother and me — about the unexpected relationship Nick Wick and Skippy shared — I knew I had the whole picture, as well as my target.

"How about that sleazoid, Nick Wick?" I suggested. "Better still if we can also torpedo him in the bargain."

"Perfect," Philly said. "Now you're getting the idea."

"So there is some advantage to having a con man in the family,"

Charlotte muttered. Her usual sarcasm was evident, but for once, it was only a whisper.

Philly seemed to take his sister's comment as high praise. He gave her a dignified tip of his head. That the helmet had made his coarse graying hair look like it'd been styled in a wind tunnel only slightly diminished the effect.

We worked out a plan and elected Vanessa to carry it off.

But Mother balked at the use we planned to make of her. "Why does Alec get to be the scandalous one? Why can't I?"

As if that hadn't happened often enough in real life. "Look, Mother, we have a secondary player who backs up our story using Dad, and we don't have enough time to scrape one up for you. Can't you let Dad win one for once?"

To my surprise, she agreed, though with a sulky nod. "But you owe me one, Alec. You too, Tracy."

Yeah. A few thousand more, and Dad and I might even the score.

Philly dragged down an assortment of electronic gear from his room, which I knew he'd used in various stings over the years.

Vanessa's blue eyes brightened at the sight of it. "Wow, this is like the stuff you see in those spy stores." She fingered a section of wire held together by duct tape. "Only...old."

"Sometimes the old stuff is the best, sweetheart," Raul said with a touching solemnity. Raul had seen Philly around here a number of times before Philly and Dad left, but I suspected he'd never viewed Drew's uncle as any more than a scruffy old man. Now he studied Philly with undisguised admiration.

We shifted to the kitchen, where Vanessa placed a call to Nick Wick, giving him to understand she had good dirt to sell.

"Why are you so eager?" he asked. "Every time I've seen you, you looked pretty tight with the old lady."

Since the call was on the speaker, I thought Mother would blow it then. But she held her tongue. Of course, her eyes bulged from the pressure.

"You can't imagine how hard Martha is to work for," Vanessa griped, as planned. "And Tracy is even more demanding."

Hey, that wasn't in the script.

Nick Wick chuckled knowingly, and they arranged a time to meet and a place, a coffee bar with a large outdoor seating area. The fish had taken the bait.

Since we had only a couple of hours prep time, Philly and Mother went to work wiring Vanessa. Mother had worn mikes in some movie shoots, so this was an area where she could actually contribute some expertise. Naturally, she really ran with it.

"Use more tape, Philly, or all we'll hear is the rustle of her clothing," she insisted.

"Martha, I've done this before," Philly said with a sigh.

"So have I."

They argued so much, I started to wonder whether we should have begun earlier. Through it all, Vanessa's creamy young face glowed a brighter pink than her hair, doubtless feeling she'd come closer to her dream of being an investigative journalist.

The weather even cooperated. The sun peeking through the clouds promised better sound transmission, since now they'd be able to sit outside.

Vanessa took her own yellow Bug to the meeting. The rest of us squeezed into Charlotte's Taurus. We parked a couple of blocks away, within the range of Vanessa's transmission, but not so close that Nick Wick would spot us.

Despite the age of Philly's well-worn gear, once Wick joined Vanessa at her table, their voices burst through the speaker, hanging from the rearview mirror, with startling clarity.

"So what's this dirt you have on the old bag?" Nick Wick's voice demanded.

Mother glared at the speaker. "If we weren't already hanging that loser out to dry, it would be my highest priority."

Charlotte shushed her.

Vanessa's laugh tinkled with the joy of holding gossip too good not to share. "Alec is having an affair with another woman. It started yesterday, right in Tracy's house. Interested?"

Nick Wick played it equally cool, as he and Vanessa negotiated, but he wanted the story. Listening in the car, we debated her tactics. Charlotte insisted that Vanessa was holding out for too much money, but I disagreed. Greed was something Nick Wick understood. In the end, it was Vanessa's determination to gouge him that sold the con.

"Okay, here's the scoop," a gleeful Vanessa said. "You're not going to believe how finely Alec shaved it. Martha went out at one o'clock yesterday to get her hair done. Alec had Nora Brady up in their room by one-thirty, and I don't think she'd been gone five minutes when Martha returned at three."

"Wait. Who's this Nora Whatever?"

"Nora Brady, the actress. You know her, don't you?" Vanessa asked, sounding appalled at his ignorance.

"Yeah, sure," Wickerson said with obvious uncertainty.

In the car, Mother groused, "Nobody who knew her would ever believe Alec would fall for someone like Nora."

"That's the point, Martha," Charlotte snapped.

We'd counted on Nora Brady, a friend of my parents, being too grandmotherly for a with-it guy like Wick to remember. Since Nora was up for a pivotal part in a picture, she jumped at the chance to help when Dad asked. Having her name associated with a scandal could only improve her chances. But Nick Wick was sure to find some egg smeared on his smarmy face when he broke that story. Between one and three yesterday, Nora had been addressing her grandson's Career Day assembly.

"Okay, that's good. What else?" Wick asked.

What else? We hadn't prepared anything else.

"Ummm...do you know Neal Eccerly?" Vanessa asked.

"Neal Eccerly, from Starline Pictures? What do you have on him?"

"What is she doing?" Mother asked with a groan.

Blasting those Sunday dinners with her dad out of the water, I'd guess.

"He was at the house last night crying that he's about to be fired. Crying literally, mind you — big, sloppy tears, like a little girl," Vanessa said. "Wiping his nose on his sleeve. So disgusting."

Vanessa embellished the story further still. When she finished and told Wickerson that was all she had, his happy chuckle didn't sound the least disappointed. We heard a chair scrap against concrete then, and Vanessa said good-bye.

"Wait. She forgot about —" I sputtered. "That was the whole point —"

"Cripes!" Vanessa said suddenly. "What time is it?" She groaned when Wickerson told her. "I forgot to do something for Tracy. She's gonna kill me."

The noisy tapping of her boots told us she'd started away again.

"Why can't she just stick to the script?" I demanded.

Her footsteps stopped and slowly walked back to the table. "Maybe you could help me. How well do you know Skippy Sullivan?"

Wickerson choked and clunked a mug heavily on the table. "Are you kidding? Sullivan has no use for me. I heard he thought about storming my set, only he figured *Scarlet Stories* would be an easier target." He snorted loudly.

"Me thinks he protests too much," Mother muttered.

Definitely. Toby Newton had been right about Wickerson and Skippy making use of each other. They might not be friends or even allies, but a connection existed.

Vanessa moaned. "Then I'm in deep shit. Tracy told me I'd only be able to reach Skippy earlier today, and I forgot all about it."

"That's too bad. What was the message?" Wick did such a bad rendition of a casual lack of interest, it belonged on one of those pseudo-reality TV shows.

Distracted sounding now, Vanessa said, "Tracy wanted him to know that he dropped something in her pool. Something important, apparently."

"Yeah? What?" the world's worst actor asked.

"She didn't say, just that it was the last thing he'd want to lose track of." We heard a faint rustle of fabric; Vanessa must have shrugged. "There must have been something about it that identified it as his. Otherwise, how would she know?" Vanessa's footsteps started off again.

But Wickerson stopped her. "Hey, I have contacts, you know? Maybe I can get the message to him."

"Could you? That'd be great," Vanessa said. "I really gotta go now. I've been gone too long as it is."

"Yeah, likewise," Wickerson said, shoving back his chair.

In the car, Philly said, "The kid did it. She played him like a harp."

I felt so thrilled, I gave Vanessa my highest praise. "I couldn't have done better myself."

Some of the weight I'd been carrying finally lifted. Once Skippy called, we'd hook him, too. We'd pull it all together then.

And he would call me, I knew. He wouldn't be able to resist.

CHAPTER THIRTY-SIX

But Skippy didn't call. Through all the seemingly unending hours of that day, Skippy stubbornly refused to take our bait.

"It doesn't make sense," I said, often enough to nauseate the others. Was I wrong about Skippy? If he had killed those men, he'd need to find out what we knew, and what we could prove about him.

Mother and Charlotte mostly ignored me, channeling their tension into sniping at each other, while Dad and Philly came up with useless solutions.

"I should rent a whirlybird," Dad said. He'd learned to fly helicopters for some movie and had kept his license in force, even if he did call them by that stupid word.

"And I should hide the Hog in the hills, in case one of us needs to make a quick getaway," was Philly's solution.

I encouraged them both to follow through on their ideas, simply to get them out of my way. Only then Vanessa started chiming in with plans of her own. "Raul and I should get his camera ready in case we need to record Skippy's confession."

As if any bad guy ever confessed on anything but *Perry Mason*.

I continued with my pointless speculations. "Maybe Nick Wick couldn't reach him."

On his way out to hide the bike, Philly shouted, "Don't believe it, kid. That sleazy clown wasn't gonna pass up the chance for a free scoop. If there was a way to reach Skippy, Nick Wick did it. And I bet he scared the bejeezus outta the guy."

Then *why* hadn't Skippy contacted us?

After they put their ridiculous plans in motion — to the extent of filling the last of the free space in my yard with a rented helicopter — we decided to move Riley to a more favorable location. More favorable to us, anyway. The empty TV station proved to be the consensus choice, though we'd probably have to break a window to get in there. I remembered to stuff Riley's wallet in his pocket, so when the cops finally found him, they'd know he had too much money to be legit. Then I rounded up Philly, Dad and Vanessa, and using the badminton net again, we wrestled from the freezer a guy who was starting to like the position he'd been left in too much to change, if you get my drift.

Though the sun shone brightly now, the rain had left the trail the consistency of hard wet sand, making hiking easier. Still, our progress wasn't fast enough for me. Stumbling along with Vanessa at my side, I groused to Dad and Philly, gripping the other end of the net, "Can you two hurry it up? I want to be there when Skippy calls."

Short of breath, Philly complained, "Give us a break, kid — this joker is frozen."

"Honey, your mother will handle Skippy better than you can," Dad said. "She's been doing it for years."

This was still *my* case. Even if I feared he was right.

I hadn't known how we were going to get Riley over the fence at the studio, other than maybe using the net as a slingshot. But sometimes a messy universe just drops the solution in your lap. Someone had left open the real estate agent's lock box, which hung from the front gate. There were only two keys in it, however, one for the gate, and the other for the radio station. Since Riley hadn't specified a preference for either TV or radio, we decided to put him there.

An exterminator's notice, posted near the real estate agent's sign, warned that they'd scheduled termite tenting for the next day.

I pointed to the notice. "This isn't gonna work, guys. The exterminator will find Riley too soon. They must do a final check for occupants before gassing the place."

Filing his lungs with a shaky breath, Philly announced, "We're not taking him back, Trace. Look at it this way. If they find him here, they're not gonna know he's been in *our* freezer. And if they don't find him, the poison ain't gonna hurt him none."

Since I wasn't any more eager than he was to carry Riley home again, I reluctantly agreed.

I peered through the dirty glass panel of the radio studio door, but I couldn't see through it. Finally, windows more filthy than mine. No Post-its, though. With the sleeve of my forearm, I rubbed away some of the dirt on the double-paned glass. When the studio beyond the glass appeared empty, Dad unlocked the door.

Though the radio studio attached to the transmission tower hadn't been intended for much use, it appeared to be fully functional. It contained an engineer's board, such as the ones I remembered seeing at the major radio stations when I tagged along on Mother's or Dad's interviews as a child, and a pair of mikes hung over the board. Several typist chairs with plastic armrests were scattered about the small studio, whose inner walls had been soundproofed.

Since Riley seemed to favor the U-shaped position he'd assumed in the freezer, we plopped him on one of those chairs and wheeled him toward the board. His feet might have stretched straight out under it, but anyone who saw him there would swear he was an engineer with his hands pressed to various levers.

While the others trudged back to the house, I ran all the way. When I burst through the door, I blurted to Mother and Charlotte, who were in the living room, "Did he call?"

"No," Mother snapped, while Charlotte gave her head a sad shake.

The evening passed at an agonizingly slow speed. Then I tossed through a sleepless night. Early the next morning, before anyone else woke up, I threw on my yellow sweats and went downstairs to feed the pets.

When the phone rang, I snatched it up on the first ring. But the caller still wasn't Skippy.

"Ms. Eaton? This is Gordon, at the Norman Club," a fussy voice announced.

Had Sir Dog been seen roaming the halls in his dirty duds?

The fawning voice informed me, "Skip Sullivan asked me to call to let you know Monsieur Chien decided to accompany him to your meeting place."

My heart froze. There was only one meaning I could give that remark — Skippy had Drew. How could he have known where to find him?

"He asked that you not bring anyone along to the meeting, though. Monsieur Chien is so reclusive, you know, he would bolt if anyone else came."

The subtle threat frightened me, and I questioned whether this guy was in on it. But his delivery sounded so straight, I decided he must be for real. This was Skippy's idea of fun.

I remembered the sign at the club announcing Skippy's talk. "Skippy Sullivan is a Norman Club member? And he told you this himself?" I asked.

"Oh, a proud member, for many years," the obsequious brown-noser said. That dump really would take anyone. But he added, "However, the message was relayed to me through our employee, Miss Bambi Franklin. Now Mrs. Sullivan," he tittered insipidly.

The fat child fiancée. Wife. A connection I should have made finally clicked into place. The girl at the Norman Club check-in desk — was the one we'd seen with Skippy outside the jail. How could I have forgotten that vapid face and great legs? They'd known all the time where we had stashed Drew. I was too stupid to live.

Good thing then that I wasn't likely to be doing it much longer.

"You won't keep Mr. Sullivan waiting long, will you?" Gordon asked. "He wanted you to know he's at the locale now."

I assured him I wouldn't and hung up. Though the meeting place wasn't specified, since Skippy committed all his murders at the studio, I was pretty sure that would be where I'd find him.

I longed to rush upstairs and wake the others up with the news. But they'd just argue about how to handle it, and maybe go off on their own. I'd underestimated Skippy — that was clear. Now that he held the trump card, I had to play it his way. All I could do was hope something I'd already set in motion paid off, even if I couldn't see how.

To the outraged shrieks of starving pets — like every moronic heroine who blithely walked into a killer's lair in all the movie thrillers I've ever hated — I opened the backdoor and went to meet my fate, and Drew's.

CHAPTER THIRTY-SEVEN

They waited for me at the unlocked gate of the studio complex, Skippy and his young wife. He held a silver semi-automatic, which he used to direct me to the radio studio. Bambi, the petulant girl, looked as she had at the jail and the Norman Club, with that straight blonde hair, fleshy body and dynamite legs.

Another connection fell into place. *"You're* the pudgy girl," I said in a tone of vicious accusation. I meant the one Garcia described as having bribed a prisoner's wife into arranging the assault on Drew at the jail.

A glint of triumph muscled indifference from her swamp-green eyes. "Look who's talking."

Hey, I'd lost weight, dammit. Despite her self-involved air, I saw more intelligence in Bambi's young face than I noticed before. More cunning, anyway. Skippy was as much a narcissistic twit as I always thought. Judging by the looks that passed between them, Bambi pulled the strings. Was she a failed actress seeking another route to prominence? No, she was too young to have failed, just unwilling to wait. But she was kidding herself if she thought she'd wrestle center stage from Skippy.

He opened the studio and shoved me in. Now that Riley had thawed some, he slumped over the board, like a guy taking a nap on the job. Drew was there as well, tied to a chair. He wore his own casual clothes, wrinkled khakis and a blue polo shirt, which Dad brought along when he checked Sir Dog into the Norman Club. Drew still needed a shave. But his golden brown eyes, while fatigued, looked pretty pissed off.

I stood fused to that spot, staring at Drew. I longed to say, *I tried to save your life, my love, so we could share more time together.* I willed him to know that. But how do you compress unlived years into mere moments?

Petty enjoyment raised Skippy's voice to a girlish level. "Take a seat, Tracy. Join your hubby."

Not that I had quit fighting. When Skippy pushed me toward a chair, I faked a stumble, colliding with Riley's body before I tumbled onto the chair. Riley's arm moved quite freely now, as I'd anticipated. None the worse for freezing, apparently; a little the worse for death.

While Bambi tied me to the chair, Skippy stood before us, loosely gesturing with the loaded cannon he held. "How I wish Martha could discover you both floating in her pool, like the others." He giggled. "But it's enough that her precious baby will be crushed like a bug."

"I understand why you'd want to wound Mother," I said. "After all, she holds your secret." I paused long enough for a knowing smile.

Skippy frowned, and quickly looked at Bambi to see whether she picked up my hint. So he still cared what other people thought about it. The fool. I'd never give anyone that much control over my life, especially someone like Mother. *Do what you do, and flaunt it proudly* — that's my motto.

Drew's eyes met mine, and a sparkle rose in them. He couldn't understand my insinuation. But he seemed to sense that I'd knocked Skippy against the ropes.

"But won't the new owner of these studios in the Simi Hills be shocked by what he finds in his radio studio?" I asked.

Skippy shrugged. "Bambi will be the new owner of this facility. We'll carry on my work together."

I was right about Bambi's ambition. While Skippy loomed over us, Bambi inched toward the door.

"Skippy, why did you kill Ian?" I asked, hoping he'd want to brag.

"Why?" he exploded. "Because he had no faith, of course. In me, or my cause. He made a sham of my sacrifice. If it got out how he rigged my acquittal, I'd be a laughingstock."

Drew rolled his eyes. But his remarks chilled me. Skippy couldn't bear for anyone to laugh at him. I was wrong — he hadn't forgotten the joke Mother had played on him. His need for dignity was too great for a guy who was basically a moron.

"And how about Riley?" I asked. "Why did you have to kill him?"

Skippy drew himself up and said, "That greedy little man didn't know who he was dealing with."

No, I'll bet he didn't. Though the studio was insulated, a soft buzzing sound from outside reached my ears. I glanced at Drew to see if he heard it, too; the barest of nods told me he did.

"I understand why you felt you had to get rid of Ian and Riley, but why Drew? How come you put out a jailhouse contract on him?"

Now anger mushroomed on Drew's face. Despite having been abducted by Skippy, he obviously hadn't put that together. A shadow of guilt passed over Skippy's tanned face. "Apparently, Drew went to that motel where they made their filthy arrangement." You'd think from his prissy tone that they'd used that room as intended. Skippy addressed Drew this time. "I couldn't be sure what you knew."

"And dead men tell no tales," Drew said, jumping in at last. Not too original, but give the guy a break — death was eyeballing him.

Skippy's nod in our direction looked nothing short of regal. "You should take pride in being martyrs to the cause."

Now that was too much. The cause of eliminating dirty words from the boob tube? Or elevating Skippy into a deity? The squeal of brakes had been added to the muffled sounds outside.

Bambi pressed her face to the glass. "Skip, the exterminators are here."

Skippy handed the gun to his devoted wife, who slipped it into the pocket of her short teal dress. He brought his hands together, as if in prayer, and inclined his head over them in a gesture that seemed to rob from both Eastern and Western religions. "Your time has come, my friends."

But while he put on his little performance, Bambi snatched the door open and rushed outside. She slammed it shut behind her — and swiftly locked the door with a key.

Skippy turned to the door. "Bambi, my dear, what —"

Bambi twisted her head toward the front of the building. "What was that?" she shouted. "No, there's nobody inside." She glanced back at Skippy. A superior twitch tugged at her bee-stung lips.

So she knew how to pull off her ambitions after all. While Drew chuckled knowingly, I said, "Skippy, something tells me your little wife is going to be the head DOLT now."

"No!" Skippy threw himself at the heavy door. "Bambi, you can't do this to me. Not to *me.*"

The fumigating tent slid down past the window. My heart began to beat in my chest like a set of bongos. Before the scant illumination was closed off, I took one last look at Drew.

Skippy continued to bang at the door, though they obviously couldn't hear him outside. His tearful beatifications to his own glory annoyed me. It was bad enough being trapped in there with his smelly cologne, without having to listen to him.

"Come on, Skippy," I said. "Grow some acorns. No wonder the girl left you."

Skippy didn't even pause in his noisy blubbering. Taking the only action I could, I kicked one of the unused chairs. It sailed into him so hard, he lost his balance. When he stumbled, I zipped my own chair aside to avoid being pinned under him. He hit the cinderblock floor and knocked himself out.

"Bet I couldn't do that again in a million years," I said with a gasp.

The room darkened as the tent pulled tightly over the small window.

"Bet you won't get the chance," Drew predicted.

Talk about downer remarks. In the silence that followed in that shadowy space, I scooted my chair next to Drew's. After putting our armrests together, I grasped his pinky with mine.

"You know, Trace..." he began. "When I was in the —"

I yanked desperately at his pinky.

"What —" Drew said. "Tracy, I'm trying to tell you something I've discovered."

"Yeah, being held within a termite fumigation tent at the tower of station KLR Radio, in the Simi Hills, sure gets you to thinking."

Drew's philosophical musings were not to be silenced. "I've always thought the destination was the point of this trip. And following all the rules, as if we're graded at the end."

Outside, the buzzing grew louder. But suddenly, it was upstaged by another sound — the hissing of gas being pumped into the tent. I told myself to hold my breath, but my heaving lungs refused to listen.

Drew continued spouting off. "But it's the journey that matters most, the adventures you experience along the way. You always understood that, babe."

"Yeah, yeah. The journey...whatever. It's a termite tent — did I say that? At the radio station, behind the old *Scarlet Stories* studio."

Drew's voice dropped to the worried part of its register. "Babe, you're not making sense. Are you getting lightheaded?"

No, but I did taste the first metallic touch of vapor on my tongue. Ooh, crap! Was this really the end? Beyond the studio, I thought I heard the sound of screeching brakes and shouting. But maybe the poison had already rotted my brain.

Then I heard a sound there was no mistaking — a shot.

The hissing of vapor stopped as suddenly as it had begun. Voices shouted, footsteps thundered to the studio. Skippy moaned, too, but I brought my foot down on him hard enough to put a stop to that. Hands tore away the tent. And a familiar voice ordered someone to "get the key."

At last, the door flew open. Detective Patti Garcia stood in the doorway. "Are you okay in there?" she cried.

A pair of uniformed deputies rushed in and cut Drew and me loose, followed by a team of paramedics.

"Who did you shoot, Detective?" I demanded. "Please tell me it was Bambi."

"If that's the leggy blonde, it went her way. She needed a shot across the bow before she understood what *freeze* meant." Garcia brought her small chin down in a crisp nod of satisfaction.

"But, Detective, how did you know where to find us?" Drew asked, as a paramedic helped him up.

She glared at Drew. "You mean other than the fact that *your* mother called me a thousand times since your wife turned up missing this morning?" Garcia tossed her thumb at me. "Other than *her* mother trying to run down a Ventura County deputy, in the mistaken belief that he worked for me, and leading a trail of patrol cars in a slow speed chase through these hills? Other than her father buzzing over in a helicopter? Or that your uncle took a motorcycle and with some dirt-bike riders he rounded up, tried to storm this building? Or that the pink-headed kid and the ex-banger have been out there doing a report for *Scarlet Stories?* Other than that, you mean?"

"Yeah," I said with a grin. "Other than that."

With a wide grin of her own, Garcia nodded to the electronic board Riley's body still slumped over. "Somehow the stiff sent out a feed of everything said in this room."

Yowza! My idea of stumbling into Riley's arm worked. "Live?"

"Not quite. It went to the main studio. But an engineer there thought he recognized your voice. Since he's losing his job once the station's sale goes through, he sent it out over the air."

The paramedics carried Skippy to the ambulance, while others helped Drew out into the sun. I followed on my own.

Garcia started to leave, but turned back. "Oh, the engineer said if you want to make any contributions to his unemployment fund, you can send them to his bookie." As if with the flick of a switch, those give-nothing-away cop eyes came back into focus. "But you didn't hear that from me."

Thank you, Toby Newton. But I didn't think he'd be facing unemployment after all. Bambi was going to be a little too busy to run a radio station and head up DOLT now.

The ambulance carrying Skippy drove away with a police escort. I watched as the paramedics helped Drew into the second ambulance.

"You did it, babe. You pulled it all together," Drew called back to me.

Standing on my own, I cocked my hip and said, "Not me, pal. Chaos did it. What did I tell you — works every time."

Then one of the paramedics insisted on helping me into the ambulance. Though I rolled my eyes, I didn't argue. I'd never admit it, but I felt a little faint. Chaos had cut it a little fine today, even for me.

CHAPTER THIRTY-EIGHT

The ER docs concluded Drew and I probably hadn't taken in enough of the bug juice to do any damage, but they admitted us to the hospital overnight for observation. I didn't know what they expected to observe — maybe that we'd scurry under the refrigerator when the light was thrown on. By the following morning, they let us go home.

The shit had already hit a mess of fans by then, kicking the media frenzy into a higher gear. This time I couldn't lament the swarm of reporters outside our house, however. Not when at the center of it all, looming large and pink, was Vanessa Eccerly, the hot new reporter for *Scarlet Stories*. Drew and I even gave her exclusive interviews on our harrowing ordeal. There wasn't a lotta truth in my account — but hey, it was for *Scarlet Stories*.

Anyway, media circuses weren't as bad without Nick Wick in the center ring. *News!News!News!* cancelled his show when Nora Brady brought her grandson's entire school to the press conference she called after Wick reported she had an affair with Dad. And Vanessa's father was said to be so furious, he threatened to buy any station that hired Wick, just for the joy of firing him.

That's not to say the media turned its back on tabloid journalism, not with Skippy and Bambi hogging the airtime, as Skippy justified his retributions in the face of such heinous betrayals, and Bambi regaled folks with her hubby's sexual tastes.

Mother got so caught up in the excitement, she considered giving Vanessa that old film of Skippy trying on her undies. But before he and Philly left to resume their Route 66 trek, Dad convinced Mother there was more grace in taking the high road. Since that seemed to be the only road she hadn't trod in her long life, she decided to give it a try.

I wished she'd start it with me. When I stepped on the scale and discovered I'd lost — not five pounds, but *seven* — she moved on to making cracks about other areas of my life.

Despite most of the loose ends having been tied up for us by Chaos, I feared a couple still might hang us. Somehow I had to explain to Garcia how we acquired Riley's photos. I could have simply thrown them away, but they sealed CeeCee's coffin. No way would I risk her getting off.

Finally, I decided to make it a simple lie. The flower must have fallen off Riley's sweater during his struggle with Skippy at the studio. And the canyon wind carried it to my yard.

Garcia's obvious anger threw that lie back in my face. But to my surprise, she fed me the right lines. "And I suppose you recognized the flower as having belonged to Riley Jacks. And naturally, when you realized it was a camera, you had to develop its film. Why did you take so long getting the pics to me?"

I hadn't even thought of an excuse to cover that question. Fortunately, with Mother's high road in mind, a pretty decent one popped into my head. "CeeCee's an old friend of Drew's. I thought I should give her the chance to turn herself in."

Garcia's lips had curled in disgust, as if she thought I should have come up with a fib with more flair. But she forgot about me once she saw the photos.

"Thanks to these, Ms. Payne won't be selling any more acquittals," Garcia promised.

"Then my work here is done," I said with a flippant air.

Garcia's gaze settled coolly on me, and for a moment, the mask fell away. With her look, she acknowledged that she knew more than she was admitting, and that to right the greater wrong, she was letting it slide. But I better not try my brand of renegade justice in her bailiwick again.

That was too bad. I expected to need her gratitude for the other sticking point that could put a noose around our collective necks. When they investigated everything, I knew they would find that Charlotte had made Sir Dog's reservation at the Norman Club. And that was going to open such a big can of worms, Garcia wouldn't be able to overlook it.

But Chaos came through again. Apparently, Bambi had worked

the desk when Dad delivered Monsieur Chien there. And she recognized the chief suspect in the murder that her dearly beloved had committed. Since she'd already decided to wash ol' Skippy out of her hair, she altered the records, so Drew's reservation appeared in the computer as having been made by Skippy. The cops concluded the DOLTs busted Drew out and kept him at the Norman Club against his will. The shiner just enhanced the story.

Sometimes Chaos is so generous.

Incidentally, Bambi Franklin Sullivan's real name was Bambi. And I complained about my parents. Jeez. But get this — The Pain's name at birth was Cornelia Caruthers Payne, which she had legally changed to CeeCee. Man, that was almost enough to make me turn in my membership to the Liars Club.

Our lives settled back into what we considered normal around here. Given the publicity my near-death garnered, my publisher decided to forgo the talk show tour. The decision disappointed Mother, but she hired a new assistant to cancel the plans Vanessa made. An ex-football player, Mother's new assistant was kinda cute, if you like 'em burly, and thicker than bricks.

Everything has its compensations — that's my motto. And now it was Mother's, too.

The only downside was that she and her new friend stayed on here. But that was okay. It gave Charlotte someone to take potshots at, since she also extended her visit.

I was too relieved to care. Anyway, guests really are the circus come to town. I sure couldn't have saved Drew's life without them.

Besides, I blew off steam by tearing up the canyon trails on Philly's motorcycle. Maybe I'd replace my totaled truck with a bike. Man, would I be a terror on city streets. Mother also threatened to get one, but I didn't mind. Drew was right — she made a better than average sidekick. Just as long as I was entitled to breaks between our partnering bouts. A little of my mother went a long way.

I came home from a trail ride to find Drew looking as satisfied as I felt. Drew had just returned from a meeting with the SCREWED higher-ups, in which both sides concluded their interests could not be less aligned. They were now officially kaput.

"Will you miss it there, Drew?" He had spent a good part of his life in that legal sweatshop.

A smile crept over his face. "Not in the least. Remember what I told you when I thought I'd never practice law again? How I finally realized I belong in criminal trial work?"

Yes! My prayers truly had been answered. Life was going to be so much fun. "Drew, you're going to love it. We can set up your office here, maybe in the dope smoking room. And Philly and I will drum up so much business —" I donned my most sanctimonious expression. "Uh...not by getting charged ourselves, you understand. By getting other people charged."

"No, Trace, you misunderstood me."

Huh? If he snatched this away from me now...

Drew grinned sheepishly. "Remember what I said about CeeCee? How she was working for the good of the people? I figured there'd be an opening now in the D.A.'s office. And...well...they have a hiring freeze at present — but the first opening is mine. Trace, what do you think about the job?"

That it wasn't as bad as telemarketing, but it fell short of working a phone sex line. I could live with it, though. He'd need an investigator, right? But if he thought my personal style rankled in the private arena, just wait till he saw how it played in the bureaucratic public sphere.

Drew's forehead contracted. "You're okay with this, babe?"

"Drew, I predict a great future for you there." Let him dream a little longer.

Charlotte and Mother chose that moment to descend the stairs together, followed by Mother's new assistant, burdened down by Charlotte's luggage. Drew shared his news.

With the most innocent of looks, Mother needled Charlotte with Drew's choice. "Are you terribly disappointed, Charlotte?"

"What I want for my son — is what makes him happy." Charlotte's serene blue eyes rested on me with a new fondness.

Standing before Mother, she lowered her head. "I must admit that you were right about so many things, Martha. And I've relaxed my views enormously with your guidance. I can do things now I could never have done before."

Mother flushed with pleasure. "So good of you to admit it, Charlotte." It wasn't often that anyone regarded Mother as a moral compass. "If you think my little bits of advice were worth something, I have loads more to tell you. We could —"

"But I still think there's some need for order and balance in the world," Charlotte said. "Don't you agree, Martha?"

Mother shrugged. "Sure, *some*."

"I'm *so* glad you think so," Charlotte purred.

With no warning, she yanked back her fist and let it fly — right into Mother's eye. Mother staggered back into the stairs, knocking the beefy assistant and the luggage to the floor.

"Arrgh!" Mother cried. She struggled ungainly to her feet and ran to the powder room, where she screamed, "My eye!"

Charlotte brushed her hands together in satisfaction.

I had to admit to feeling pretty satisfied myself. Now *that* was my kind of order.

Pandemonium broke loose. Mother screamed at Charlotte. Charlotte's response was a wicked laugh; I might have created a monster there. Buddy barked. A taxi outside, waiting to take Charlotte to the airport, honked louder than a marching band. Harri spat. I shouted to Mother where she'd find the aspirins. And the new assistant demanded hazard pay.

Drew seemed unfazed by any of it. He led me to the stairs, where we sat to watch the show.

"Drew, did you ever think, when I ran into your roommate's car, that any of this would happen? That you'd be accused of murder, break outta the slammer, and hole up in the Norman Club, of all places, dressed like a bum?"

He answered with a happy laugh. "Quite a journey we're having, eh, Trace?"

Boy, had he changed. "Wait till you see the adventures that await us, Drew. If you think this —"

Right before my eyes, as his confident posture deflated, the old Drew overtook the new one. "Uh...you mean — soon? You know, I always thought adventures should be —"

I remembered what he'd told me at the Norman Club: Change was hard. I jumped away from that suggestion as if it had caught fire. "No, not soon. Are you kidding? Anyway, I've been thinking… before you start your new job, maybe we should take a trip. You know, catch up with Dad and Philly and I could show you all our old Route 66 haunts." Dad and I had taken regular trips along Route 66, but I'd never shown it to Drew.

Drew's gutsy new spirit took hold once more, now that it wouldn't be tested. But I noticed he still sighed with relief.

I bit the insides of my cheeks to keep from looking too smug. But really — he was gonna love it.

Kris Neri

Kris Neri is the author of the Agatha, Anthony, Macavity Award-nominated Tracy Eaton mysteries, *Revenge of the Gypsy Queen*, *Dem Bones' Revenge* and *Revenge for Old Times' Sake*.

Her other books include *Never Say Die*, *The Rose in the Snow* and *High Crimes on the Magical Plane*.

She is a two-time Derringer Award winner and a two-time Pushcart Prize nominee for her short fiction.

And with her husband, she owns The Well Red Coyote bookstore in Sedona, Arizona.

Readers can reach her through her website: www.KrisNeri.com

Acknowledgements

One of the most gratifying aspects of sending a book onto publication is that it gives the author the chance to thank all the people who generously shared their expertise, or lent support, or went out of their way to do something for her. These are some of the special people my gratitude goes out to:

- Gayle Triolo, who hosted exquisite parties to share my books with her friends. Gayle, you are a dear and generous friend.

- Kenette Faulkner, for proofreading my manuscript and catching my most embarrassing goofs. Kenette, it's only right that you appear in the book you worked on. I hope you like what I did with your name.

- Elaine Paulette and her mother, Juanita Irene Jones. At a time when I needed it, Elaine shared with me something her mom liked to say, and after tweaking it a bit, I made it into one Tracy's mottoes. Juanita and Elaine, thanks for the wisdom.

- A number of attorneys, and others working in the legal field, or associated with it, offered advice about the law and lawyers. Thanks to Leslie Budewitz, C. Hope Clark, Krista Davis, Reece Hirsch, Audrey Liebross, Sheila Lowe, Debbi Mack, Phil Mann, Mary O'Gara, Judy Smith, Triss Stein and others.

- My beloved pets, Jake and Morgan, for lending their appearances to Buddy and Harriet Houdini, Tracy's dog and cat. Though they've gone on to pet-heaven now, by writing Harri and Buddy, I'm able to keep them with me.

- My Girls Night Out group, for the good times and good talks.

- Greg Lilly, Cherokee McGhee publisher, for giving Tracy and the gang a new home and for sharing my vision for this series; and Lisa Kline, my editor, whose insights helped me to make this a better book.

- And, as always, Joe, to whom this book is dedicated, my soul mate on this journey, whose belief in me is great enough to fill a Sedona sky.

TRACY EATON MYSTERIES

Revenge of the Gypsy Queen

" ... a hilarious debut mystery... Neri's sleuth offers
a sharp eye, a smart mouth, and an irrepressible
sense of humor...in an intricately plotted, surprise-
in-your-face, don't-put-it-down mystery."
— Carolyn Hart, author of the *Death on Demand* series

Dem Bones' Revenge

"Kris Neri has written another winner. Fasten your
seatbelts and enjoy this sly, smart Hollywood roller
coaster, which should appeal to mystery and movie
buffs alike."
— Laura Lippman, author of *Life Sentences*

Revenge for Old Times' Sake

"Kris Neri's cool-under-pressure protagonist and
her witty narrative voice are the reasons this series
is an award winner. The clever plot twists and
vivid characters bring to mind what might result
from the unholy coupling of Mel Brooks and Janet
Evanovich."
— Bill Fitzhugh, author of *Pest Control* and *Highway 61
Resurfaced*

From **Cherokee McGhee** Publishing
& available from fine bookstores everywhere.

LaVergne, TN USA
13 January 2010
169921LV00002B/38/P